Author, playwright, translator, and theater and film director Roger Pulvers received his MA in Russian Studies at Harvard Graduate School and did post-graduate work at Warsaw University in Poland before arriving in Japan in the summer of 1967. He has published more than fifty books in Japanese and English, including novels such as *The Death of Urashima Taro*, *General Yamashita's Treasure*, *Star Sand*, *Liv*, *The Dream of Lafcadio Hearn* and *Peaceful Circumstances*.

In 2017 the feature film of *Star Sand*, written and directed by him, had wide release throughout Japan and screened on primetime Japanese television. He is also the author of two memoirs: *My Japan: a cultural memoir* and *The Unmaking of an American*, both published by Balestier Press.

Roger has worked extensively in radio, film and television. He was assistant to director Oshima Nagisa on the film "Merry Christmas, Mr. Lawrence" and co-wrote the script for "Ashita e no Yuigon" (Best Wishes for Tomorrow), for which he won the Crystal Simorgh Prize for Best Script at the 27th Fajr International Film Festival in Tehran.

Roger received the prestigious Miyazawa Kenji Prize in 2008 and the Noma Award for the Translation of Japanese Literature in 2013; in 2018, Japan's highest honor, the Order of the Rising Sun; and in 2019, the Order of Australia. Over the past fifty years he has translated prose, drama and poetry from Japanese, Russian and Polish, and his plays have been widely performed in Australia, Japan and the United States.

ALSO BY ROGER PULVERS

Liv
Half of Each Other
The Honey and the Fires
The Dream of Lafcadio Hearn
Peaceful Circumstances
The Unmaking of an American
My Japan: a cultural memoir
The Charter—and Thirteen Other Stories about Japan

TRANSLATIONS

Night on the Milky Way Train and Nine Other Stories
by Kenji Miyazawa
The Illusions of Self: Tanka by Takuboku Ishikawa
Wholly Esenin: Poems by Sergei Esenin
Poems 2020: Translations from Russian, Polish and Japanese

THE BOY OF THE WINDS

with other stories and poems by
Miyazawa Kenji

and works by Mori Ogai, Ishikawa Takuboku,
Akutagawa Ryunosuke, Dazai Osamu
and Inoue Hisashi

Translation from Japanese and Commentary by

ROGER PULVERS

BALESTIER PRESS
LONDON · SINGAPORE

Balestier Press
Centurion House, London TW18 4AX
www.balestier.com

The Boy of the Winds
with other stories and poems by Miyazawa Kenji
and works by Mori Ogai, Ishikawa Takuboku,
Akutagawa Ryunosuke, Dazai Osamu,
and Inoue Hisashi
Translation from Japanese and Commentary
Copyright © Roger Pulvers, 2022

The Water Letters used by permission.

All Japanese names are given in Japanese order with
surname before given name.

A CIP catalogue record for this book
is available from the British Library.

ISBN 978 1 913891 20 6

Cover illustration by Lucy Pulvers

Contents

Introduction

Miyazawa Kenji was born in the late Meiji era (1868-1912), lived through the Taisho era (1912-1926) and died in the early Showa era (1926-1989).

His birth, in August 1896, came a little over a year after Japan's victory in the Sino-Japanese war. It was in this war—the first major war that Japan fought in its modern era—that Japan established itself as a nascent world power. His death, in September 1933, came two years, almost to the day, after the Manchurian Incident, in which the Japanese imperial forces staged an incident of blatant aggression in order to "justify" the invasion of China.

As such, Kenji lived in what was the most tumultuous and dramatically fluid era in the history of Japan since the Heian period (794-1185). This was an era of imperial growth and the awareness among the Japanese people of the meaning and significance of Japanese nationhood. Japan was, for most of its history, a collection of clans and an assemblage of provinces, just as Italy during the time of the Renaissance had been a conglomeration of powerful city-states.

By the time Kenji was born Japan was unified and well away on the path of genuine and profound modernization in its educational system, its industry and its legal institutions. The result was the creation of the first Asian model of a democracy, with the determination to join the Kaiser's club and stand shoulder to shoulder with the Western empires. In the ongoing process, Japan was also turning into a highly polemical society where vibrant intellectual dialogue played out in the public arena. After all, Japanese literacy rates, particularly in the bigger towns and cities, had always been higher than those, for instance, in Europe. Interpersonal relations may have remained largely hierarchical and feudal; but headspinning transformations in the cities, especially in the new capital Tokyo, spurred the development of democratic social mores similar to those in Europe and the United States. Later, in the Taisho era, fashion, design, the graphic arts, music, literature and theater contributed to a sense of freedom the likes of which was not to be seen again until after the Second World War.

Kenji, being from the backwater small town of Hanamaki in Iwate prefecture in Tohoku, was filled with wonder at this development. He was just becoming an adult when he encountered this modern world and he wanted to absorb it all, not only as an observer but as an active participant. He studied geology and astronomy, in addition to his primary field of research, agronomy; he drew and painted; he played the cello and the harmonium, and composed music; he learned how to use a typewriter, the rough equivalent of the word processor. He did all this with an obsessive enthusiasm and unbridled passion.

But by the time he was an adult his country was turning its back on the freewheeling democracy of the Taisho era and leaning heavily toward the repressions of early Showa. These repressions were both political and social. They were thorough. They quashed intellectual and artistic expression; they brutally excised and purged liberal political ideas; and they widened the rift between the older and younger generations, making real dialogue laborious and, eventually, futile.

In such an era artists, writers and intellectuals had to choose which side they were on. Even Kenji, from an upstanding and exceedingly well-to-do family, was investigated by the police for his supposedly questionable ideas, though he was by no means a political radical. By the time the war in China was being waged in earnest Kenji was dead, and the vast majority of writers and intellectuals were bending over backward to spruik their support for their military's bellicose actions. Once Japan had committed itself to a full-scale war with the United States and its allies, the writers, artists and intellectuals had only two choices: vocally support the war effort or remain silent.

In a day when Japanese people were obsessed with their identity in the world and their position in Asia and places farther afield, Kenji was totally out of step with his people. There is virtually no mention of Japan or the Japanese in his stories and poems. He is not in the least concerned with those issues of nationhood that his compatriots were shouting out from on high or increasingly keeping silent about as they meekly crouched down in the shadows. It is no wonder that editors and readers ignored him. His profound concerns were totally different from those of almost all other Japanese people at the time, as well as from those of contemporary people around the world.

In his entire being he sensed another battle looming. This battle was one that was going to be waged by every single human on Earth. It was only long after the Second World War had ended that some people began to identify the vision that he had seen and described decades earlier. One of those people was Rachel Carson, who in 1962 published her book *Silent Spring*. She warned in it of the consequences of human pollution of the air, land and water. Over the years people heeded her advice, and many laws were enacted in her country, the United States, and elsewhere to protect our natural elements.

Much later, people began to become aware of human cruelty toward animals. Again, laws were enacted in some countries to protect animals against their most cruel and *inhumane* enemy, the human being. In 2008 Spain's parliament announced that great apes would have their rights respected. These rights included the freedom to have a life free of any kind of torture. This was the first time that any country recognized rights for non-humans.

It is very easy to kill off a species. When Europeans settled in North

America there were upwards of five billion passenger pigeons in the eastern and mid-western regions of the United States and southern Canada. It is estimated that this was about one-third of all the birds in North America at the time.

I would have loved to have witnessed what some people in Ontario Canada saw in 1866. A flock of passenger pigeons was seen flying across the sky. The flock was one-and-six-tenths kilometers wide and four hundred and eighty kilometers long. Scientists have calculated that there were some three and a half billion birds in that flock.

Fifty years later, there was not a single passenger pigeon in existence. They had been hunted down for their meat, first to feed to slaves before the Civil War and subsequently as a cheap foodstuff. The last passenger pigeon to die was an individual in the Cincinnati Zoo on 1 September 1914. Her name was Martha. She was named after Martha Washington, the first president's wife.

Cruelty to animals is a major theme in Kenji's literature, the main theme in his story "The Frandon Agricultural School Pig," which is included in my earlier anthology of his stories titled *Night on the Milky Way Train*. We're good at it, much better and more systematic now than we were in Kenji's time. Miyazawa Kenji may have been out of step with his contemporaries, but he is completely in step with those of us who are rebeling against extinction. This makes him a writer of our era.

Human degradation and destruction of the Earth continue in all spheres and on all levels. Carbon emissions have made the planet hotter; and this is going to have disastrous effects on our production of food and on the liveability of our land, from the coasts to the outback. Wanton human destruction of plant and animal life has led to the extinction of countless species of plants and animals. We are on the crest of an enormous wave right now that is gradually rolling forward. This wave may crash over everything we have and wash away the sustainability of our own life. Human greed has led us to prosecute wars of mass destruction, to take from other people what we consider "rightfully" ours, or to ensure that what is theirs can be freely exploited by us.

Kenji addressed three concerns in his life and writing. He begged us to nurture the Earth's natural endowments, not to exploit them for temporary gain. He implored us to be kind to animals and respect them. He pleaded with us to embrace evil in order to smother it and cancel it out; to dedicate our lives to others, to take on their burden of grief and anger as our own, so as to nullify and ameliorate that burden for the aggrieved. How could such messages have been understood in an era such as the one he was born into, when Japan was "on the move" and intent on becoming a colonial superpower? How could he, obsessed as he was with sharing, be taken seriously in the era of rapid growth after the war, when Japanese people were blinded by the acquisition of wealth and the lure of luxury? He was loved by many after the war as a children's story writer of eccentric genius, but not appreciated for being the revolutionary social thinker that he was.

It was only after the Great Hanshin Earthquake in January 1995 and the sarin gas attacks on the Tokyo subways two months later that people in Japan started to take another look at this "offbeat writer of bizarre children's fantasy tales." The Japanese asset bubble had burst some five years earlier. Both the Meiji model of geographical expansion and the postwar model of rapid economic growth, seemingly for its own sake, had proven, at worst, a costly miscalculation and, at best, a plan for the future that was sorely wanting. Japanese people were now asking themselves: Was our nation truly acting in and for our *welfare*?

The First Kenji Boom of the mid-nineties petered out quickly. Japanese people withdrew into their own little worlds. Japan began to lose its competitive edge to Korea and China. Young people became less interested in going overseas to study. All that Japanese people wanted was to be happy in little, strictly personal ways. Social and moral ideals, pursued during earlier eras, lost out, and Japanese people lost their way. That is why the two decades following the shriveling and collapse of the asset bubble in 1990 and 1991 are called *ushinawareta nijunen*, or "the lost two decades." Actually, it should rightfully now be *sanjunen* ... three decades and counting.

In the middle of it all came the triple disaster in Tohoku on 11 March 2011: the earthquake, the tsunami, and the meltdowns at the Daiichi Nuclear Plant on the Fukushima coast. Japanese people were thrown into an abyss of confusion deeper than the one stretching back for the previous two decades. Where are we going? How can I live my own life with joy and hope? Is it possible to make a difference to other people?

Kenji had the answer. Find joy in the happiness of others and you will have hope. Our survival on this planet depends upon social cooperation, he constantly tells us. This was true tens of thousands of years ago too, when our ancestors lived in smaller groups and set out for other lands.

Kenji's message is: It is easy to exclude others who are "different" from your circle, but if you exclude others, you exclude yourself, because you are inextricably linked to them; it is easy to be unkind to others, but if you are unkind to others, you are unkind to yourself; it is very easy to kill, but if you kill another person, the person who dies within is yourself.

The smile and the open hand are more powerful than the frown and the fist. Kenji uses—dare I say, overuses—the word *warau* (smile, laugh). His goal is that all of us will live a content life in harmony by looking after each other. He is, in many senses, a utopian thinker. But he is realistic in his means. He always starts on a feasible individual level, where good deeds are magnanimous in spirit but small in scale. His stories are generally about only a few individuals. This is not *War and Peace*. It is about the war with oneself. That's what makes his take on morality credible, plausible and achievable.

Kenji purported to achieve a morality based on compassion by teaching us that it is our link with nature that holds the key to harmony. For him it is the natural environment, both organic and inorganic—he makes little distinction between the two and considers them both "alive"—that enlightens us as to how to treat each other. We communicate and commune with each other by virtue of nature.

One of my most prized possessions is a little walnut shell given to me by Kenji's younger brother Seiroku more than fifty years ago now. It is not an ordinary walnut shell, but the shell of a walnut that was dug out of the bed of the Kitakami River in Hanamaki. The outside of the shell has pointy ridges and the hollow for the nut inside is smaller than that of the usual walnut shell. The shell given to me is, in fact, a fossil of a *batakurumi*, a Japanese walnut related to the butternut walnut of North America.

During the summer Kenji would take his agricultural students on walks and excursions. On one of these he records "picking up forty-odd half-fossilized walnuts" on the banks of the Kitakami River.

Many people would probably have just tossed them back into the river. But Kenji's curiosity was piqued. Since then these walnut shells have become a symbol of the city of Hanamaki; and the walnut logo featured on the cover of the postwar edition of his complete works.

So, the narrative of the distant past—what the rivers, lakes, seas, mountains, deserts and forests were like before there were humans roaming the Earth—is still locked up in the Earth's present. We have accepted that now. That's why we study fossils. For Kenji this study was a mania. He may be the only poet anywhere who believed that you could not describe what you see in the present without keeping in your mind's eye what existed at that spot in the remote past and what is likely to be there in the distant future. Most poets are content to crystalize an instant of vision. Kenji is convinced that humans are only one minute unit in the chaos of an entire universe, both on Earth and beyond. He strives to take it all in when detailing a single perception.

Now, finally, we humans seem to have accepted the fact—and a fact it is—that the Earth's future exists *right now* before our eyes, under our feet and above our heads, and that we can take no step without compromising or bettering it. We have to realize that every action we take today, from the simplest ones such as cutting down a tree for wood or killing an animal for food to the more complex ones such as cutting into a mountain or building a fossil-fuel-powered plant to provide energy ... that all our actions, every breath we take, every step we take, every object we touch will affect the future of our planet.

It is this awareness that permeates nearly every story that Miyazawa Kenji wrote. This is the era when we most need to listen to him.

But what is Kenji's true vision for the future?

Much of his vision is enveloped in a rather esoteric, and often fanatical, religious fervor. Other aspects of the morals of his stories may now seem rustic, old fashioned and excessively idiosyncratic.

It is natural that the messages of writers and artists date. Consider the paintings of Johannes Vermeer. Some of them depict women reading or writing a letter. The women are naturally dressed in the attire of seventeenth-century Holland. A letter from a woman to her husband who has gone, say, on a long sea voyage might take up to a year to reach him; and his reply, that she is now holding in her hand, may have taken just as long to reach her.

In our era of click and send we expect to hear from someone almost instantly. And we can skype, zoom or facetime them, wherever they are, in real time, and not only talk to them but see them. When we look at a Vermeer painting, we take out of it what we need now. It may be difficult for us to comprehend the sense of yearning, longing and heartache of a woman who communicates with a loved one over such a long span of time. But we haven't lost the ability to have such feelings.

Similarly with Kenji, the cruelty of human to human or animal to animal may come in parables that appear quaint. But coursing under that surface are ideas and cosmic concepts that are as essential to our wellbeing today as they were a century ago in Japan. This is what makes Kenji's message universal, in both senses of the word.

Kenji tells us that our future lies in seeing all nature, animate and inanimate, as the primary link to our fate.

What is water? Most people would answer, something we must drink to stay alive, a liquid that is essential for all life. That is why our search for life in the solar system is first and foremost a search for water. To Kenji water is a scientific medium that brings change to nature. Water is also a medium for the flow of time: It carries an instant in its flow from one place to another.

What is wind? We would answer with something like "moving air." But to Kenji, wind is also a medium, a medium of communication between humans and nature, where nature encompasses the lives of all people, as well as all animals and plants, that have ever existed. This is evident in the title story of this book, "The Boy of the Winds." The winds from the past contain omens that will transpose into the future.

What is light? Well, people might define this in a number of ways. To Kenji it is a medium that contains a catalogue of all phenomena that exist in a space-time continuum. It is the medium that allows us to see the past, present and future simultaneously. It allows us to see the future, because our future is bound to be like the past on other planets and stars.

These three media—water, wind and light—can be used for the good of humankind if they are "properly" understood ("properly" being a word Kenji turns to often).

When the hero of one of his stories, Penen Nolde, wanted to provide energy for the people, he went all the way up to the sun to get the "black thorns" (read sunspots) in the sun and bring them back to Earth "with the thought in mind that this would make everyone's work less laborious." When Matasaburo appears among the children, he comes on the wind.

But it is water, perhaps, that is the most sacred thing of all to Kenji. After all, he was an agronomist. The water in the River in the Sky (the Japanese name for the Milky Way) binds all of the properties of time and space together. It comes down to Earth as rain and sleet and snow, and, as he wrote in his beautiful poem "The Morning of Last Farewell" about the death of his little sister Toshi, "as heaven's ice cream." Water is a symbol of the love we have for each other, a medium that transmits to us an existence that has passed on to another level. Toshi, burning with fever on her deathbed, asks her brother, in local dialect, to "fetch me the rainlike snow." To me this simple phrase is one of the most poignant lines in all of Kenji's works. She wants it to refresh and cool her; but at the end of the poem, Kenji foresees that her very being, though passed on, will come back to Earth in this form. Toshi died some three weeks after her twenty-fourth birthday. Kenji, at her bedside, was bereft. He stuck his head into a closet, weeping and wailing. The last lines of "The Morning of Last Farewell" are these …

I now will pray with all my heart
That the snow you will eat from these two bowls
Will be transformed into heaven's ice cream
And be offered to you and everyone as material that will be holy
On this wish I stake my every happiness

Kenji takes a scientific approach to these elements: He dissects light; he analyzes the wind; he examines the properties in the water. It is all done to find out how these media carry messages from the past through the present to the future, so that we may continue to live on the Earth in peace, harmony and mutual love. (There are very few poets who observe natural phenomena in this way. Kenji was a rare breed of poet who was a practicing scientist, an author and a deeply religious scholar.)

The crises that Japan and the world are facing today may destroy these very media. The wind and the water carry deadly toxins and radiation, not to say destruction in the form of surging typhoons. The light from the sun is creating heat on Earth that will destroy the delicate balances in nature. In other words, we have been manipulating these media, thinking that this is bringing us progress, convinced that we are bettering our lives by doing so.

But this manipulation has caused us to reverse the role of the wind, the water and the light. These media are now working against humankind. We can take all of the "advanced" measures—scientific, political and economic—to arrest the destruction, but these may have little effect on the climate crisis in the long run if we do not transform ourselves.

Kenji was not a romantic who believed that we should put a stop to economic development. His goal was to help the farmers of Iwate prosper. He was a professional agronomist and a teacher of agronomy, a progressive scientist who thought constantly about ways to improve the harvest. Anyone who believes that we should give up on economic development and go back to some supposedly "natural" way of life totally misunderstands the needs of the future. We require efficient and productive development of energy, particularly in Japan, where people are still so dependent on foreign resources. But we must add something to that "mix," something that goes beyond the realm of economics; and that is the understanding that nature is the repository of our morality. Destroy nature in any or all of its qualities and we destroy human goodness, compassion and love.

No Japanese understood this more profoundly than Miyazawa Kenji, and the people of the world need to know that.

Roger Pulvers
Sydney 2022

PART ONE

Written by Miyazawa Kenji

The Boy of the Winds

Taneyama-ga-Hara is a plateau, or tableland, ranging from six hundred to eight hundred and seventy meters above sea level. It is fifty-five kilometers southeast of Kenji's hometown of Hanamaki and was one of his favorite places in his native Iwate prefecture. Several of his works were inspired by the nature there. One of these is a play written in Hanamaki dialect that is set there. Another work inspired by this place is the story "The Boy of the Winds."

I went to Taneyama-ga-Hara in October 2011 and spent many hours there. (This was to film a four-part NHK television series on Kenji.) The thistles, the pampas grass and the bamboo grass that appear in Kenji's stories were all there, just as in Kenji's day. The sweep of the meadow on the plain is vast, taking it right up to the sky. I had never been in a place where I felt so close to the sky, as if you could reach out and touch it with your palm. It wasn't windy that day; but it is said that the winds that rush over the tableland are fearsome.

Matasaburo himself is a recognizable type in Kenji's stories: the misfit kid; in today's parlance, the weirdo, the geek, the nerd. He is also otherworldly, with his glass mantle and red hair, the latter being all but impossible for a Japanese. Many of Kenji's characters have foreign names, but the names in this story are both Japanese and countrified. The *mata* in this boy's name means "again," indicating that he, in the form of wind, is a frequent visitor to many places. In this case, we learn that Matasaburo has lived in Hokkaido, in Kenji's day not the prefecture with developed urbanized locations that it is today. He is an outsider. To the boys in their local school, he may as well be from the moon. He also speaks standard Japanese, while the other boys use the local Tohoku dialect. He is dressed in Western clothing and shoes; they, in a Japanese garment, below which they would wear a loin cloth, and *geta*, or wooden clogs.

Kenji added the mata to a name that existed traditionally in the region to personify the winds that blow across the northern prefectures of Japan: "Kazenosaburo", or "Saburo of the wind." (*Kaze* is the word for "wind," and Saburo is a common boy's name, reserved primarily for the third-born boy, seeing as the first part of the name is the character for "three.") The sound of the name that Kenji created, Kaze-no-mata-sa-buro, has a lyrical rhythm, more so than the shorter Kaze-no-sa-buro. Kenji is the poet and author in Japan who uses the most onomatopoeia. He went so far as to coin many mimetic words himself. The sounds of words, and the sounds that natural phenomena produce, are an essential element that is pervasive in both his stories and poems.

Bullying is a theme in this story, as it is in many of his other works, including his longest piece of fiction, *Night on the Milky Way Train*. In a society that puts such a premium on maintaining harmony, often in the form of enforced conformity in the group, the bullying of someone different is all too common, and, of course, by no means limited to Japan. Matasaburo becomes an obsession for all the children from the moment they spot him in the classroom. He is a quiet boy who does not readily participate in group activities; and it doesn't take long for some of the other boys to cotton on to his supernatural powers, making him an object of envy as well as one for sly deprecation.

A word or two about Kenji's style may be appropriate here.

No one wrote Japanese, or does so now, like Miyazawa Kenji. The best word to describe his style might be "strange" ... or "bizarre" ... or "wonderous" ... all contained in the Japanese word *fushigi*. His sentences are often ungrammatical, so much so that a reader or translator can agonize over which character this author is talking about and which adjective goes with which noun. His non sequiturs are legion; his mixture of scientific jargon and colloquial patter, unnerving; his use of Chinese characters and the hiragana alphabet, seemingly wanton and befuddling. Though he published two books during his lifetime, both were self-edited. Had he been discovered then by a Japanese publisher, he would have been assigned an editor who would assuredly have "cleaned up" his act. That we have him in the illogical raw is a blessing. He has left us a style that is inimitable. He has had many would-be imitators, but just as no one can paint like Van Gogh, no one can write like Miyazawa Kenji. I'm sorry but grateful that he wasn't recognized in his lifetime, regardless of the sweet agony I have experienced in translating him.

"The Boy of the Winds" is an accessible story of Kenji's with a clear linear narrative and very little religious content, though it is, in its own way, a morality tale, as all other works of his are.

It was the first story of his to be filmed. The major film company Nikkatsu produced a film version in 1940 at its Tamagawa studios in Tokyo, releasing it on 10 October of that year, seven years after Kenji's death. It is in black and white and is ninety-seven minutes long. Saburo was played by Katayama Akihiko, who was thirteen at the time of the shoot. He went on to act in dozens of films and television dramas, passing away in 2014 at the age of eighty-eight.

I have chosen this as the title story because of its setting in Kenji's locality and for its personification of the wind as a fusion of human being and natural element. Kenji's brother once told me that Kenji always talked of the wind as the medium that blew out the flame that is one's life and transports that life to the next realm. The story refers to the Tuscarora Deep, a submarine feature in the Japan Trench. In Kenji's day it was thought, at eight thousand five hundred and thirteen meters below sea level, to be the world's deepest spot, but was surpassed with the discovery of the Mariana Trench, which is more than two kilometers deeper.

THE BOY OF THE WINDS
by Miyazawa Kenji

> *Howl and thunder … howl roar HOWL!*
> *Wind, blow off the fresh-green walnuts*
> *Wind, blow off the sour quinces*
> *Howl and thunder … howl roar HOWL!*

A little school was located by a riverbank in a ravine.

It consisted of a single classroom for pupils from years one to six, except that there were none in year three. The yard was only about as big as a tennis court with a grotto in one corner that spurted out ice-cold water. There was also a beautiful mountain right behind the yard covered in grasses and weeds and dotted with chestnut trees.

On the invigorating morning of the first of September the wind was howling in the blue sky and the yard was bathed in sunlight. Two first-year pupils came around from the embankment into the yard dressed in black winter work pants.

"Wow, we're the first ones in … the first!" they shouted, very pleased with themselves, as they passed through the school gate. But they were stopped dead in their tracks when they peered with alarm into the classroom. They stared at each other, trembling and quaking. One of them burst into tears. The reason for this outburst was a funny red-haired boy that they didn't recognize sitting up at the desk in the front row of the otherwise empty room. And if this wasn't the desk where the boy who was bawling always sat!

The other boy was on the verge of tears too but forced himself to keep his eyes peeled on the new boy when he heard someone yelling from upriver.

"Caw-rattle-coo-click! Caw-rattle-coo-click!"

Kasuke, smiling big and holding onto his school bag, came flying into the yard like an enormous crow, followed hot on his heels by the likes of Sataro and Kosuke.

"What ya blubberin' about, crybaby?" said Kasuke, grabbing the shoulder of the boy who was doing his best to hold in his tears. "You stickin' yer nose in where it don't belong?" This caused the boy to snivel and sob. All the boys looked into the classroom and saw the weird little redhead boy sitting up straight as a pin at the desk. They all fell silent. The girls arrived, one after another, joining them … and there wasn't a peep out of any of them.

The redhead boy was as calm as a cucumber as he sat very properly at the desk, staring at the blackboard. That's when Ichiro, who was a year-six pupil, showed up.

"What's goin' on?" he said to the others, striding at a leisurely pace, just like an adult, to where they were milling about.

They all babbled at the same time, pointing to the weird boy in the classroom. Ichiro, holding his school bag to his chest, rushed to a window and stood below it. All the others felt the urge to follow him.

"Who would dare to go to class before it's time to, eh?" said Ichiro, as he crept up the wall and poked his face in the window.

"Anyone who goes inside early on a nice day like this'll get the book thrown at 'em by the teacher!" said Kosuke from below.

"It's no skin off my back if some kid gets in the teacher's bad books," said Kasuke.

"Get outta that room! Get outta that room right now!" cried Ichiro.

But the boy in the classroom just looked in their direction as if a bit startled, sitting with his hands primly on his knees.

The boy's demeanor was, in a word, truly bizarre. He wore a weird grey baggy jacket, white short pants and low red leather shoes without an ankle strap. As for his face, it looked like a ripe apple, and his googly eyes were jet-black. He didn't seem to understand what they were all saying, and this left Ichiro entirely stumped.

"The guy's a foreigner!"

"This must be his first day."

They all jabbered away until Kasuke, who was in year five, suddenly screamed out.

"Oh, I got it, he's goin' into year three!"

"Yeah, that's it!" said the little children.

Ichiro just stood there puzzled, with his head cocked to one side, as the weird new boy sat in his seat all prim and proper, staring back at them.

A strong gust of wind howled through the classroom and its glass doors rattled loudly, all the grasses and weeds and chestnut trees turned strangely pale, swaying back and forth, and the boy in the classroom started fidgeting in his seat with a big grin on his lips.

"Oh, I got it. He's Matasaburo, the boy of the winds!" shrieked Kasuke.

They all seemed to be agreeing with this, when Goro yelled out from behind.

"Ow! That hurts!" They all looked back. Kosuke had stepped on Goro's toes, and Goro blew his stack and was clobbering him. This sent Kosuke into a rage.

"Ow!" shouted Kosuke, slugging Goro. "It was you who started punching me!"

Goro was bawling and his face was streaming with tears. He was doing his best to grapple with Kosuke. Ichiro wedged between them, and Kasuke took hold of Kosuke.

"Stop fighting," said Ichiro, looking through the window. "The teacher's already in his office."

But a cloud suddenly came over Ichiro's face. The strange boy who had been in the classroom but a moment ago had vanished into thin air. They all felt as if a pony they had just got to know had escaped to an unseen place or a little titmouse that they caught had flown away right between their fingers.

The wind was still howling raucously, rattling the glass doors, and pale waves rippled the grasses and weeds on the mountain behind the school.

"It's your fault for fighting and sending Matasaburo away!" said

Kasuke, fuming.

Everyone agreed with this. Goro too felt it was all his fault. He forgot all about his pain and just stood there shrugging his shoulders.

"So that guy was Matasaburo, you mean?"

"Yeah, 'cause it's two hundred and ten days after the first day of spring."

"Yeah, an' he wore shoes."

"Yeah, an' he wore Western clothes."

"But he was a real weirdo with that red hair."

"Wait. He put stones on the desk!" said a second-year pupil.

Sure enough, a bunch of small dirty stones had been left on the desk. "Yeah. Wait! He's smashed some of the glass in the doors!"

"Naw. That's from when Kasuke threw a rock at it before the summer break."

"Hell no! I didn't!" cried Kasuke.

By coincidence, that's just when the teacher came out the front door of the school into the yard. He held a shiny whistle in his right hand, getting ready to blow it to get the pupils to line up, and right behind him was none other than that red-haired boy, putting on airs, as if he was the loyal follower of some great spiritual leader, strolling all puffed up with a white cap on his head.

None of the children let out so much as a peep.

"Good morning, teacher," said Ichiro after a pause.

"Good morning, boys and girls," said the teacher, blowing hard on the whistle. "You all seem in high spirits today. All right then, let's line up." The whistle's whistle echoed off the mountains on the other side of the ravine right back to them as they lined up by class year, just as they did before the summer break. One pupil in year six. Seven in year five. Six in year four. Eight in year two and four in year one lining up together in the same row.

The weird little new boy stood all the while behind the teacher, staring at the other pupils with the sides of his tongue between his teeth, as if terribly amused by the spectacle.

"All right, Takada," said the teacher, taking the boy to the year-five row and, after comparing his height with Kasuke's, pointing to the space between him and Kiyo behind him, "line up here."

All the other pupils turned their gaze on him.

"Now, fall in!" commanded the teacher.

Everyone immediately fell into straight lines, but they were all so curious about what the weird new boy would do that they half turned around or tried to glimpse him out of the corner of their eye. But the new boy seemed to know exactly what to do and put out his hands to stand precisely at arms' length from Kasuke. As for Kasuke, he was all jerks and fidgets, as if his back was itchy or he was about to be tickled.

"Eyes to the front!" commanded the teacher again. "Now, forward from year one on!"

The year-one pupils started to march forward, followed by the pupils from year two, passing before all the others and entering the school from the right where the shoe cupboard was located. When the year-four pupils were walking, the new boy, looking exceedingly pleased with himself, followed Kasuke. The pupils in front of him turned around to steal a look at him, while the ones behind couldn't stop staring at him.

Before long everyone's wooden clogs had been placed in the cupboard and all the pupils were sitting at their desk according to class, just as they had lined up outside. The new boy, looking all puffed up with himself like before, was sitting behind Kasuke. But that's when all hell broke loose in the classroom.

"Hey, someone's put rocks on my desk!"

"Hey, this isn't my desk!"

"Hey, Kikko, did'ya bring your report card? I forgot to bring mine."

"Listen, gimme your pencil, lend it to me, will ya?"

"Keep your mitts off my pencil!"

When the teacher walked in they all stood up noisily.

"Bow to the teacher!" said Ichiro from the very back.

The pupils stopped jabbering while they bowed but started blabbing to each other once standing straight again.

"Quiet, boys and girls!" said the teacher. "That's enough chattering!"

"Shhh!" said Ichiro to the loudest of them. "Etsuji, shut up. That means you too, Kikko."

This hushed them up.

"Boys and girls, I'm sure that you enjoyed your long summer vacation," said the teacher. "You all went swimming first thing in the morning and shouted in the woods louder than the hawks and helped the older boys with their mowing up at the fields. But today marks the end of your vacation and the beginning of the autumn term. It has always been the case that the autumn term has been thought of as the best one for concentrating on your studies. So, let's all buckle down and really study hard from now on. And, you've got a new classmate since the summer break. It's Takada who's sitting right there. His father's company has sent him to work up at the front of the field on the mountain. Until now Takada has been in school in Hokkaido, but from today he'll be your classmate, so I want you to ask him to study with you and to pick chestnuts and go fishing with him. Is that clear to everyone? If it is, please raise your hand."

All the pupils raised their hand right away. The new boy, Takada, raised his hand right up into the air too, bringing a faint smile to the teacher's lips.

"I see you all agree," he said. "We'll leave it at that."

They all lowered their hand as fast as a flame goes out.

"Teacher?" said Kasuke, raising his hand again.

"What is it?" he said, pointing to him.

"What's Takada's given name?"

"It's Saburo."

"Wow, I guessed it! He really is Matasaburo!"

Kasuke clapped his hands and was all but dancing at his desk. This made the older children burst into laughter, but the littler ones just stared at Saburo in silence, as if he was somehow scary.

"Now, boys and girls," said the teacher, "you were all supposed to bring your report card signed by your parents and your homework. Please place them on your desk and I'll come around and pick them up."

All of them hurriedly opened their school bags or undid the knots on their furoshiki cloths and put their report card and homework on their desk. The teacher went around collecting them, starting with the year-one pupils. But, without warning, they were given a jolt. A man who wasn't there before was seen at the back of the class. He was just standing there smiling faintly while gazing over the pupils. He was dressed in a loosefitting white linen suit, had a glossy black bandana around his neck instead of a necktie, and in his hand he held a white fan that he was lightly fanning his face with. The sight of him quietened down all the pupils and they just stood where they were like statues. The teacher acted as if the man was not there at all. He just went around from desk to desk picking up the report cards. When he came to Saburo's desk he saw that there was neither report card nor homework on it. The only thing on Saburo's desk were his two clenched fists. But the teacher walked right on by without speaking and, after finishing his round, straightened out all the papers in his hands and returned to the front.

"So, I'll be giving you back your corrected homework this Saturday, so those who didn't bring it today please bring it without fail tomorrow. And I'm talking about Etsuji, Yuji and Ryosaku. That will be all for today. Please come prepared from tomorrow as you always have. Year four and year six, please stay behind and assist with cleaning the classroom. Class dismissed."

"Attention!" said Ichiro, as they all stood up together. Even the man in back lowered his fan and stood up straight.

"Bow!"

They all bowed, including the teacher and the man in back, who did so with a nod. The littler children dashed out of the room. Those in years four and six were fidgeting in their seats. Saburo made his way to the man in the baggy white suit in the back, and they were joined by the teacher.

"All I can say is thank you very much," said the man, politely bowing to the teacher.

"I'm sure that Saburo will become good friends with everyone right away," said the teacher, returning the bow.

"I'm grateful for everything you are doing for him," said the man, bowing again. "We'll be off now."

He signaled to Saburo that they should go, walked over to the entrance and out, waiting by the door for Saburo to follow. Saburo, wide-eyed and aware that everyone was looking at him, took himself to the side entrance and left, then followed the man across the yard. He took one more look back at the school and the children, who were glaring at them from the edge of the yard, then rushed to catch up with the man in the white suit on the path that led downriver.

"Sir, is that man Saburo's dad?" asked Ichiro with a broom in his hand.

"That's right, he is."

"What does he do here?"

"He's here to get things ready to dig out molybdenum, which is a kind of metal, that's in the ground around the front of the field up the mountain."

"Whereabouts up there?"

"I'm not sure myself, but you know the old horse path that everyone uses? I think it's a bit downriver from that."

"What does that molybdenum stuff do?"

"Well, it's used in steel alloys and it can apparently be a medicine as well."

"Does that mean Matasaburo's diggin' it up too?" asked Kasuke.

"Don't call him Matasaburo. His name's Takada Saburo," said Sataro.

"No, it's Matasaburo. Matasaburo!" insisted Kasuke, his face now red as a beet.

"If you're just standin' around like that, give us a hand here," said Ichiro.

"No way. It's the kids in the fourth and sixth year whose turn it is today!"

At that, Kasuke flew out of the classroom.

A wind rose again, the window glass rattled and the black surface of the water in a bucket with a wiping cloth in it rippled and swished.

Ichiro was dying to get to school to see if that weird new boy was there doing his schoolwork, and he went over to Kasuke's really early so they could go together. But Kasuke had the same thought and, having wolfed down his breakfast, was already standing in front of Ichiro's house with a furoshiki full of books. They couldn't stop talking about the new boy on their way to school. Several of the little children were playing hide-the-stick in the school yard. The new boy apparently hadn't been through there yet. Maybe, they thought, he was already in the classroom like the day before, but when they peeked into the room there wasn't a soul there. All they saw was hazy white stripes left on the blackboard by the wiping cloth from the day before.

"The kid from yesterday hasn't come yet," said Ichiro.

"Yeah," said Kasuke, looking through the window all around the room.

Ichiro went under the horizontal bar and, pulling himself up by huffs and puffs until he finally made it up, managed to sit himself up on the side bar by gripping it with both hands together, determined to stay right there so that he could keep a close watch on the path that Saburo left school by the day before. The river glistened as it flowed, and the weeds and reeds rose in white waves as the wind blew over the mountains.

Kasuke stood by the poles that propped up the bar. He also had his eyes peeled on the path that Saburo had taken. It didn't take long before Saburo was running up the path, clutching his grey school bag in his right hand.

"He's here!" blurted out Ichiro to Kasuke below him.

Saburo was already making his way around the embankment and through the school gate.

"Morning," he called out in a clear voice. They all looked his way, but no one said a thing in return.

They had all been taught from the very beginning that you had to say "Good morning" to each other every day. Even so, none of them felt like doing it today, and they were really flustered by Saburo saying it and in such a nice high-spirited way to boot, so they somehow managed to mumble some garbled words, but it was definitely nothing resembling a "Good morning."

Saburo was totally unfazed by this. He took a couple of steps forward, stopped and gazed all around the yard with those jet-black eyes of his. It seemed like he was looking for someone to play with. The others stared at him but somehow continued to busy themselves with things like playing hide-the-stick at the same time. Not one of them went up to Saburo. He just stood there as if frozen to the spot and out of place, gazing around the yard.

He then started taking big strides across the yard, as if measuring how far it exactly was from the gate to the front door of the school. Ichiro abruptly jumped down from the bar and stood beside Kasuke. They both held their breath and stared at Saburo. When Saburo made it to the front door he turned toward them and cocked his head to the side, like you do when you're doing mental arithmetic. None of the children could take their eyes off him. Finally, he put his hands together behind his back as if troubled by something and started to walk past the teacher's office toward the embankment on the other side.

Just at that moment a strong gust of wind passed through the yard, sending whirlwinds of dust into the air, and the grasses on the embankment rustled in waves. When the gust struck the front door of the school, little whorls of wind wound around, climbing higher than the roof in what looked like yellow dust coming out of jars turned upside down.

"That's him doin' it!" screamed Kasuke. "It's all because of him, Matasaburo! Whenever he does something, the wind blows."

"Yeah," said Ichiro, though he really wasn't sure and looked back at Saburo again.

As for Saburo, he was simply walking at a brisk pace toward the embankment as if nothing at all had happened.

"Good morning," said all the little children to the teacher, who was coming out of the school with his whistle in hand.

"Good morning," said the teacher, looking around the yard. "Well, line up, please," he added, blowing his whistle.

All the children lined up straight, just as they had done the day before, and Saburo, too, was standing where he was supposed to be. The teacher gave out his instructions, squinting from the light of the sun that was shining right into his eyes, and after that all the children went to the classroom through the side entrance. "So, today we begin our studies in earnest," he said, after the standing and bowing formalities were over. "You've all brought everything you need, I trust. Now, year one and year two, take out your penmanship textbooks and your inkstones, also years two and four, your arithmetic and general exercise books and pencils, years five and six, your Japanese textbooks."

But the class broke into an unbelievable commotion. Sataro, who was in year four and whose desk was right next to Saburo's, stuck his hand over to second-year Kayo's desk and snatched her pencil off it, and she was his little sister!

"Sataro, gimme back my pencil!" she said, reaching out to get it.

"No, it's mine!" he said, slipping the pencil into an inside pocket and, putting both hands in his sleeves like the Chinese do when they bow to each other, leaning forward to lay his chest over his desk.

"You lost your pencil in the back shed yesterday," she said, standing up and trying as hard as she could to get it back. "Give it back!"

But Sataro was sprawling over his desk like a fossilized crab, and all Kayo could do was stand there with a big twisted grimace on her face as if she was about to bawl her eyes out.

Saburo, who had been staring at his Japanese textbook and

wondering what to do, noticed that Kayo was sobbing and, reaching over to Sataro's desk with his right hand, put his half-worn-down pencil on it. This suddenly brightened Sataro's mood and he bolted up.

"You givin' me this?" he asked.

"Uh-huh," said Saburo, after a moment's fluster.

Sataro smiled, reached into his inside pocket, took out the pencil and placed it in Kayo's little pink palm.

The teacher was putting water on a year-one pupil's inkstone some desks away so he didn't see what happened, and neither did Kasuke, who was sitting in front of Saburo, but Ichiro had seen it all from his seat in the very back of the room and was overcome with a strange feeling and at a total loss for words.

"Now, I want the year-two pupils to review subtraction that you did before the summer break," said the teacher, writing "25 minus 12" on the board. "I want you to solve this."

All of the year-two pupils, including Kayo, stuck their face right into their exercise book.

"Year four, this is for you," he said, writing "17 times 14" on the board.

All the year-four pupils, including Sataro, Kizo and Kosuke, copied the problem in their notebook.

"Now, year-five pupils, read to yourself from your readers from where we left off last time. Make sure you write down any characters you don't know in your notebook." The year-five pupils started reading to themselves.

"You too, Ichiro. Look through your reader from where you left off and pick out the characters you don't know."

Having said that, the teacher stepped down from the board and went around the desks of the year-one pupils, checking their penmanship.

Saburo held his book properly in both hands on his desk and concentrated intently on reading from where he was supposed to. But he wasn't writing down any characters in his notebook, and it was hard to say if it was because he knew all of them or because he had given his only pencil to Sataro.

The teacher returned to the board and wrote the right answers to the problems he had given the pupils in years two and four on it, before giving them new problems to solve. Then he wrote the characters that the year-five pupils had copied into their notebook on the board and, next to them, the readings and meanings of those characters.

"All right, Kasuke," he said, pointing to a page in the textbook, "read from here."

Kasuke faltered on a few characters, but the teacher gave him a hand. Saburo just sat there taking it all in. The teacher, with book in hand, listened to Kasuke read, but stopped him after about ten lines.

"That will do," he said, starting to read aloud himself.

He read through that part and then told the pupils to pack their things in their bags.

"All right, we'll stop here now," he said from the board.

"Attention!" said Ichiro from the back.

They all bowed and filed outside. But now instead of forming rows they ran about in all directions and played.

During the second hour they practiced choir. The teacher brought out a mandolin and accompanied them in all five songs they had learned. Saburo knew the songs too and sang along at the top of his lungs. The time flew by in no time.

During the third hour the year-two and year-four pupils studied Japanese, while years five and six did math, with the teacher writing problems to solve on the blackboard. Ichiro wrote down his answers while stealing glances at Saburo. For his part, Saburo produced a little chunk of charcoal from out of nowhere and furiously began his calculations.

The next morning the sky was translucent and clear, and the river in the ravine murmured as it flowed along. Ichiro went around to Kasuke's and Sataro's and Etsuji's before they all proceeded to Saburo's house.

They crossed the river a bit downstream and all broke off a branch from the willow tree on the bank and made whips by peeling off the green bark as they would the skin of an apple and whirring them around in the air as they made their way in a flurry up the road to the field on the mountain. Before long they were out of breath.

"D'ya think Matasaburo's really waitin' for us by the spring?"

"Sure he is. Matasaburo wouldn't lie."

"It's so hot. I wish a wind would blow."

"There's a wind comin' from somewhere."

"Yeah, Matasaburo's bringin' it on!"

"Gee, the sun's gone all dim."

A gauze of cloud now covered the sky. The boys had made it quite a ways up the mountain. Everyone's house down in the valley looked minute and the shed roof at Ichiro's house was reflecting a white light. The road had turned into a forest and for some time was all soggy. They couldn't see far through the dark. But they were soon approaching the spring where Saburo had promised to meet them. That's when they heard him shout out to them.

"Hullo! Is that you guys?"

At this they all hustled up the road toward him and, when they turned a corner, Saburo was there watching them with his thin lips clamped tightly shut. They finally made it to him but they were panting so hard they couldn't get a word out. Kasuke, for one, was really impatient to speak, but all he could do was look up at the sky and loudly expel a "Whew!"

"I've been expecting you for ages," cried Saburo with a laugh. "And, you know, they say it might rain today too."

"We all better beat it then. I just wanna have a drink from the spring first."

The four boys wiped the sweat from their brow, crouched down and, cupping their hands, drank the cold water that was bubbling out from the white boulder.

"I live right near here," said Saburo. "It's just above that valley over there. It'd be great if you all stopped in."

"Great. But first we gotta go to the field."

The five of them started on their way. The water in the spring creaked and rumbled, as if trying to tell them something, and all the trees around them roared and rumbled. They crossed through the thickets and groves, passing many places where the boulders had tumbled into stones and pebbles, until they finally got close to the gate at the field. They all turned around to view the road they had taken and the western sky. The fields and meadows that skirted the river spread out hazy blue in the distance beyond the countless hills piled one onto the other, and it all was bathed in brilliant light and again in gloom.

"Wow, I can see the river!"

"It's like the cloth that hangs down on the rope from the bell at Kasuga Shrine," said Saburo.

"Like what?" asked Ichiro.

"Like the cloth that hangs down on the rope from the bell at Kasuga Shrine."

"You mean, you've seen the cloth that the gods got?"

"Yep. I saw it in Hokkaido."

They all had no idea at all what he was talking about and found themselves at a total loss for words.

There was a single huge chestnut tree in the neatly cut grass by the gate to the field. Its trunk grew from roots rising out of a large burnt-black hole, and hanging from its branches were shreds of old rope and tatters of straw sandals.

"There're people cuttin' the grass up there," said Ichiro, as he forged ahead on a path that ran through the mowed grass. "An' they got horses up there too."

"They can let the horses run free up here," said Saburo, who was right behind him. "Because there are no bears up here."

Tall oak trees lined the path up from there, and under the trees hemp bags were lying about and bundles of grass were scattered around.

"Hey, is my brother up there?" snorted Ichiro, wiping the sweat from his brow and yelling in the direction of two horses with a load of grass bundles on their back. "Tell him his little brother's here!"

"Yup!" shouted Ichiro's brother from a hollow beyond the horses. "I'm here! Stay there, I'll be there in two shakes of a lamb's tail!"

The sun came blindingly out and Ichiro's older brother emerged from the tall grass beaming.

"Thanks for comin'. You got all your friends there? They're all welcome," said his brother, looking back at them. "Take the horse back with you, okay? It's gonna cloud over later today for sure. I'm gonna stay here a bit and get this grass bundled up. You all go down to the embankment if you're gonna play. Still about twenty horses from the farm up here. But don't stray from the embankment. It's dangerous if you lose your way. I'll join you all around noon."

"We'll stick close to the embankment."

Ichiro's brother disappeared. A thin veil of clouds hung over the sky and the white mirror of the sun seemed to be coursing away from them. The grasses that hadn't yet been mowed were a sea of waves in the spiraling wind.

Ichiro walked ahead of the others on the straight path until he came to the embankment. Two logs lay where the embankment had broken away. Etsuji was about to go around them when Kasuke spoke up.

"I can lift these off any day," he said.

Kasuke took hold of an end of one of the logs and sent it tumbling down, as the others jumped over it. Some seven shiny brown horses with freely waving tails were milling about a slightly elevated place on the other side.

"Those horses are all worth more than a thousand yen a head," said Ichiro, nearing them. "They're all gonna be put in the horse races next year."

The horses trotted over to where Ichiro and the others were, as if longing for human company. They stuck their noses out as far forward as they could, hoping to get something from the boys.

"Aw," they said, putting their hands out to pet the horses, "they want salt."

Saburo, who it seemed was not used to horses, shoved his hands uneasily into his pockets.

"Look," said Etsuji, "Matasaburo's afraid of horses."

"Who's afraid of horses?" said Saburo, taking his hands out of his pockets and reaching for a horse's nose. But when the horse thrust its head toward him and put out its tongue to lick him, he suddenly turned pale and stuck his hands right back into his pockets.

"See," said Etsuji again, "Matasaburo's afraid of 'em after all."

Saburo turned beet red and just stood there fidgeting.

"Okay then," he said, "you all want to have a horse race?" None of them had a clue as to how you held a horse race.

"I've seen lots of horse races," said Saburo. "But none of these horses has a saddle so you can't ride them. So, we'll all each chase a horse, and the first one who gets to that big tree over there … see it? … he'll be the winner."

"Oh, that's fun," said Kasuke.

"If the herdsman sees us we'll be in big trouble."

"It'll be okay," said Saburo. "It'll give some practice to the horses who are racing next year."

"Great. This horse's mine."

"An' this one's mine."

"Well, I guess I gotta settle for this one."

They all lightly swatted the horses with their willow bark whips and tufts of reeds.

But the horses acted with total indifference. They just lowered their head to the ground and munched on the grass, occasionally raising their eyes as if nonchalantly taking in the scenery.

"Giddyup!" said Ichiro, whipping his horse with both hands gripping his whip.

This sent all seven horses running away with their manes lined up in the air.

"Goodee!" cried Kasuke, bolting after them. But there was no way that this could be seen as a horse race. First of all, the horses ran absolutely neck and neck the whole way and in no way fast enough for this to be called a race. Even so, the boys were having a ball, trotting behind the horses and screaming "Giddyup … giddyup!" The horses seemed to be stopping up ahead, but the boys, though panting and out of breath, pushed on to follow them. Finally, the horses went around the slightly elevated place where they were before and came to the embankment that the boys had crossed.

"The horses are getting away, they're getting away!" shouted Ichiro, turning pale. "Catch 'em, quick, don't let 'em get away!"

The horses were crossing over the embankment. They started to run again and were about to jump over the log that was still there.

"Whoa … whoa whoa whoa," said Ichiro as he ran as fast as his legs would take him, almost falling over but finally getting to where the horses were and reaching out to them. But by then two of the horses had already made it to the other side.

"Get over here!" hollered Ichiro out of breath, putting the log back where it was. "Quick, we gotta catch 'em!"

The boys ran like the devil, avoiding the logs, but the two horses had stopped on the other side of the embankment and were yanking grass out of the ground with their teeth.

"Don't rush, take it slow and easy," said Ichiro, grabbing one horse by the bit.

But when Kasuke and Saburo tried to get a hold on the bit of the other horse, it bolted as if alarmed and ran at full speed south along the embankment.

"The horse's getting away!" shouted Ichiro at the top of his lungs in the direction of where his brother was. "It's getting away … away!"

Kasuke and Saburo ran after the horse, and this time it really looked like it was trying to get away. It galloped through grasses that were as tall as it was, raising and lowering its head and never about to stop. Kasuke's legs got all numb and he hadn't a clue where the horse was now. Everything went all blue around him, he got dizzier and dizzier and, in the end, fell right into the tall grass. The last thing he caught a glimpse of was the red mane of the horse and the white shirt of Saburo running after it. He was flat on his back. He looked up at the sky. The sky was like a radiant white pinwheel and the dull grey clouds in it were streaming far into the distance. He heard a loud clanging noise, finally got up and, breathing in fits and starts, started to walk in the direction that the horse ran in. There was a kind of opening in the grass where, it seemed, the horse and Saburo had gone, and he thought, laughing to himself, "Sure, the horse's scared and has stopped somewhere in his tracks." He followed through that opening in the grass, but before he went even a hundred steps the opening branched out into two other openings where honeysuckle and strangely tall thistles were growing. He had totally lost his bearings and didn't know which way was which.

"Hullo!" he hollered.

"Hullo!" shouted Saburo from somewhere.

Hearing this, Kasuke forged ahead down an opening in the middle. But he just came upon places that were overgrown and steep inclines that a horse could never walk over.

The sky turned fiercely dark, layer by layer, and the surroundings were enveloped, by degrees, in a dim mist. A cold wind began to traverse the grasses, and both the clouds and the mist fragmented, rushing straight into his eyes.

"Ah, I'm really in trouble now," thought Kasuke. "It's an omen of one bad thing after another that's gonna happen."

And he was right. In a flash, the opening that the horse had gone through disappeared in the grass. Kasuke's heart raced. "We're in for it. Everything's going to go to the devil now," he thought.

The grasses bent at their stalks, clicking and clacking as they rustled in the strong wind, the fog grew milky and thick, and his clothes hung on him like a damp blanket.

"Ichiro, Ichiro," screamed Kasuke at the top of his voice. "Get over here!"

But there was no reply. Tiny dark cold globules of mist, like chalk dust falling off a blackboard, danced through the air, a hush fell over everything, all there was around him was misery and gloom, and all that could be heard was the trickling and dripping of water falling off the grass.

Kasuke turned back to join Ichiro and the others as fast as he could. But the place he was running through was not the same as before. First of all, there were way too many thistles in the way and jagged rocks hiding below the grass that weren't there before. Besides that, a huge valley that no one had ever talked about appeared right before his eyes. The pampas grass rustled and the space in front of him just vanished into the fog like a bottomless ravine.

The fronds of the pampas grass lengthened their myriad thin fingers into the wind, furiously waving as if to say, "Ah, West … ah, East … ah, West … ah, South … ah, West…."

Kasuke was mortified and he turned sideways, rushing back from where he came, coming across a narrow black path through the grass that was made by thousands of horses' hoofs. He let out a little laugh and raced down the path for all he was worth. But he couldn't trust the path because it kept getting narrower down to five inches then wider up to three feet and then going what seemed like around in circles, before branching off into the haze in several directions when it reached a burnt chestnut tree with spreading branches at the top. It was probably a place where wild horses gathered, because he could see what looked like a corral through the fog.

Kasuke, crestfallen, started to retrace his steps on the black path. Fronds and tufts that he had never seen before were all around, swaying in silence, and when a strong wind began to blow, the body of grass around him bowed down, as if on signal from somewhere or other to make room for him. The sky creaked with light.

A huge black object shaped like a house appeared out of the fog right before his eyes. Kasuke stood there for a time disbelieving his own eyes, but it definitely looked like a house. He took one reluctant step after the other toward it until he realized that it was a huge frigid black boulder. The sky swung and swayed, revolving around itself, and the grass shook off all its droplets in one fell jolt.

"If we go wrong here and descend from the other side of the field," thought Kasuke, half saying it in a whisper, "both Matasaburo and I are goners."

Then he screamed out …

"Ichiro, Ichiro, you there? ICHIRO!"

It brightened up again, all the grasses heaved a happy sigh of relief, and he clearly heard words that someone had once said to him.

"The child of the electrician at Isado had his hands and feet tied by a giant woodsman."

That's when the black path vanished again and everything around went quiet as the grave and a ferociously strong wind blew in. The sky fluttered in light, like a flag, and sparks crackled and burned in the air.

Kasuke finally fell into the grass and was soon dead to the world.

*

It all seemed like things that happened somewhere far away.

Matasaburo had remained silent. He was looking up at the sky with outstretched legs and was now wearing a glass mantle over his usual grey jacket. His shoes too were made of gleaming glass. The blue shadow of a chestnut tree fell on his shoulders, and his own shadow, in turn, fell blue into the grass. And the wind whistled higher and higher.

Matasaburo was neither speaking nor smiling. He was merely gazing up at the sky with his thin lips clamped shut like a vice. All of a sudden he flew up in the air just like that, his glass mantle glittering and gleaming with him.

*

Kasuke suddenly opened his eyes. The grey fog was sailing far far away, and the horse was standing solidly right in front of him, looking askance as if wary of him. Kasuke bolted up and held him by the name tag, as Saburo came from behind with his colorless lips shut tight. Kasuke shook like a leaf.

"Hullo!" called Ichiro's brother from a bank of fog, as thunder rolled over them.

"Hullo!" cried Ichiro. "Kasuke, you there? Kasuke!"

"Hey, I'm here, I'm here. Ichiro, hullo!"

Before he knew it Ichiro and his brother were standing in front of him, and he started bawling his eyes out.

"We looked for you everywhere," said Ichiro's brother, cradling the horse's neck with a practiced hand while skilfully attaching the bit in its mouth. "We were worried about your safety. Oh, gosh, you're soaking wet."

"Let's get outta here."

"You must've been really spooked, Matasaburo," said Ichiro to Saburo.

But Saburo just stood there with his lips clamped shut like before.

They all followed Ichiro's brother as he climbed up two gentle slopes and took the big black path for a while. A couple of lightning flashes dimly lit the white sky and the smell of burning grass filled the air that flowed in billows, like smoke, through the fog.

"Granddad," shouted Ichiro, "we found him, we found him. We're all here!"

"Goodness, I was worried, worried sick," said his grandfather, standing against a bank of fog. "Thank goodness. Oh, Kasuke, you must be freezin'. C'mon, get on in here."

Ichiro's grandfather was just like a grandfather to Kasuke too.

There was a little enclosure made of grasses at the root of a tall halfburnt chestnut tree, with a crackling red fire ablaze in it. Ichiro's brother tied the horse, who was neighing, to the trunk of an oak tree.

"Aw, poor kid, you must've cried yer eyes out. That boy's the miner's boy, ain't he. Now, all of you, dig into these dumplings. C'mon, don't be shy. I'll grill these ones here for ya. So, where on earth did you all get to?"

"Down to the place that leads to Sasanagane," answered Ichiro's brother.

"Aw, it's not safe down there, not safe at all. We've lost horses and people down there. Now, Kasuke, eat up that dumpling. You, too, kid, have one. Come on, don't leave any."

"Granddad, should I leave the horse here?" asked Ichiro's brother.

"Hmmm. When the herdsman gets here he's bound to make a fuss. Hold on here a bit longer, will ya? It's bound to clear up soon. Aw, I was worried sick. I went down the mountain to look for ya. Yup, well, anyway, thank goodness, that's all I gotta say. Rain's clearin' up too."

"If only we'd had no rain and fog this mornin'...."

"Yup. Anyway, it's clearin' up now. Damn, rain's leakin' in."

Ichiro's brother left. The roof of the enclosure was swishing and humming in the wind. The grandfather looked up at it with a big smile, as Ichiro's brother returned.

"Granddad, it's all bright out. The rain's stopped."

"Hmm, right. Now all of ya get yerself close to the fire. I'm goin' out to cut some more grass."

Bright rays of sunshine cleaved the fog. The sun had sailed on to the west. Radiant bands of fog lingered in the air, like wax. Droplets glittered as they fell from blades of grass and all the leaves and stalks and flowers sucked up the sun near the end of day. The blue fields far away in the west had stopped their crying out and were now beaming, and the chestnut tree in the distance was giving off a light blue aura.

They were all exhausted as they followed Ichiro down to the field they had come from. Saburo, his lips together as before, separated from the others when they came to the spring and went off by himself to his father's cottage.

"He's gotta be the god of the winds," said Kasuke, walking along. "I mean, the child of the god of the winds. He and his dad are livin' up here."

"You're wrong, he's not," insisted Ichiro.

The next day it had stopped raining by morning and by the second hour of school the sky was getting brighter and brighter. By the time the ten-minute recess came in the third hour you could see blue patches of sky etched between the clouds. Layers of bright white cirrocumulus cloud were sailing swiftly toward the east, where a vapor of cloud remained and, rising up from the reeds and the chestnut trees, blanketed the mountains.

"Wanna go pick grapes after class?" whispered Kosuke to Kasuke.

"You bet I do! Maybe Saburo wants to come with us," said Kasuke.

"No! Don't let Saburo know about that spot."

"I'll go with you," said Saburo, not having heard what Kosuke had just said. "I picked heaps of grapes in Hokkaido. My mum pickled up two barrels of them."

"If you're goin' grape pickin', take me too!" piped in Shokichi, a year-two pupil.

"No way! There's no way we'd tell you where it is. I found this new place last year myself."

They all couldn't wait till school ended. Six of them—Ichiro, Kasuke, Sataro, Kosuke, Etsuji and Saburo—went upriver from the school to where there was a house with a straw roof behind a small tobacco field. The bottom leaves had already been picked from the tobacco bushes, and the boys thought that the blue-green stalks, all lined up like trees in a forest, looked weird. "What's going on with these leaves?" blurted out Saburo, ripping off a leaf and showing it to Ichiro.

"Hey, Matasaburo," said Ichiro, turning pale and alarmed. "If you rip off leaves the Tobacco Monopoly Bureau will skin you alive. What did you go and do that for, Matasaburo?!"

They all turned on Saburo.

"Hell, the bureau records every single leaf they got here. Don't come to me."

"And don't come to me either."

"And not to me either."

"I didn't know that, I just took it," said Saburo hesitantly, blushing and somewhat miffed as he waved the leaf about.

They all looked toward the house, terrified that someone had seen them. But it seemed that no one was in the house, which they could see through the steam puffing up from the field.

"That's little Kisuke's house, the year-one boy," said Kasuke to calm everyone down.

Kosuke had been really against Saburo and everyone tagging along to the thicket where the grapes grew that he had discovered.

"It's not good enough that you didn't know," he said nastily to Saburo. "So, you gotta put it back were you tore it off from and pay the damages."

"Well, if that's the case," said Saburo, trying to find the right words after a long pause, "I'll just put it back down here."

He gently laid the leaf at the root of the bush.

"Okay, let's get outta here," said Ichiro, walking ahead.

They all followed him, except for Kosuke, who turned to Saburo.

"It's all on your head, Matasaburo," he said, before catching up with the others. "That's *your* leaf under there."

They climbed part way up the mountain on a narrow path running through the weeds and reeds, with chestnut trees dotting the hollows on the south side of the path, below it a big thicket overgrown with grape vines.

"I found this place first," said Kosuke. "So you can all take just a handful each."

"I'll pick chestnuts instead," said Saburo, picking up a stone and throwing it at one of the branches, bringing down a burr.

He peeled the burr with a stick and took out two chestnuts that were still white, as the others were busying themselves by the vines. But Kosuke was soon off to another thicket, passing under the chestnut tree, when all of a sudden a big splash of water fell right onto him, and it looked like he'd been dunked in the river from his shoulders down his back. He looked up in shock to see Saburo on a branch with a funny little smile on his lips, wiping his face on his shirt cuff. "Hey,

Matasaburo," said Kosuke, bitterly, "what the hell d'ya think you're doin'?!"

"The wind came up," said Saburo, sniggering.

Kosuke walked away, went to another thicket and began to pick grapes. He picked much more than he himself could handle, stuffing some into his mouth, which now was purple and bloated.

"Well," said Ichiro, "I think I'll call it a day with this much."

"I'm not through yet here," said Kosuke.

Just then Kosuke's head was drenched in big drops of cold water. Taken by surprise again he looked up to the branches above him. This time Saburo wasn't there at all, but he did glimpse Saburo's grey elbow on the other side of the tree. Saburo was still sniggering at him and it made him furious.

"Hey, Matasaburo! You throwin' water on people again?"

"No, it was from the wind."

Everyone found this hilarious … except, that is, Kosuke, who didn't look happy and was staring daggers at Saburo.

"You went and shook the tree, Matasaburo."

Again the others found this hilarious.

"Listen good, Matasaburo. There's no place in this world for the likes of you!"

"All right, little Kosuke," said Saburo in a mean voice. "Well, excuse me for living."

Kosuke was so furious that he wasn't able to say what he wanted to and couldn't think of anything new to say either.

"Listen good, Matasaburo, and watch yer step!" he shrieked. "We don't need wind like you comin' into our world, you hear?"

"Well, then, I am truly sorry," he said, blinking over and over and feeling a bit sorry. "What can I do? You're just so awful to me."

But this in no way assuaged Kosuke's anger, and he repeated what he said for the third time.

"Hear me, Matasaburo! There's no place in the world for any wind. Get it?"

"What do you mean by no place for wind in the world?" said Saburo, sniggering again and now drawn into the discussion, raising a finger in the air like a teacher. "Okay, then. Would you please itemize what you want to say, one by one? *Get it*?"

Kosuke felt like he was being tested and he really didn't like it one bit.

"You are just up to mischief all the time," he said, gritting his teeth. "You ruin everyone's umbrellas."

"And what else, what else?" said Saburo, clearly enjoying this.

"An' you break apart trees and turn them topsy-turvy."

"Okay, and what else?"

"You rip apart people's homes."

"Okay, what else, what else do I do?"

"You snuff out people's lights."

"Okay, is that all? Is that all I do? Come on."

"You send people's hats flying."

"Uh-huh, and what else, what else do I do?"

"You send people's umbrellas flying too."

"What else, what else?"

"You … you … you bring down telephone poles."

"Tell me more, tell me more, tell me more."

"And you take people's roofs off people's houses."

"Ha ha ha, roofs should be included in the earlier part about the houses. Okay, so do you have anything else? Come on, what else?"

"What else? You … you put out people's lamps."

"Ha ha ha, lamps should be included in the part about the lights. So, are you through? Hey, come on, what else can you come up with?"

Kosuke was stumped. He had said just about everything and he couldn't come up with anything else.

"Come on, what else? Eh? You can do it. What else?" said Saburo, with a finger in the air, thoroughly enjoying himself.

"You … you smash up windmills," said Kosuke finally, his face reddening from ear to ear.

Saburo found this funnier than all the others and burst out laughing. All the others followed suit, giggling and chortling and guffawing.

"So, you finally got to the windmills," said Saburo, ceasing to laugh. "There isn't a windmill that doesn't love a wind. There may be the odd time that they are broken by the wind, but much more often it helps them go around. I tell you, windmills look up to the wind. And besides, the way you listed those things a moment ago was really weird. 'You … you … you' … you kept repeating that. And then you got to the windmills at the end. Ah, it really makes me laugh!"

And having said that, Saburo howled with laughter until his eyes were running with tears. As for Kosuke, he gradually stopped thinking about how angry and bothered he was and started to laugh himself.

"Kosuke," said Saburo, now in a good mood, "sorry about the mischief."

"Well now, how about we set off," said Ichiro, handing Saburo five bunches of grapes. Saburo shared two white chestnuts each with the other boys and they all walked down the sloping path together, separating and going to their own home in the end. A mantle of fog hung over the morning of the next day and the mountain behind the school was virtually lost in the haze. But once again the day began to brighten up around the time of the second hour and soon the sky was clear and the sun was beating down so that by noon it was as hot as any day in the middle of summer.

By early afternoon the teacher was having to wipe the sweat off his brow in front of the blackboard. It was so muggy that the year-four pupils doing their penmanship and the year-five and year-six pupils their drawing were all but dropping off with pencils in their hand.

They all filed down to the river right after class.

"Hey, Matasaburo," said Kasuke, walking in front of Saburo. "Wanna join us for a swim? These days everyone from the littlest up goes."

They weren't going where they went before. This time they went to a stream flowing off the right side of the river where there was quite a wide dry bed and further down a huge gleditsia tree grew out of the side of a cliff.

"Hey there!" hollered some half-naked little boys who had arrived before them, waving both their hands in the air.

Ichiro and the others ran like the wind through the silk trees on the dry riverbed and, in a flash, they had stripped down to their loin cloth and were splashing about in the water, crouching down and spurting water at each other, and lining up on an angle to swim to the other side. The boys who were there earlier swam after them. Saburo was the last to take off his clothes and get into the water. He swam for a bit then laughed out loud.

"Hey, Matasaburo," shouted Ichiro from the other bank, shivering with purple lips and slicking his hair down like a seal's, "what's so funny?"

"This water's freezing," said Saburo, shivering as he came out of water.

"So, what were you laughin' at, Matasaburo?" asked Ichiro for a second time.

"At the way you swam," said Saburo, now all giggles. "I mean, why do you slosh your legs around like that?"

"Hey, huh?" said Ichiro, feeling awkward, but then, picking up a white stone, adding, "Wanna play find-the-stone?"

"I do, I do," shouted all the children on the bank.

"Okay, so I'll go above where that tree is and drop it down."

Ichiro easily climbed halfway up the cliff to where the gleditsia was.

"Okay, it's comin' down. Ready, set, go!" he said, dropping the white stone with a splash into the deep pool in the river.

They all plunged headfirst into the river, each one determined to get to the stone first, diving right down to the bottom like bluish-white otters, aiming for the stone. But not all of them could make it to the bottom, and some had to come up for air, as a mist blew in waves over the river. Saburo had been closely watching the others dive down, and, after they returned to the surface in happy spirits, he himself plunged in, as four adults who had stripped to the waist by the silk trees on the far bank were coming toward him carrying a net.

"Hey, everyone, they're gonna be blasting!" hollered Ichiro in a low voice from his place just above where the tree was. "Pretend you didn't know but just leave the stone and get downriver right away!"

All of the children did their best to not look at the adults but still continued to pick up grindstones and chase wagtails, pretending not to be at all concerned about any blasting.

Shosuke, who was a miner downriver from there, peered about from the bank of the pool for a while then suddenly sat down on the pebbles and crossed his legs. He methodically took a tobacco pouch from around his waist, filled his long-stem pipe and smoked. He reached into his work vest and pulled out an object.

"They're gonna blast, they're gonna blast!" cried all the children.

But Ichiro waved his hands, gesturing for them to stop screaming. Shosuke put the little bowl of his pipe to the object, as a man behind him entered the water to prepare the net. Shosuke, as calm as could be, rose and, with one foot in the water, flung the object to a point in the river right below the gleditsia tree. At that there was an awful boom, the water there swelled up and for a time a ringing sound lingered in the air. That's when the other adults got into the water.

"They're floatin' past. Grab 'em!" said Ichiro.

Kosuke grabbed a brown sculpin the size of a pinkie that was floating belly up down the river, and right behind him Kasuke with a beet-red face shouted like he was slurping melon when he snagged a carp about six inches long. All the other children were catching fish too, jumping up and down in the water with glee.

"Pipe down, pipe down!" said Ichiro.

Several adults, some with shirts on and some without, came running from the bleached dry riverbed, and a man in a see-through shirt came galloping bareback headlong toward them, just like in the movies. The adults were attracted by the explosion.

"Slim pickin's," said Shosuke, folding his arms over his chest and looking at the fish that the children were gripping onto.

"You can have these back," said Saburo, standing next to Shosuke and putting two medium-size carp on the ground for throwing back into the river.

"Who's this kid, eh? Some weirdo?" said Shosuke, staring Saburo up and down.

Saburo went back to the others without saying anything. Shosuke gave him a dirty look and all the others just laughed. Then Shosuke went upriver and the other adults followed him, including the man in the see-through shirt, who was still on horseback. Kosuke swam to the place where Saburo had put the two fish down and brought them back to where the other children were, and they all had a good laugh.

"Let's scatter the small fry!" shouted Kasuke, hopping up and down on the sandbar.

They all made a little circular tank with rocks in the shallow water to keep the fish alive and from swimming away, then ran to the cliff face and started to climb up to the gleditsia tree. The sun was blazing hot now, the silk trees looked all droopy like they did in the middle of summer, and the sky was like a bottomless pool.

"Oh no, someone's bustin' up our fish tank!" shouted one of the children.

Sure enough, a man with a weirdly pointy nose, dressed in a suit and straw sandals, was stirring up the fish with what looked like a stick. Then he started to slosh his way right along the bank toward the boys.

"He's from the Monopoly Bureau, the Monopoly Bureau," said Sataro.

"Hey, Matasaburo," said Kasuke, "he's come to get you for rippin' off that tobacco leaf."

"So what, I'm not scared," said Saburo, biting down on his lip.

"Let's all surround Matasaburo," said Ichiro. "Make a circle around him."

They all sat in a circle on the branches of the gleditsia tree with Saburo on a branch in the middle.

"He's here, he's here!"

They held their breath. But the man apparently didn't have his sights on Saburo at all and just walked right past them, stepping into the shallows next to the pool. He stopped in the middle of the river and walked back and forth, washing the dirt off his sandals and cloth leggings. The children felt less anxious about him but didn't take to him at all.

"I'm gonna yell first," said Ichiro, "and then I want you all to yell on my count. Got it? 'Don't dirty up the river! We'll tell our teacher on you!' Okay … one, two, three!"

"DON'T DIRTY UP THE RIVER! WE'LL TELL OUR TEACHER ON YOU!"

The man looked their way and spoke but the children couldn't catch what he said.

Once again they screamed out what they had screamed out before.

"You people here drink this water, do you?" said the man with the pointy nose, pursing his lips like someone puffing out cigarette smoke.

"Don't dirty up the river! We'll tell our teacher on you!"

"So, a man's not allowed to walk in the river, huh?" he said, a bit miffed.

"Don't dirty up the river! We'll tell our teacher on you!"

The man continued to ford the river at a leisurely pace, as if to hide the fact that he was somewhat rattled, then climbed up the blue clay and red pebble bluff on an angle, just like an Alpine mountain climber, disappearing into the tobacco field above.

"What's the big deal?" said Saburo. "He wasn't here to get me at all."

Saburo jumped straight off the branch, splashing into the pool, and all the others followed one by one, feeling both a little sorry for the man and Saburo but also a little drained inside. They swam to the dry riverbed, wrapped the fish in hand towels and took them home.

The next morning all the children were having fun in the yard before class, hanging off the bars and playing hide-the-stick. Sataro arrived a bit late, carrying a basket with something in it.

"What'cha got? What'cha got?" said all the children, rushing up to him and peeking into the basket.

Sataro put his sleeve over the top of the basket and hurried off to the cave in the rock behind the school. The children ran after him. Ichiro took one look in the basket and turned as white as a ghost. Sataro was carrying prickly-ash powder for poisoning and killing fish, and, like blasting them, you can get arrested for using that. After hiding it in the weeds by the cave, Sataro went back to the yard without a care in the world. And that's all the children talked about in whispers until it was time for class.

By about ten o'clock it was as hot as blazes like the day before. All the children could think about was the end of the school day. When the fifth hour was finished at two, they all flew out of there. Sataro went back to furtively covering the top of his basket with his sleeve, followed by Kosuke, as they all traipsed down to the dry riverbed. Saburo went with Kasuke. They brushed past the silk trees that were giving off a fusty smell, like gas at a town festival, till they got to the cliff face by the pool where the gleditsia tree was.

An immense bank of summer cloud was towering over the eastern horizon and the gleditsia tree was shining blue. They all quickly slipped out of their clothes and stood by the side of the pool.

"Stand in a straight line, okay?" said Sataro, looking right into Ichiro's eyes. "If you see a fish floatin' up, swim out and grab it. Just catch it, that's all. Got it?"

The little children were jumping with joy and, with bright red faces, they pushed and shoved each other to get a good place around the pool. Pekichi and a few of the others were already in the water waiting at a spot below the gleditsia tree. Sataro, totally pleased with himself, went to the shallows upriver and dipped the basket in the water over and over again, as they all stared into the pool in silence. Saburo was not looking at the water at all but had set his sight on a black bird that was flying over the bank of cloud. As for Ichiro, he was plopped down on the dry riverbed knocking rocks together. But no matter how much time passed not a single fish came floating up to the surface.

Sataro stood straight up and down peering into the water with a very serious expression on his face. They had all seen about ten fish floating up after the blasting the day before and continued to wait there without saying a word for the same thing to happen. But again, not one fish showed up on the surface.

"They're just not floatin' up, are they," shouted Kosuke.

Sataro gave a start, but it didn't stop him from peering constantly into the water.

"Not even one's there," said Pekichi from below the tree.

They all began gabbing away and jumping into the pool.

"How about playin' tag?" said Sataro, crouching by the side of the water and feeling pretty ashamed of himself.

"Yeah, let's play!" they all said, raising their hand in scissors or rock or paper out of the water to decide who goes first, with those in water too deep to stand swimming to a shallower place so they could join in.

Ichiro came from the dry riverbed and put his hand up too. He set the blue soggy clay place under the bluff that the weird man with the pointy nose had climbed up as the home base. If you got to there before the person who was "it" did, you were safe. Anyone who got tagged before was "it." Etsuji lost and was made "it" by everyone. Etsuji ran about the dry riverbed until his lips turned purple. He touched Kisaku and now there were two who were "it." They all ran helter-skelter over the sandbar and around the pool, tagging and being tagged by each other. In the end, Saburo too became "it." He soon caught up with Kichiro, as all the others looked on from home base below the tree.

"Kichiro," said Saburo, "you should chase everyone from upriver. You understand?"

Kichiro opened his mouth, spread his arms out and chased

everyone over the blue clay earth. They all got ready to jump into the pool, except for Ichiro, who climbed up a willow tree. But Kichiro's feet had got all muddied in the clay and he slipped and tumbled down in front of everyone. They all yelled and screamed as they hurdled over Kichiro and plunged into the water or dashed for home base.

"Matasaburo, get over here!" said Kasuke with his mouth wide open and his arms outstretched, trying to fool him.

"If that's how you're going to play," said Saburo, clearly angered, "just watch me."

Saburo was determined this time. He splashed right into the water and swam with all his might toward Kasuke. His red hair splashed around and his lips turned purple from being in the water, so much so that all the other children were alarmed. For one thing, the place that was set as home base was much too cramped for all of them to get to safety there and the ground was like a slippery plate. Four or five children below had to hold onto someone above or they would slip and plop right into the pool. Only Ichiro, who was at the highest point, was calm and collected. The others were involved in a discussion, wracking their brain as to what to do. Saburo, kicking and splashing, was getting close to them.

They were all huddled together whispering to each other when Saburo started splashing them with both his arms. They did their best to flap their arms about trying to keep dry, but the wet clay started to slip and slide down, falling apart as it did. Saburo sent even more sheets of water their way.

The result was that they all came tumbling down with the clay. Saburo did his best to catch some of them and Ichiro pitched in too. Only Kasuke went around to the river and swam away. Saburo swam after him and caught him, grabbing his arms and pulling him around several times. But it looked like Kasuke was choking. He had swallowed a lot of water and was trying to spray some out of his mouth.

"I've had enough," he said. "I'm not goin' play tag anymore."

All the littler children jumped onto the pebbles. Saburo remained alone under the gleditsia tree.

All of a sudden the sky was filled with black clouds, the willow tree shone strangely white, and the grasses and weeds on the mountains dimmed and darkened. Everything they could see had taken on an indescribably terrifying air. Soon thunder was rumbling about the fields on the mountains, where what sounded like a landslide was in progress, a sudden shower was drenching them and the wind was whistling and whirring in the air. The water in the pool started whirling around ferociously and you couldn't tell the waves from the rocks.

All the children picked up their clothes from the dry riverbed and started to run under the silk trees. Even Saburo seemed scared for the first time. He jumped into the water where the gleditsia tree was and started to swim in their direction. Then … they all heard someone say …

Rain, pitter-patter, Rain-Saburo
Wind, howl-bellow, Mata-Saburo

And they all joined in …

Rain, pitter-patter, Rain-Saburo
Wind, howl-bellow, Mata-Saburo

Matasaburo was in a panic. He jumped right out of the pool as if something was pulling down on his leg and ran for dear life, shivering and trembling, to where the others were.

"Is it you who just shouted out now?" he asked.

"Not us, no, not us," they all cried in unison.

"Not us," said Pekichi, stepping out.

Saburo, feeling really awkward and uncomfortable, looked back at the river, tightening his pale lips as he always did.

"What's going on?" he said, shaking as before.

All the children went to their home until they thought it had cleared up.

Howl and thunder ... howl roar HOWL!
Wind, blow off the fresh-green walnuts
Wind, blow off the sour quinces
Howl and thunder ... howl roar HOWL!
Howl and thunder ... howl roar HOWL!

Ichiro heard that very same song in a dream that he had heard Saburo sing. He bolted up, startled, to find the wind raging ferociously outside, the forest virtually roaring, and the whole house, from the paper sliding doors to the lantern box on the shelf, bathed in the pale blue light of the dawn sky. He quickly tied his belt, slipped into his clogs and stepped off the dirt floor outside and into the stable. When he opened a side door, the wind, reeking of rain, rushed in. A back door of the stable thudded down loudly and the horses were snorting up a storm.

Ichiro felt that the wind had made its way right into his heart, and he blew out a rush of breath and dashed outside, where it was already bright and the earth was soaked through. The chestnut trees all in a row in front of the house were strangely glowing pale blue, buffeted and tossed about, as if being washed and wrung out by the windy rain.

The earth was strewn with countless fresh green leaves and burrs that had been ripped from the blue-green chestnut trees, and the clouds, grey and foreboding in the light, were being carried at great speed northward. The forest in the distance was roaring like a raging sea. Ichiro stood fast, gazing up at the sky and listening to it all as his face was being battered by the cold rain, and it seemed as if his clothes were about to be torn right off him.

He felt waves rippling through him and his heart started drumming and thumping as he watched and listened to the rushing wind groan and roar. The wind that had once been placid as it passed, lucid, over the hills and the fields below the sky had now in the dawn moved onto another plain as that sky coursed rapidly toward the northern edge of the Tuscarora Deep. Ichiro's face flushed feverishly, his breath caught in his throat and he felt as if he too was sailing with that wind over the sky. He rushed back into the house and only when there was he able to heave his chest and breathe out.

"Ah, this is a terrifying wind," said his grandfather, standing by the side door and peering into the sky. "With a wind like this, the tobacco plants and the chestnuts have had it."

Ichiro ran to the well, filled a bucket with water and went to the kitchen to mop and clean it up. Then he got out a metal basin and scrubbed his face, took some cold rice and miso from the cupboard and wolfed it down like there was no tomorrow.

"Ichiro, miso soup'll be ready in a jiffy so why don't you wait a minute," said his mother putting logs into the stove to make feed for the horses. "What's the rush to get to school this morning?"

"Uh, Matasaburo might be in the air."

"What's Matasaburo, some bird or something?"

"Uh, he's a boy named Matasaburo," said Ichiro, swallowing down the last mouthful of rice, washing up the bowl and, putting on a rain-proof jacket that he took down from a hook in the kitchen, darting barefoot over to Kasuke's house with his clogs in his hands.

"I'll just eat a quick breakfast," said Kasuke, who had only then woken up.

Ichiro was waiting for him by the stable when Kasuke came out with a little straw rain cape over him. The two of them were soaked to the bone by the fierce windy rain by the time they reached school. They went in by the side entrance, but the classroom was deserted. Rain had made its way in through gaps in the windows and the floorboards were covered in a slippery film of water.

"Kasuke," said Ichiro, looking around, "let's sweep away the water together."

He got hold of a hemp-palm broom and started sweeping the water into cracks in the floor below the windows. They heard someone come in and saw the teacher, who, for some inexplicable reason, was wearing a single unlined garment and held a red fan in his hand.

"You boys are here early," he said. "Are you cleaning the classroom for us?"

"Good morning, teacher," said Ichiro.

"Good morning, teacher," said Kasuke, immediately adding, "Is Matasaburo coming to school today?"

"When you say Matasaburo, do you mean Takada Saburo?" he asked, after a short pause. "Well, he went with his father somewhere else yesterday. As it was a Sunday, he didn't have time to go around and tell everybody he was going."

"Sir, did he fly away?" asked Kasuke.

"No. His father received a telegram from his company headquarters to go. He plans, it seems, to return here but his son will be going to a school over there from now on. That's where his mother is, for one thing."

"Why was he called away by his company?" asked Ichiro.

"It seems that the vein of molybdenum here is not ready to be mined for some time."

"That can't be true," shrieked Kasuke. "It's because that boy was Matasaburo, the boy of the winds!"

Just then there was a clatter coming from the night-duty-man's room, and the teacher, holding his red fan, rushed into it.

Ichiro and Kasuke just stood there in silence for some time, staring into each other's eyes, as if seeking to read the other's thoughts.

The windows continued to rattle away, clouded over in raindrops sent by a wind that wasn't about to stop.

The Wildcat and the Acorns

This is a simple story and one of Kenji's earliest. The hero is, as in many of Kenji's stories, a little boy who goes on a journey, in this case one prompted by the receipt of a postcard sent by a wildcat. Wildcats are native to Japan but generally associated with the southern parts of the country rather than Kenji's native Tohoku. In general they are exotic animals for the Japanese. As for acorns, they are everywhere in Japan, even making it into an expression known to all Japanese, "like comparing the length of acorns," which means "there's not much to choose between (them)" or "much of a muchness." Ichiro is intrigued by the postcard's message, especially by what the wildcat could mean by "troublesome."

Right off the bat there is a lucid (or, more literally, transparent) wind that sends chestnuts scattering here and there, a sure sign in a Kenji story that there is more afoot than what meets the eye. Personification of nature abounds here; and it is not only animals that can speak but also trees, mushrooms and a waterfall. (The mushrooms have even formed a band.) Some of the onomatopoeia that Kenji applies to natural phenomena are those that might normally apply to people. He makes no distinction in his world. In our Judeo-Christian world it is only humans who possess a soul. In Kenji's world humans are no different, neither higher nor lower, than any other thing in nature. In fact humans are often taught valuable lessons by other forms of nature; so it could be concluded that we are not as intelligent, and that the notion of intelligence itself needs to be redefined. Kenji alludes to this when Ichiro tells the wildcat judge that "the greatest ones here are the stupidest, the most confused and the ones who've got the longest way to go. I once heard someone who preached that." I believe that Kenji is referring to himself, in a little self-reflexive joke, when he refers to the person who preached that. In his poem "Strong in the Rain" he comes right out and says that the kind of person he wants to be is the one people call "Blockhead."

Kenji harbored an innate disdain for pomposity, conceit and those who flaunted their wealth in order to wield power over the weak and defenseless. This and the inner drive to negate it came from his childhood.

The Miyazawas were one of the richest families in Iwate prefecture and major landowners. Kenji's father, Masajiro, owned and operated a pawn shop, where he also dealt in old clothing. In the more remote regions of Japan, banks did not maintain a significant presence. Iwate was a poor agrarian prefecture. Pawnbrokers provided ready cash to farmers, who would come into the Miyazawa shop with whatever they possessed of value. As a little boy Kenji watched this and nurtured a guilty conscience and a compassionate ardor for helping the miserable farmers as best as he could. This ardor was the impetus for him becoming an agronomist and runs, in the form of a number of themes, through all of his written work.

The Japanese name for Flute Blowing Falls is Fue-fuki-no-taki. Kenji created this by modifying the name of a real waterfall called Fue-nuki-no-taki. The *nuki* is the same character in the old name for the district in which Kenji lived, namely Hienuki (see page 209). It is said that the name of the falls preceded that of the district and that the latter took its name from the former. The water in these falls comes out of a row of seven holes of various sizes in the boulders. The holes are lined up like those in a flute.

"The Wildcat and the Acorns" was made into an anime film of

twenty-five minutes' length and released on 30 September 1988. It was created by the anime production house Mad House, the same animators who made the full-length animated version of "The Diary of Anne Frank" for which Michael Nyman composed the music and I wrote the screenplay in 1995.

Playwright and novelist Inoue Hisashi (see page 250) wrote in an issue of his theater troupe's magazine "the Za" in 1986 that "The Wildcat and the Acorns" was the first book he ever bought with his own money. The price was seven yen and fifty sen. I'm not sure which edition of this Chuo Koronsha "Tomodachi Bunko" story he bought, but my guess, from the price, is that it was the second edition in 1946, before Hisashi turned twelve. He said of this story: "It taught me how to form a relationship with nature."

THE WILDCAT AND THE ACORNS

by Miyazawa Kenji

A weird postcard arrived at Ichiro's home one Saturday evening.

To Master Ichiro Kaneta The 19th of September
I trust that you are in high spirits.
I am conducting a troublesome trial tomorrow
so please be present. Kindly leave all weapons
at home.
Yours truly, Wildcat

That was all. The handwriting was as clumsy as it gets. The ink was all patchy and smeary, as if made from charcoal and glue, and it looked like it was sure to get all over your fingers. But that didn't bother Ichiro one bit. He was beside himself with glee. He slipped the postcard into his school bag and jumped for joy around the house.

Even after snuggled into his futon, all he could think about was the wildcat's face doing a big meow and what a troublesome trial would look like. He thought so much that he couldn't fall asleep until the wee hours of the morning.

So, it was all bright by the time he woke up and he went right outside. The surrounding mountains were drippy and dewy, rising, as if they too just got up, into a pure blue sky. Ichiro wolfed down his breakfast and started off toward the north, up a trail running along a mountain stream.

A translucent gust of wind was sending chestnuts on a chestnut tree sailing in all directions.

"Chestnut tree, chestnut tree," said Ichiro, looking up, "you didn't see a wildcat pass by here, did you?"

The chestnut tree became still for a moment.

"Wildcat?" replied the chestnut tree. "Yeah, one definitely flew by here in a carriage early this morning, heading east."

"Oh, that's just where I'm heading too, east. That's weird. Anyway, I'll go a bit further and have a look. Thank you, chestnut tree!"

And once again the chestnut tree stood still, silently strewing its nuts about the ground.

It was not at all long before Ichiro found himself at Flute Blowing Falls. Now, Flute Blowing Falls is where water gushes out of little holes in the middle of a pure white rock cliff, whistling like a flute before roaring down as a waterfall into the valley below.

"Hey, Flute Blowing Falls, you didn't see a wildcat pass by here, did you?" hollered Ichiro up to the waterfall.

"A wildcat flew by here in a carriage going west just a little while ago," whistled the waterfall.

"That's weird. West's back toward my home. Anyway, I'll go a bit further and have a look. Thank you, Flute Blowing Falls."

And the water resumed its whistling down the falls.

It wasn't long before Ichiro found himself under a beech tree where lots of white mushrooms had formed an offbeat little band, tooting and honking away for all they were worth.

"Hey, mushrooms, you didn't see a wildcat pass by here, did you?" asked Ichiro, bending down.

"Wildcat?" replied the mushrooms. "Yeah, one definitely flew by here in a carriage early this morning, heading south."

Ichiro twisted around.

"That'd take you right into those mountains. That's weird. Anyway, I'll go a bit further and have a look. Thank you, mushrooms."

And all the mushrooms went on tooting and honking in their offbeat little band.

Ichiro soon came to a walnut tree, where a squirrel was hopping among its topmost branches.

"Hey, squirrel, you didn't see a wildcat pass by here, did you?" asked Ichiro, waving his hand until the squirrel stopped hopping.

"Wildcat?" said the squirrel, looking down from the treetop at

Ichiro with its paw against its forehead. "Yeah, one flew by here in a carriage before the sun came up, heading south."

"That makes two who said he was heading south. That's weird. Anyway, I'll go a bit further and have a look. Thank you, squirrel."

But the squirrel was nowhere to be seen. All you could see was the swaying of the topmost branches of the walnut tree and the leaves of the beech beside it flickering and glittering.

As Ichiro went farther, the trail that ran along the mountain stream narrowed until it disappeared altogether. There he found a new little track leading south from the stream into a pitch-black nutmeg-yew forest. He took that track until it turned into a frighteningly steep rising slope where the branches of the nutmeg-yew trees were so overlapping and intertwining that you couldn't see so much as a sliver of blue sky between them.

Ichiro made his way up the slope. His sweat was dripping off his beet-red face. Then out of the blue everything went all bright, and his eyes twinged. Before him lay a beautiful golden-yellow grassland. The tall grasses, surrounded by a dense forest of olive-colored nutmeg-yew trees, rustled and swished.

A short and oddly shaped man was kneeling smack in the middle of the grassland. He held a leather whip in his hand and was staring silently in Ichiro's direction. Ichiro was more and more astonished as he gingerly approached the man and stood before him. One of the man's eyes was white, blinking with a nervous twitch, and he wore what looked like a funny cross between a Western jacket and a Japanese livery coat. Above all, his legs were crooked like a goat's and his feet were as flat as spatulas. Ichiro did his best to keep an eerie feeling inside him.

"Do you happen to have seen a wildcat?" he asked calmly.

The man looked at Ichiro out of the corner of his eye.

"The wildcat will be hightailin' it right back here before you can say jack rabbit," he said with a smirk. "You'd be Ichiro, ain't you?"

"Uh-huh, I'm Ichiro," said Ichiro, taken aback and stepping back a step. "But, how do you know that?"

"Right, so you got the postcard then, didn't ya," said the curious little man, grinning from ear to ear.

"I did. That's why I'm here right now."

"It was written pretty ungrammatical, I guess," said the man, peering sadly at the ground.

"Well," said Ichiro, feeling sorry for the man, "I'd actually say that the style was pretty polished."

The man perked up at this and, panting as if out of breath, turned bright red right up to the back of his ears. He opened the collar of his jacket to let the wind cool him down.

"And didya find the penmanship up to scratch?"

"Pretty polished penmanship, I'd say," replied Ichiro, his lips growing into a smile. "I mean, not even somebody in year five could write as good as that."

"Year five?" said the man in a miserably feeble voice, once again looking like a sourpuss. "You mean like someone in year five in grammar school?"

"No, no … I mean like somebody in year five at university!"

Once again the man perked up no end, his face beaming with a smile that all but covered his entire face.

"It's me who wrote that postcard, y'know," he chortled loudly.

"So, who on earth are you?" said Ichiro, stifling a laugh.

"Why, I'm in charge of Mr. Wildcat's carriage, that's who."

Just then the wind roared around them, the tall grasses waved like a choppy sea, and the little odd man promptly bowed politely to Ichiro.

Ichiro turned about, feeling that this was all a bit too weird for words. Behind him stood the wildcat, donned in what looked like a sleeveless yellow battle jacket. He had googly green eyes and, as you would expect, a wildcat's straight pointy ears. He bobbed his head in a bow to Ichiro.

"Oh, good day," said Ichiro, as politely as he could. "Thank you for the postcard which I received yesterday."

"Good day," said the wildcat, pulling on his taut whiskers and thrusting out his belly. "It's kind of you to come. To tell you the truth, a most troublesome dispute has cropped up since the day before yesterday and we are in somewhat of a pickle with the trial, and I was anxious to get your opinion on it. For now, please take a short breather. The acorns will be here posthaste. Ah, every year I have to put up with the same trial and it's driving me mad."

The wildcat took a box of cigarettes out of an inside pocket and slipped a cigarette into his mouth.

"Want one?" he asked, offering a cigarette to Ichiro.

"Uh, no thank you," replied Ichiro, somewhat startled.

"Hmmm," said the wildcat with a big toothy smile, "sure, you're not old enough."

At that he struck a match and blew out a puff of blue smoke with a firm frown on his face. The little odd man in charge of the carriage stood to attention and, stifling his desire to have one of the wildcat's cigarettes, sobbed like a baby.

It was then that Ichiro heard a crackling noise at his feet, like big grains of salt grating against each other. He crouched down, wondering what could be making the noise, and saw glittering round golden-yellow objects scattered throughout the grass. On closer look they were acorns sporting red trousers. There had to be over three hundred of them, all blabbing and squealing about something or other.

"Ah, they're here already," said the wildcat to the little odd man in charge of his carriage, tossing aside his cigarette. "They're coming toward us like ants. Hey, so, ring the bell, quick! Cut down that grass over here! It's going to be sunny today."

The man in charge of the wildcat's carriage took ahold of a big sickle that was attached to his belt and chopped away at the tall grass in front of the wildcat. The acorns rushed out of the surrounding grass into the clearing, gleaming and glinting, blabbing and squealing.

The man now rang a big bell. Its clashing and clanging echoed throughout the nutmeg-yew forest so resoundingly that the golden-yellow acorns were all but silenced. And in the blink of an eye the wildcat, now decked in long black robes, took a seat in front of the acorns with a highly pompous air. It looked to Ichiro like a picture of pilgrims gathered in the presence of the Great Buddha at Nara. The man in charge of the wildcat's carriage snapped and cracked his leather whip a few times. The gleaming and glinting acorns composed a truly beautiful picture below the perfectly clear blue sky.

"Now, we've come to day three of the trial, so why don't you all do the right thing and make up," said the wildcat with a mixture of concern and dignified pride in his voice. But this didn't stop the acorns from clamoring.

"Out of the question! We acorns with the pointy heads are the greatest of all. And I'm the pointiest of the pointy here!"

"Rubbish! We round ones are the greatest of all. And the roundest of the round is none other than me!"

"It's size that counts. We biggest ones are the greatest of all. And since I'm the biggest of the big, I'm the greatest here!"

"You must be kidding! Just yesterday the judge judged me to be the biggest here."

"Ridiculous! It's length that counts. It's how long you are that decides who's the greatest."

"It's the one who wrestles best that's best. Let's wrestle and see who wins."

They went on and on like that, jabbering and prattling away, like a hive of buzzing bees that someone had poked into, until you couldn't make hide nor hair of what they were trying to say.

"Silence!" screamed the wildcat, fed up with the racket. "Do you realize where you are? Order! Order!"

The little odd man in charge of the wildcat's carriage snapped and cracked his whip until the acorns fell silent.

"Again, we are already into our third day of this trial," said the wildcat, tweaking his whiskers. "Don't you think it's high time for you all to bury the hatchet?"

"No, no, no way! We pointy ones are …"

And the raucous buzzing went on and on like that.

"Silence!" shrieked the wildcat. "What do you take this place for, eh? Order! Order!"

The little odd man snapped and cracked his whip again until the acorns said no more.

"You see what I have to put up with," he said, softly, turning to Ichiro. "Can you tell me what I should do here?"

"In that case," said Ichiro, smiling, "how about passing down this judgement? The greatest ones here are the stupidest, the most confused and the ones who've got the longest way to go. I once heard someone who preached that."

The wildcat nodded with satisfaction and, affecting a most prim and proper air, parted the lapels of his robes, revealing a strip of his yellow battle jacket.

"That settles it," he said to the acorns. "Silence, please. You may have my judgement. The ones among you who are the stupidest, the most confused, who've got the longest way to go and whose heads have been cracked open … you're the greatest of all!"

A hush came over the acorns. Not one of them was budging an inch. The wildcat removed his black robes, wiped the sweat off his brow and took Ichiro's hand in his paw. The little odd man in charge of the wildcat's carriage snapped and cracked his whip several times until the air crackled around it.

"I thank you from the bottom of my heart," said the wildcat to Ichiro. "In a minute and a half you managed to wrap up this very thorny case. I would be grateful if you would consider being an honorary judge of my court. Do you think you could come here whenever you receive a postcard? If you do, I will give you a token of my gratitude."

"I agree to your request," said Ichiro. "But I am unable to accept gifts."

"I ask you, please accept a token of my gratitude. That is the kind of wildcat I am. Henceforth, I shall address postcards to 'Master Ichiro Kaneta', and, by your leave, I would be most pleased if you would grace this court with your presence."

"Yeah, that's okay," said Ichiro.

The wildcat tweaked and twisted his whiskers, as if he was mulling over something he dearly wanted to say.

"And, in addition to that," he finally said resolutely, blinking his eyes over and over again, "as for the wording of the postcard, henceforth it shall state: 'Your presence is humbly requested on the morrow.' How would you like that, eh?"

"Well," said Ichiro, smiling again, "it strikes me as a bit over the top. I'd rather not get a notice like that."

For a while the wildcat just tweaked and twisted his whiskers while staring at the ground, as if he really regretted saying something that left a bad taste in Ichiro's mouth.

"In that case," he said, accepting the situation, "I shall retain the previous wording. Now to the token of my gratitude. Which would you prefer, a two-kilogram box of golden acorns or the head of a salted salmon?"

"I prefer the golden acorns."

The wildcat seemed relieved that Ichiro had not chosen the salmon head and barked a swift order to the little odd man.

"Bring me a box of acorns right now! If there aren't enough golden ones to make up two kilograms, mix in some gold-plated ones. Now, shake a leg!"

The man gathered up the acorns that were there and weighed them.

"It comes to exactly two kilograms!" he shouted.

The wildcat's sleeveless battle jacket flapped loudly in the wind.

"Good," he said, stretching in all directions and half-stifling a yawn with closed eyes. "Get my carriage ready immediately." The little odd man in charge of the wildcat's carriage produced a carriage made from a huge white mushroom pulled by funny-looking light-grey horses.

"Well then, I shall take you to your home," said the wildcat.

The two of them climbed into the carriage, while the little odd man put the box of acorns on a seat beside them.

The carriage sailed and soared, cutting through the tall grasses of the grassland. The woods and the groves trembled and whirled as if their trees were made solely of smoke. Ichiro kept his eyes on the golden-yellow acorns, while the wildcat stared wildly into the distance, looking as if butter wouldn't melt in his mouth.

But as the carriage made its way ahead, the acorns gradually lost their shine, turning a garden-variety brown by the time it came to a stop. And as for the wildcat's sleeveless yellow battle jacket and the man in charge of the wildcat's carriage and the mushroom carriage itself, they all vanished in a flash into thin air, and Ichiro found himself standing in front of his home with a box of acorns in his hands.

After that, he never received a postcard signed "Yours truly, Wildcat."

Ichiro thought, from time to time, that in the end he really should have told the wildcat that it was all right to write, "Your presence is humbly requested…."

The Wild Pear

Children in Japan generally read "The Wild Pear" in their year-six school textbooks. This is a fascinating choice, for there is much that is puzzling and inexplicable about this story.

This is one of the very few stories that Kenji published in a newspaper or periodical during his lifetime. It appeared in the "Iwate Mainichi Shinbun" (not affiliated with the national Mainichi) on 8 April 1923.

One of those puzzling aspects is the names used in the story. There are at least nine authoritative explanations given for the origin of the name Clambon. Theses have been written on the subject. It has also bothered many scholars and ardent fans of Kenji's literature that there is no sign of the crab mother, especially disconcerting to some because Kenji was so close to his mother and she always protected him against his hard-headed martinet father.

Almost all transliterate the name with an "r" as Crambon. This is because the name may have derived from the word "crab" or, perhaps, from the ice cleat that acts as a traction device on a shoe or boot to assist those climbing in ice or snow, a crampon. But either "r" or "l" are possible, and I prefer the latter, not only for its sound but also because the first syllable denotes another animal that lives in the water. The pear here is the so-called Chinese white pear, native to northern China, quite juicy, whitish yellow in color and shaped more like a Western pear than a nashi. In Japanese it is called an *iwateyamanashi*, or "Iwate wild pear", or a *koringo* (literally, small apple); while in China, its name is written with the characters for "duck" and "pear," for its resemblance to a mallard. The fascinating thing about this plant is that it is also called "Siebold's crab." (The crab name in Siebold's crab derives from "crab apple.") Philipp Franz von Siebold was the remarkable nineteenth-century Bavarian physician and botanist who collected, studied and classified thousands of Japanese animals and plants. I believe that Kenji was inspired by Siebold's name of this wild pear to write the story.

The opening line refers to the color blue, the most often used color in all Kenji's works. He even opens his poetry collection *Spring and Ashura* with the lines …

The phenomenon called I
Is a single blue illumination
Of a presupposed organic alternating current lamp

Blue is the color of the sky, which itself is a space between this world and that. Bear in mind that all things can transmigrate on this two-way celestial street. The use of the word *aoi*, which means "blue," is complicated for the translator by the fact that it also can correspond to "green" in English. A green traffic light in English is an aoi one in Japanese. So sometimes this may be translated blue-green or greenish or, in the case of young leaves or shoots, fresh green. If all words meant the same in every language, then I would gladly give up my role to my artificially intelligent counterpart. They may beat a human at the board game go, but they'd be a dead duck in the water in translating Miyazawa Kenji.

The blue flames emitted on the ceiling of the river (the inside surface) tell of the transience of all life, be it plant—in this case the wild pear—or animal. The pear will become sweet wine, attesting to natural and positive transformation. Not that Kenji enjoyed sweet or any other kind of wine. He was a teetotaller all his life, though I have been told by people who knew him that he did, on the odd occasion, steal away and down a glass of cider. Even those we have come to consider saints have their innocent vices.… The two months themselves—May and December—symbolize the seasons of things coming to life and those things departing it.

THE WILD PEAR
by Miyazawa Kenji

This is a picture from a little mountain stream bed as seen through a blue magic lantern.

ONE MAY

Two crab brothers were chatting away on the bed under pale-blue water.

"Clambon laughed!"

"Clambon was all bubbles!"

"Clambon spattered and splashed when he laughed!"

"Clambon was all bubbles!"

Everything above and to the sides of them looked dark and steely blue.

Darkish foam trembled as it flowed along the velvety ceiling.

"Clambon was really laughing."

"Clambon was all frothy."

"So why on earth was Clambon laughing?"

"Search me."

The foam was still trembling as it flowed. The crab brothers continued to bubble away, sending froth into the water. The froth rolled as it rose on an angle, gleaming like mercury.

In a flash a fish, flipping its silver belly up, passed over their head.

"Clambon's died!"

"Clambon's been killed!"

"Clambon's dead and gone...."

"He was murdered!"

"So why on earth was he killed?" asked the elder crab brother, plonking two of his four right legs on his little brother's flat head.

"Beats me."

In the blink of an eye the fish was sailing back downstream.

"Clambon was laughing!"

"So he was."

A flash of light came out of the blue and, as it happens in a dream, the gold of a sunbeam streamed down through the water.

The shining net produced by the ripples swayed exquisitely as it stretched and contracted over the white rocks on the bed. Shadows cast by the wavy net and speckles of dust formed perfectly straight slanted pillars in the water. The fish was making its way upstream, spluttering through the water's golden light, now flowing along in its steel-grey and iron-blue sheen.

"Why's the fish going back and forth like that?" asked the little brother crab, moving its eyes from the dazzle of light.

"He's being naughty an' he's catching something."

"Catching something."

"Uh-huh."

The fish returned from upstream. But now it came toward them slowly, calmly, moving neither fin nor tail, simply gliding through the water with its open mouth as round as a ring. Its shadow, black, slid silently over the bed's net of light.

"That fish is…."

That's when it happened. In the blink of an eye, the white foam ceiling stirred and something like a bullet, a glaring blue light, shot down through the water.

The elder brother crab definitely caught sight of something black and as sharp as a compass needle at the point of that blue light. In an instant the white belly of the fish flashed and flipped over, and it appeared to fly upward. But then neither the thing that flashed blue nor the fish were anywhere to be seen. The golden net just tossed and swayed, and froth bubbled in a flow.

The two brother crabs crouched and cowered on the bed without making a peep.

Their father showed up.

"What's up? You're both shaking like a leaf."

"Dad, something really weird was just here."

"What kind of thing?"

"It was blue and it was shiny too. Its tip was pointy and black. It just came and then the fish went straight up."

"Did it have red eyes?"

"Don't know."

"Hmmm. Well, it's definitely a bird. Called a kingfisher. It's okay. No need to get all worked up. It's nothing to do with us."

"Where did the fish go to, Dad?"

"The fish? The fish went to a scary place, that's where."

"I'm scared too, Daddy!"

"Forget about it. It's all fine. Nothing to worry about at all. Look, wild cherry blossom flowers are floating this way. See how lovely they are?" A slew of petals came gliding along the ceiling, encased in foam.

"I'm so scared, Daddy!" said the little brother crab.

The net of light swayed, stretching and contracting, as shadows cast by the petals slowly skated over the sand.

TWO   DECEMBER

The crab brothers had grown considerably and the lightscape on the bed of the river had changed markedly from summer through the autumn.

Smooth white round rocks had rolled onto the bed and crystal grains the shape of little drills and slivers of bronze mica had floated down and come to rest.

Lemonade-bottle moonlight shone transparent and crystal clear all the way down to the cold bed of the river, the pale-blue foam on the ceiling now burned like fire, now died out, and there was a hush all about, save for the sound of echoing ripples originating, seemingly, very far away.

The crab boys couldn't sleep a wink for the moon's brightness and the water's beauty, so they went out and just gazed up at the ceiling for a while, bubbling away in silence.

"My bubbles are bigger than yours," said the elder brother crab.

"That's because you're making them big on purpose. I could make my bubbles bigger if I wanted to."

"Okay, so let's see 'em. Eh, that the best you can do? Look here, watch your big brother. See? Pretty big, wouldn't you say?"

"You call that big? Same as mine."

"Yours just look big to you 'cause you're closer to 'em. All right, then, let's blow bubbles together. Ready, set, go!"

"Mine are bigger!"

"Bigger, are they? Okay, watch this one."

"That's not fair. It's no fair standing on tiptoes."

Their father showed up again.

"Time for bed now, boys. It's late. Or I won't take you to Isado tomorrow."

"Daddy, which one of us has the bigger bubbles?" asked the little brother crab.

"Your big brother's are bigger."

"No they're not. Mine're bigger!"

Just when the little crab was saying this on the verge of tears, something plopped into the water. It was big black and round, and it fell from the ceiling and sunk right down, but then bounced up again, giving off little golden specks that glistened in the water.

"It's the kingfisher!" said the crab brothers, ducking down.

The father crab bulged his eyes like binoculars as far out as they would go and peered intently upstream.

"Not this time," he said. "That was a wild pear. It's being taken by the stream. Let's follow it. Ah, smells like heaven!"

Sure enough, the heavenly scent of wild pear filled the moonlit water. The three crabs followed the wild pear as it skated over the bed of the river, their three black shadows dancing what looked like six dances, sidling sideways along the bed and chasing, hot on the heels, the shadow of the wild pear.

The water was soon babbling, the ripples on the ceiling emitted blue flames, the wild pear rolled over until caught in the branch of a tree, and knobbly rainbows of moonlight floated in clumps above it all.

"Didn't I tell ya? It's a wild pear an' really a ripe one too. Smells amazing, doesn't it?"

"It looks delicious, Dad."

"Hold your horses! In a couple of days it'll sink back down here and then it'll naturally turn into sweet wine. Now, let's be gettin' back home and to bed. Come along."

The father crab and his two crab boys went back to their burrow.

The ripples emitted pale-blue flames as they swayed and trembled, and they, in turn, seemed to be bubbling out the dust of diamonds.

This brings my magic lantern show to a close.

The Fire in the Opal

The Japanese title of this story, "Kai no Hi," translates literally as "Shell Fire" or "The Shell's Fire," the shell in this case being the kind found in the sea. But it is clear that Kenji was using the word "shell" as a time-related substitute for the opal.

From childhood Kenji was obsessed with rocks, so much so that his friends called him "Rocky Kenji." This obsession lasted his entire life. After all, rocks are time capsules that speak of the Earth's past and the many geological processes that went into forming its features. There is a museum dedicated to the rocks that feature in his literary works in the small town of Ichinoseki, some sixty kilometers south of Hanamaki. The museum's location is the old crushed stone and gravel factory where Kenji held his last job. (His last trip to Tokyo not long before he died was taken for the purpose of selling the crushed stone that the factory produced. He fell ill on the trip and had to return home early, and never really recovered after that.) The museum, also called "The House of Sun and Wind," carries, as a kind of preamble, this Kenji exhortation: "Prick up your ears, why don't you ... Ever so quietly, quietly ... You will hear the sound of the rocks whispering to you...."

Opals appear in his writing, as does the adjectival form of the word, "opaline." In his poem "A Fine View at the Laboratory" he writes ...

The snow's reflection and the poplar trees ...
And crossing the sky are opaline clouds
Or are they delicate slivers of ice?

Kenji, who delved deeply into the study of minerology and petrology, was well aware of both the opalescent beauty of this jewel and the attitudes and stories that have historically surrounded it. The opal is, paradoxically, eternally beautiful yet fragile in that beauty, considered in some countries as a stone of bad luck for the fickleness of its sheen and colors. It was Sir Walter Scott who related the jewel to dark forces in his 1829 novel *Anne of Geierstein*, in which a princess who adorned her hair with an opal comes to a tragic end when the stone is sprinkled with holy water. It seems, however, that Scott chose the opal merely for its lustre and did not believe that this jewel, as opposed to another, brought bad luck. It was only a chance detail, but the devil was, in this case, definitely in the detail. (Contrary to what may be generally thought, the British did not widely consider the opal as an omen of misfortune. Queen Victoria was very fond of opals and gifted them to her five daughters.) I bring up the reference to Scott because Kenji was an admirer of his literature, particularly of his poetry, from which he borrowed imagery.

I have called the magic jewel in the story the "Flame King Opal" after what is judged to be the world's most famous example of this gem, the "Flame Queen Opal," found in 1914 at Lightning Ridge in outback New South Wales, Australia. When viewed from one perspective, this "eye-of-opal" as it is known—so called when an opal in-fills a cavity—is a fiery red.

Though this story wasn't published in the collection that Kenji published during his lifetime and didn't appear in print until 1934, one year after his death, there is a record of him reading it to his students at the Hanamaki Agricultural School in November 1922. What they would have made of it was anybody's business.

The theme of the first part of the story centers on the virtue of self-sacrifice, the most important virtue in Kenji's mind. After all, it is through self-sacrifice that a human can achieve Enlightenment. This can take a rather gruesome form. The Buddha, in his birth as King Sibi, went so far as to gouge his eyes out in order to give them to a man who was blind. To Kenji, following on from this in some of his stories, giving your body for the sake of others is a major theme. The scorpion in *Night on the Milky Way Train* is a prime example. He would gladly set himself on fire if the heat and light could serve the wellbeing of others. The red star in the southern sky in "The Fire in the Opal" is, most certainly, Antares, the brightest star in Scorpio, a crossreference to the scorpion in *Night on the Milky Way Train*. One of the two main characters of that novel, Campanella, gives up his life in an attempt to save the life of another boy, and one, significantly, who is actually a bully.

Homoi's immediate and instinctive action that saves the life of the little skylark prompts the birds to bestow on him the reward of the jewel. He put his own life in danger and was almost washed away in the river. The name Homoi is Kenji's Esperanto version of the Latin word denoting the genus of primates of which we are the present-day representative, namely "Homo."

The second part of the story, however, finds Homoi all puffed up with himself. His conceit gets the better of him and seals his fate, insofar as the possession of the magic jewel is concerned. He foresees this in a dream, when he finds himself standing atop a mountain shaped like an ice pick. This is a not-so-clouded reference to a feature of the Buddhist hell, the mountain of needles that exists there to cause sinners to suffer.

Homoi's father seems like a decent chap and a kind parent. He accomplishes the good deed himself of freeing the birds. He admonishes Homoi for bringing stolen goods into the home. (The bread that grows on the "kitchen tree" is the sole symbol of a human presence in this story.) But it has puzzled Kenji scholars for decades as to why he eagerly consumes this contraband the next day. Perhaps he merely had a soft spot for white bread. Though it was introduced into Japan in the mid-sixteenth century by missionaries (hence the Japanese word for bread, *pan*, borrowed from Portuguese), it didn't become a popular food until the Meiji era. It was sold first in Yokohama and thought of as an exotic food eaten daily by nonJapanese. After all, the Japanese staple was rice, though the poorer people's staple was millet. The first Western-style bakery to appear in Kenji's region was in the capital of Iwate prefecture, Morioka, as early as 1885. Children in Kenji's time and hometown of Hanamaki, some forty-five kilometres from Morioka, would have considered bread a rare treat, as do the inhabitants of the humble rabbit hutch in this story.

THE FIRE IN THE OPAL

by Miyazawa Kenji

The rabbits all wore their short brown pants at this time of year. The grass in the meadow gleamed brightly and the sprinkling of wild cherry blossom trees were adorned in white flowers. The entire meadow gave off a truly fine fragrance. "Wow," said Homoi, the little boy rabbit, dancing and prancing around with glee, "that really smells good. Love it, just love it. And the lilies of the valley are all crisp and fresh!"

The leaves and flowers of the lilies of the valley were clinking together in the wind, tinkling little bells.

Homoi was beside himself with delight, so much so that he hopped as he sailed over the grass without stopping to take a breath. But then he stopped in his tracks.

"I guess I've got a real gift," he said, folding his arms on his chest and chuckling to himself. "I could just glide over the waves of a river."

And before he knew it he had come to the bank of a narrow stream where cold water was gurgling up and the sand on the bed was all aglitter.

"I guess I could just hop right over this river," he said to himself, cocking his head to one side. "Piece of cake. But the grass on the other side isn't good for me."

He heard shrill sounds coming from upstream, like trilling and chirping and twittering and warbling and cheeping, and he saw a scruffy dull black birdlike creature writhing and fluttering its wings as it flowed toward him. Homoi rushed to the bank to wait for it to reach him.

It certainly looked like it was a skinny little baby skylark floating toward him. Homoi plunged right into the water and grabbed hold of it with his front paws. But this seemed to frighten the daylights out of the skylark, who opened its yellow beak wide with a shriek so loud that it rang deafeningly in Homoi's ears.

"Everything's okay, you'll be fine," said Homoi, frantically paddling the water with his hind paws as hard as he could.

He held onto the skylark for dear life, almost letting go once. The bird's beak was very big for its face, and as for the face itself, it was all wrinkled up and bore a strong resemblance to a lizard's to boot.

But Homoi was a strong little rabbit and not about to let go of the skylark. His lips were clamped shut, if a bit askew, from the hair-raising task of getting the skylark to safety, but he managed to hold it tight and high above the water.

They were swept away together. Homoi was twice washed under and had swallowed a lot of water. And yet he didn't let go of that baby skylark for an instant. They came to a bend in the stream where a small willow branch was sticking out making little eddies of water that sloshed around it. Homoi quickly bit down on the branch, making a gash so deep that you could see the greenish inner bark, and flung the little skylark with all his might onto the soft grass on the bank. After that he made a big hop himself right out of the water.

The little skylark, its eyes as white as bone, lay plopped down on the bank, shaking and trembling. Homoi was so drained and sapped of strength that he felt wobbly on his legs, but he nonetheless managed to rip off some white flowers from the weeping willow and use them as a blanket for the skylark. The skylark lifted its grey head in thanks. But this sent a shudder down Homoi's spine and he sprung back and ran off, yelping.

In an instant something came shooting out of the sky, whistling like an arrow. Homoi stopped running away and looked back to see the mother skylark, herself shaking and trembling, silently embracing her child tightly with her wings. Homoi ran like the wind back to his father's house, relieved that the little skylark would be safe now.

Homoi's mother was making rows of little bundles of white grass.

"Oh good grief, what happened to you?" she said, startled, as she took the medicine box off the shelf. "You look like you've seen a ghost."

"Mummy," said Homoi, "I saved a scruffy little mangy little bird from drowning."

"Scruffy little mangy little bird, you say?" asked his mother, taking medicine powder out of the box and handing it to Homoi. "Was it a skylark?"

"Most likely, I think," said Homoi, taking the powder. "Oh no, I'm so dizzy. Everything looks so weird, Mummy."

And having said that, Homoi fell right into a little heap and was soon burning up with fever.

*

The lilies of the valley were decked with fresh green berries by the time Homoi had fully recovered, thanks to his father, mother and Dr. Coney. He went out the front door of the house for the first time on a tranquil cloudless evening. He was spellbound as he watched a red star angling across the southern sky, when suddenly he heard a flutter of wings and caught sight of two little birds descending toward him.

"Master Homoi," said the bigger of the two, bowing respectfully after carefully putting something red and shiny in the grass, "we owe the life of the little bird here to you."

Homoi could clearly see the faces of the birds in the red light coming off the object in the grass.

"You're the skylarks from the other day, aren't you," said Homoi.

"That's correct," said the mother skylark. "We are eternally grateful to you for what you did, for saving the life of my little boy here. I understand that you even fell ill as a result of your good deed. Have you made a full recovery?"

Mother and son bowed to him over and over again.

"We've been flying around here every day hoping you would eventually come out," she continued. "This is a gift from our king." The mother skylark picked up the red object in her beak and placed it before Homoi. It was wrapped in a gossamer-thin handkerchief, so thin that it looked like just so much smoke. She undid the handkerchief. Inside was a perfectly round jewel about the size of a chestnut. A red flame glimmered and flashed inside the jewel.

"The is a miracle jewel called 'The Flame King Opal'. Our king wishes to convey to you that it can accomplish miraculous things, depending on how you care for it. Please be so kind as to receive it."

"Mrs. Skylark," said Homoi with a smile on his lips. "I wouldn't know what to do with something like this. Please take it back. Just looking at it is enough for me, it's so beautiful. I'll go to where you are if I feel I want to see it again."

"We ask you, please don't give it back. Our king truly wishes it to be yours. If you give it back, my son here and I will have to commit harakiri. Now, son, we should take our leave. So, bow to the kind rabbit. We bid you farewell."

The mother and son skylarks bowed several times to Homoi and flew off in a flurry. Homoi picked up the jewel and gave it a close look. It was really cold and exquisitely clear, and yet it gave off red and yellow flames that made it look like it was burning inside. He held it up to the sky and peered through it. The flame vanished and the Milky Way appeared all the more lucid in it. He took it away from his eye, and the magnificent flame flashed and glimmered once again.

Homoi went into his house, holding the jewel gently at eye-level. Before anything, he showed it to his father.

"This is the world-renowned treasure called 'The Flame King Opal'," said his father taking off his glasses and inspecting the jewel at close range. "This is one amazing jewel. It is said that up to now the only ones who have been able to hold onto this, as they wished, for a lifetime have been two birds and only a single fish. Listen. You must see to it that the flame never goes out."

"You mustn't worry about that, Daddy," said Homoi. "I wouldn't let it go out in a million years. The skylark told me that too. I'm going to breathe on it a hundred times a day and polish it up a hundred times with a strawberry finch feather duster."

"This jewel is extremely fragile," said his mother, holding it and staring into it. "Aquila the late-Eagle Cabinet Minister used to have it and a huge volcano erupted, and he flew around giving orders and directions to all the birds so that they could evacuate in time. They say that the jewel was battered by a mountain-lode of rocks and inundated by tons of hot lava but that it came out of it all not only without a single scratch or clouded over but even more beautiful than before."

"Yep, that's right," said Homoi's father. "Won't find a soul who hasn't heard that famous story. And you're bound to become as famous as Aquila someday too, Homoi. Listen, you've got to make sure you're never mean or unkind to any creature, you hear?"

Homoi was dog tired and very sleepy.

"You mustn't worry about that, Daddy," he said, rolling onto his side in his bed. "I promise I'll be someone everybody will look up to. Give me the jewel so that I can sleep with it."

His mother passed the jewel to him and, holding it close to his chest, he soon fell into a deep sleep.

*

That night he dreamed a beautiful dream. Yellow and green fires were burning in the sky, and from one end to the other the grassy fields turned bright and golden. Myriad tiny windmills sailed through the sky, buzzing faintly like bees, and Aquila the late-Eagle Cabinet Minister performed his duties, making waves in the air by flying around the fields with his silver mantle streaming behind him.

Homoi sensed that he was shrieking over and over with joy, "Heavens above, he's doing us proud … he's doing us really proud!"

*

Homoi woke up at around seven the next morning and took a look at the jewel before doing anything. It was even more captivating than it was the night before.

"I see it, I do see it," he whispered to himself. "It's the mouth of a volcano and it's spurting out fire. There it goes, another spurt! Oh, this is so much fun. It's just like fireworks. Oh … oh … oh … it's gushing out fire! The fire's splitting in two! Gorgeous sparks … and more sparks … like lightning! They're streaming out! They're streaming out all gold! Amazing, just amazing. Oh … it's gushing out fire again!"

Homoi's father had already gone out.

"Now, Homoi, get your face washed," said his mother, bringing in some delicious-looking white grass roots and blue-green rose hips. "You're going to be doing a bit of exercise today. So, show me the jewel now. Well, well, if that isn't the most beautiful thing I've ever seen! Do you mind if I just look at it while you wash your face?"

"Of course I don't, Mummy. It's our family treasure, so it's just as much yours as mine."

Homoi brushed six big drops of dew off the leaf tips of the lily of the valley by the front door and washed his face from ear to ear. Once he'd finished breakfast he breathed on the jewel a hundred times and polished it a hundred times with the strawberry finch feather duster. He then meticulously wrapped it in a strawberry finch feather cloth, placed it for safe keeping in an agate box that held a telescope especially made for rabbits and put it in the care of his mother.

He went outside. The wind was blowing, scattering droplets of dew all around and everywhere. The dotted bellflowers were jingling and jangling their morning bells. Homoi hopped over to the wild cherry blossom trees and, when he got there, an aging wild horse came trotting up to him. Homoi was about to take his first hop toward home when the horse bowed formally to him.

"Could you possibly be Homoi?" asked the horse. "I understand that you are now in possession of the Flame King Opal and I take my hat off to you. A good one thousand and two hundred years have passed since that jewel has come into the possession of an animal. To tell you the truth, I could not hold back the river of tears that flowed from my eyes when I heard about it just this morning."

The horse started bawling his eyes out. This made Homoi somewhat uncomfortable and, seeing the tears flowing down the horse's nose, felt a trifle sniffly himself.

"You are our mentor," said the horse, wiping his tears with a light-yellow handkerchief about the size of a furoshiki. "Do please make sure that nothing happens to you."

And having said that, the horse again bowed formally to Homoi before setting out in the direction from which he came. Homoi walked in a daze, not sure if he was happy or just felt odd. He came to the shade of an elderberry tree, where two young squirrels were munching happily away together on white rice cakes. They took one look at Homoi and, almost jumping out of their skin, straightened their collars and, with eyes like saucers, gulped down their rice cakes whole.

"Good morning, squirrels," said Homoi, as he always did.

Both squirrels stiffened and didn't squeak a word.

"Hey, you two," Homoi hastened to say, "won't you come play with me somewhere today?"

But the squirrels just exchanged glances as if there was no way in the world they would join him and, holding up their nose, turned the other way and ran away as fast as their legs would take them. Homoi was staggered. He plodded home looking like death warmed over.

"Mummy," he said, "I don't know why but everyone seems really offput by me for some reason. "I mean, the squirrels really gave me the cold shoulder just now."

"What do you expect, Homoi?" said his mother, smiling. "You're in a different class now from the others. The squirrels are simply embarrassed, that's all. So, from now on you have to be really careful or else you may become a laughingstock."

"I'll be okay, Mummy. If that's the case, does it mean that I've become the boss, like a general?"

"Well, in a manner of speaking," she said, delighted with this turn of events.

"That's great, that's great," said Homoi, prancing around gleefully. "That means I've got a following an' everyone's below me. Even the fox an' things don't scare me one bit. Mummy, you know what? I'm going to make the squirrels my rear admirals. And the horse, you know, the horse is going to be my colonel. Yeah."

"Well, maybe," said his mother, still smiling. "But don't let it all go to your head."

"I'll be fine, Mummy. I'm just going out for a bit," he said, hopping off toward the fields.

He caught sight there of that sly nasty old fox rushing like the wind by him.

"Wait up, fox!" called Homoi, shaking but none the less determined. "I'm a general now, you know!"

"So I've heard," said the fox, startled as he turned toward him. "Yes, so I've heard. All right then, what's on your mind?"

"You really used to give me a hard time, you know," said Homoi, putting on a commanding air. "From now on you'll be under me, in my entourage."

"Your entourage … I have nothing to say for myself," said the fox, holding his paws in the air and about to fall flat on his face. "I beg your indulgence and forgiveness in all things."

"I make a special exception and forgive you," said Homoi, his heart thumping with joy. "From hereon forth, you shall be my second sublieutenant. Please step up to the tasks of that rank."

"Your wish is my command, sir," said the fox, running after his tail four times. "Thank you from the bottom of my heart. I will do your bidding. Would you like me to steal some corn for you, for instance?"

"Nope," said Homoi. "That's a crime. There's no way you should do that."

"Yessir, yessir," said the fox, scratching his scalp. "I give you my word that I will never do that again. Just tell me what your wishes are.

I am at your disposal."

"That's right," said Homoi. "I'll call you if I need you for something. Just beat it for now."

The fox went around in circles again, bowed to him and flew off. Homoi couldn't contain himself for his delight. He roamed over the fields talking to himself, laughing his head off and thinking of one merry thing after the other. And as he was doing that, the sun fell beyond the wild cherry blossom trees like a shattered mirror.

Homoi went home. His father was back already. That night his mother had prepared a feast of different foods ... and that night Homoi dreamed the most beautiful dreams.

*

Homoi's mother told him to go out into the fields the next day and gather lily of the valley berries.

"Gee," said Homoi to himself, picking the berries, "it's pretty weird for a general to have to gather lily of the valley berries, if I do say so myself. If someone sees me, I mean, gee, talk about being a laughingstock! I wish the fox would show up."

No sooner had he said that than did the ground under his paws start to bulge. He could tell that a mole was tunneling right past him.

"Hey, mole, mole in the hole! You know that I've really come up in the world now, don't you?"

"Ah," said the mole from below the ground, "is that Gen. Homoi up there? Certainly, I am aware of this."

"Well, then I'll look favorably down on you," said Homoi, feeling all bloated up. "I'll ... I'll make you a sergeant. But in turn you'll have to do a little job for me."

"Um, what sort of job might that be?" asked the mole, jittery and on edge.

"Pick lily of the valley berries for me."

"Ah, dear me, but I beg to inform you," said the mole, a cold sweat streaming down his face as he scratched his scalp, "when it comes to doing work in bright places, I am all thumbs."

"Is that so?!" hollered Homoi, fuming. "All right then, fine. I won't put the hard word on you. But don't come to me when you meet the awful fate that awaits you."

"Please find it in your heart to forgive me. I'll die if I'm forced to see the light of day for more than a short time."

"I said that's fine. No skin off my back," said Homoi, thumping the earth. "So just shut your trap, will ya?"

Just then five squirrels came tumbling toward him from the shadows of the elderberry tree.

"Gen. Homoi, sir!" they said, bobbing their head up and down. "Please find it in your heart to allow us to gather the berries for you."

"Why not," said Homoi. "Get on it right this instant. You'll all be my rear admirals. How's that?"

The squirrels took to the task, squeaking with glee. Then six ponies came galloping toward Homoi. They came to an abrupt stop in front of him and the biggest among them spoke up.

"Gen. Homoi, sir! We humbly request that you give us an order."

"Why not," said Homoi, exceedingly pleased. "I'll make you all my colonels. You are to come galloping whenever I give the call."

The ponies were delighted and leapt into the air.

"Please, Gen. Homoi," begged the mole, weeping under the earth, "please give me an order that I can carry out. I promise you that you won't be disappointed in the result."

But it was clear that Homoi was still furious with the mole.

"You're totally useless," he said, thumping on the earth. "The fox will show up soon enough and take care of you, and your like, once and for all. Just you wait!"

There wasn't a peep from under the earth, where it was as quiet as the grave.

The squirrels spent the entire day gathering lily of the valley berries, making an uproarious fuss when they brought them to Homoi's house.

"Good gracious!" said Homoi's mother, when the squirrels barreled noisily into the house. "What's come over all of you squirrels?"

"Mummy," piped in Homoi from the side, "see what I'm capable of? There's no end to the things I can accomplish."

His mother was plunged into thought by this and she didn't give out so much as a whimper. That's when Homoi's father walked in.

"Homoi," he said, surveying the scene, "are you sure you're not running a fever? I hear that you gave one hell of a fright to the mole. They're all bawling like there's no tomorrow down at his place. And, tell me, who's going to eat up this many berries, eh?"

Homoi burst into tears. The squirrels looked at him with great pity, after which they creeped out of there and ran away like nobody's business.

"You've made a mess of everything," said Homoi's father. "You take a look now at the Flame King Opal. I bet it's all clouded over."

Even Homoi's mother was crying now. Quietly wiping her tears on her apron, she went to the cupboard and took out the agate box with the jewel in it. His father took the box from her and lifted the lid. But he was shocked to see that the jewel was far far redder than it was two nights before and, not only that, its flame was flaring, flashing and flittering like wildfire.

The three of them were, for a time, lost in that flame. Then Homoi's father handed him the jewel and they all sat down for supper. Homoi's tears dried and he was soon smiling happily as they finished eating and called it a day.

*

Homoi went out into the fields early the next morning. It was a beautiful day. The lilies of the valley were no longer jingling their leaves, for there were no berries to jingle them on.

The fox came hurtling headlong from the blue fields in the remote distance.

"Gen. Homoi," he said, screeching to a stop in front of him, "I've heard on the grapevine that you permitted the squirrels to gather lily of the valley berries for you. I've got a proposition for you. I'll bring you somethin' you'll really and truly savor. It's yellow and it's rich and fit for a king. Pardon my rudeness, but you've never set eyes on the likes of anythin' like it. Now, you said that you were goin' to see to it that the mole got his just deserts. That lazybones is a cheeky bigmouth, and I'm plannin' on chasin' him right into the river."

"Don't take anything out on the mole," said Homoi. "I'm forgiving him this morning. However, I would like some of that delicious thing you just talked about. Bring me some."

"At your disposal, sir, at your disposal. Give me ten minutes. Just ten little minutes!"

And having said that, the fox flew away like the wind.

"Mole, mole, you little mole!" shouted Homoi. "I pardon you for all your sins, so dry your tears now."

But it was so quiet down there you could hear a pin drop. And the fox came flying again out of the blue.

"Put this in that mouth of yours, sir," he said, placing a slice of bread that he had run off with by Homoi's paws. "They call this 'Heavenly Tempura'. It can't be topped."

Homoi ventured a bite and found it truly mouth-wateringly delicious.

"What tree does this grow on?" he asked.

"Ah," chortled the fox under his breath, "this grows on the kitchen tree. That's kitchen spelt ki-tch-en! I'll bring some to you every day if you find it to your liking."

"Very well," said Homoi. "Fetch me three slices every day. Is that clear?"

"Yessir!" said the fox, blinking his eyes obsequiously. "Nothing would please me more. In return, I ask you to give me a free claw in catching chickens."

"It's a deal," said Homoi.

"And now I will fetch you two more slices, to make up today's harvest."

The fox once again flew away like the wind. Homoi considered taking the slice of bread home with the idea in mind of giving it to his parents. "After all," he figured, "dad has probably never had anything as good as this. Gee, I'm a good son."

Soon the fox was back with two slices of bread between his teeth. He put them down in front of Homoi, bid a hasty farewell to him and darted off.

"I wonder what on earth that fox does with himself every day," grumbled Homoi to himself as he headed for home.

At home, his parents were drying lily of the valley berries in the sun.

"Dad," said Homoi, holding out the bread, "I've got something I think you'll like. Would you like some? Have a little bite and see if you like it."

"The fox gave you this, didn't he," said his father, taking off his glasses and examining the bread. "This is stolen goods. I wouldn't touch it with a ten-foot pole."

Without warning his father grabbed the slice of bread that Homoi had brought for his mother, flung it with his own slice on the ground and thumped on it till it was a mushy mess. Homoi burst into tears and his mother burst into tears with him.

"Homoi," said his father, pacing over the earth, "what am I going to do with you? Take a look at the jewel. It must have crumbled into dust by now."

His mother, with tears still in her eyes, took out the box and his father lifted the jewel out. The jewel burned so radiantly in the sun that it seemed like it was about to rise up itself like a star. Homoi took the jewel from his father, who had nothing more to say. Homoi forgot why he was crying and stared at the jewel.

*

The next day found Homoi in the field again.

The fox rushed up to him and gave him three slices of bread, which Homoi immediately took home and placed on a kitchen shelf before returning to the field where the fox was still waiting for him.

"Gen. Homoi," said the fox, "I've got a great idea for something you'll really get a kick out of."

"What is it?"

"Giving the mole what for, that's what. That mole's the vermin of these fields. An' he's a no-good lazybones to boot. You've let him off the hook already, so you can just sit here idly by while I browbeat an' torment the hell out of him. Whadda ya say, eh?"

"Yeah," said Homoi. "It never hurt to browbeat and torment vermin a little."

The fox pranced around sniffing the ground, tapping it to hear where the mole might be. He then turned over a big rock. A family of eight moles were snuggling up together, shivering and shaking, in a hole under the rock.

"Scram!" said the fox, stomping on the earth. "If you don't beat it, I'll make mincemeat outta you!"

"Have mercy on us, have mercy," they cried, doing their best to run away. But they couldn't see in the bright light. All they could do was paddle their legs against the grass. The littlest of the children moles turned flat on his back and fainted.

The fox ground his teeth, seething, and even Homoi thumped the earth loudly.

"Get lost, get lost!" said Homoi to the mole family.

"Hey you! Whadda ya think yer doin'?" came a loud voice.

This sent the fox chasing his tail four times and making tracks as fast as his legs would carry him.

It was Homoi's father. He quickly put the mole family back in their hole and covered it with the rock. Then he took Homoi by the scruff of his neck and hauled him home. His mother came out of the house already weeping and clung onto his father.

"Homoi," said his father, "what on earth am I going to do with you? Today of all days the jewel will be pulverized into dust. Get it out for him!"

His mother wiped her tears and brought out the box. His father lifted the lid. But again he was flabbergasted. The Flame King Opal was more beautiful than it had ever been. It looked like there was a veritable war between the fiery colors going on in there … red and green and blue … all fighting with each other to burn the brightest, detonating land mines, shooting out flares, and amidst it all, lightning was flashing and the blood of fire was gushing and, to top it off, light-blue flames seized and encircled the jewel, and what looked like sheets of red poppies and yellow tulips and purple gromwells quivered in the wind inside it.

Homoi's father gave him the jewel and, again, said nothing. Homoi forgot all about his tears as he stared at it with delight. His mother started to prepare lunch, finally feeling some peace of mind. They all sat down and ate the bread.

"Homoi," said his father, "you've got to watch out for that fox."

"Dad," said Homoi, "there's no need to worry about me. A fox like that is no match for me. I've got the Flame King Opal, you see. It won't crumble or cloud over in a million years."

"It's so true," said his mother. "It's amazing, that gemstone."

"Mum," said Homoi, all puffed up with himself, "I … I was born to own it and will never be parted from it. I mean, the Flame King Opal wouldn't fly away to somebody else no matter what I did. It just won't happen. Besides, I'm still breathing on it and polishing it up a hundred times a day."

"I just hope you're right," said his father.

Homoi dreamt that night that he was standing on one paw at the very top of a huge tall mountain shaped like an ice pick. He cried so much that it woke him up.

*

The next day found Homoi in the fields again.

A gloomy marshy fog had descended over everything. The trees and bushes and grasses were mute. Even the leaves of the wild cherry blossom trees were still in the dreary air.

The only sound breaking the silence and resounding throughout the sky was the loud morning pealing of the dotted bellflowers. They jingled and jangled into the sky until a final gong echoed off the distant mountains.

The fox came running in short pants with three slices of bread between his teeth.

"Good morning, fox," said Homoi.

"Geez," said the fox with a sly and sinister smile on his face, "I got the jitters yesterday, I did. Your dad's as stubborn as a mule, you know. What was he like after that? His mood brightened up right away, I trust. I've got an idea for something really fun today. Do you have anything against zoos?"

"Nope," said Homoi, "nothing in particular."

"Look," said the fox, taking out a little net from his inside pocket. "If we hang this up somewhere, dragonflies and bees and even sparrows and jays and even bigger ones'll get themselves all tangled up in it. All we gotta do is collect 'em up and, presto, we'll have our own little zoo."

Homoi conjured up the zoo and felt like it was the most fun thing he had ever heard.

"Let's do it," he said. "But are you sure this net will work?"

"Work?" said the fox, chuckling at Homoi's harebrained question. "Like magic! Hurry now and take the bread home. I'll catch a hundred or more things for our zoo in two shakes of a lamb's tail."

Homoi rushed home with the bread, put it on a shelf in the kitchen and was back in a jiffy. The fox was laughing his head off in the fog by the wild cherry blossom tree where he had hung the net.

"Ha ha ha ha ha! Look at that. We got ourselves four little ones caught already," he said, pointing to a large glass box that he had brought out of nowhere.

Sure enough, a jay and a bush warbler and a strawberry finch and a field sparrow were flapping about in the box. Yet, they all calmed down the instant they set eyes on Homoi. "Gen. Homoi, sir," said the bush warbler through the glass, "please find it in your powers to save us. The fox caught us and will surely eat us up tomorrow. We beg of you, sir."

Homoi didn't waste a minute in reaching out to open the box, but the fox's brow wrinkled up in black wrinkles and he glared at him angrily.

"Homoi!" he barked, with his mouth cloven up to his ears. "Don't you dare! Put one little toe on that box and I'll tear you from limb to limb, you little robber!"

Homoi ran home, terrified, as fast as he could. His mother had gone to the fields and was not there. Homoi's heart was thumping, so he decided to take a look at the Flame King Opal. He got the box out and lifted the lid. The jewel inside was burning like fire. It may have been his imagination, but he saw a teeny-tiny patch of white cloud on the jewel and it bothered him no end. So, he blew his breath on it like he always did and rubbed it ever so lightly with a cloth made from the chest feathers of a strawberry finch.

But no matter how many times he rubbed the cloudy patch, it wouldn't come off. His father walked in and saw how pale he was.

"Homoi," he said, "did the Flame King Opal cloud up? You look like you've seen a ghost. Give it here, I'll have a look."

He held the jewel up to the light.

"No problem," he said, chuckling. "We'll get this off in no time flat. The yellow fire's burning even brighter than it did before. Here, hand me that cloth, will ya?"

He began to polish the jewel as if his life depended on it. But not only didn't the cloudy patch come off, it just got bigger and bigger. Homoi's mother walked in, took the jewel from him without saying a word, held it up to the light herself, sighed a big sigh and started to polish it with her breath. The three of them, sighing and sighing and sighing, took turns in breathing hard on it to polish it up.

Night fell.

"Anyway, let's have something to eat," said Homoi's father, suddenly rising as if he was on to something. "I think we ought to soak it in oil overnight. Apparently that's the best thing to do."

"Oh, good grief," said his mother, startled, "I plum forgot to prepare supper. I've got nothing made. You think you'll have enough with the lily of the valley berries from the day before yesterday and this morning's bread?"

"Sounds pretty good to me," said Homoi's father.

Homoi sighed and replaced the jewel in its box, staring at it for a while, and they all ate in silence.

"So, time to get the oil out?" said his father, taking down a bottle of oil made from the seeds of the nutmeg-yew tree. Homoi took the bottle from him and poured oil into the box with the Flame King Opal. Then they turned off the light and, much earlier than usual, were soon lost to sleep.

*

Homoi woke in the middle of the night. He sat up with trepidation and looked at the Flame King Opal that was beside his pillow. The jewel glistened silver in the oil, looking like a fish's eye. Its red fire was out. Homoi sobbed, wailed and howled. His father and mother woke with a fright and turned on the light.

The Flame King Opal had turned into what looked for all the world like a lump of lead. Homoi, through tears, told his father about the fox's net.

"Homoi," said his father, putting on his outdoor clothes in a panic, "how could you be so stupid? And I'm just as stupid as you. You were given that jewel because you saved the life of that skylark, isn't that right? And a few of days ago you went and said that you were born to have it. All right, off we go to the fields. The fox's net may still be hanging there. You've got to put your neck on the chopping block and fight that fox. Of course, I'll give you a helping paw."

Homoi cried again and stood up. His mother also cried as she followed the two of them. The day was breaking but a dense marshy fog was hanging low over everything.

The fox was standing under the wild cherry blossom tree where his net was still hanging. But he simply burst into a raucous laugh, with his mouth askew, when he saw the three of them.

"You, fox!" hollered Homoi's father. "You got a cheek leading Homoi by the nose like that! We demand satisfaction!"

"Satisfaction, is it?" said the fox, now looking truly like the villain he was. "You know, I could do away with the three of you and gobble you up right this instant, but I don't fancy getting scratched in the bargain. Besides, I've got much nicer things to eat."

In a flash the fox had the glass box on his back and was about to dart off with it.

"Hold yer horses!" said Homoi's father, grabbing the box.

The fox tottered and staggered, finally managing to get the box on the ground before hightailing it out of there.

All the hundred-odd birds in the box were crying, from the sparrows to the jays, from the bush warblers to the bulky owl. Homoi's father lifted the lid of the box. The birds immediately flew out and, bowing down low to him, sang out in chorus.

"Thank you very much. Where would we be without you?"

"Don't mention it," said Homoi's father. "We have nothing to say for ourselves. We cast a thick cloud over the jewel that your king had bestowed on us."

"Good grief," they cried. "Perhaps we could take a look at it for you."

"A look? Please follow me."

He led them all in a stream to his house. Homoi, crying, crestfallen and dejected, brought up the rear. The owl threw scary glances back at him from time to time, plodding along with weighty steps. They all entered the house together.

The birds perched themselves on every available spot, on the floor, the shelves and the tables. The owl peered about with the most ludicrous and preposterous look in her eyes, while time and time again clearing her throat with one "ahem" after another.

Homoi picked up the Flame King Opal, which was now no more than an ordinary white stone.

"This is what it's come to," he said. "I wouldn't blame you for laughing your head off at this turn of events."

But no sooner had he said that than did the Flame King Opal crack right in two and, right before their very eyes, crackle loudly and crumble into a cloud of dust.

Homoi collapsed by the front door. Dust from the jewel struck his eyes. All the others were struck with fear. They rushed to him. Now there was a popping sound, and a smoke-like cloud of particles rose in the air. The particles smashed into smithereens. Then the minuscule pieces imploded, becoming two halves again, these in turn smacked together and the Flame King Opal took on its previous form. The jewel burned like a volcano, and, shining like the setting sun, flew out the window on a high-pitched whistle of air.

The birds, feeling like they had now come back down to earth, filed out of the door one after the other, leaving only the owl in the house.

"It only lasted six days, ho ho, a mere six days, ho ho," she said, looking about the house with googly eyes. Then she shook out her shoulders and strided out with a sneering grin.

Homoi's eyes were dull and clouded over, just like the jewel, and he couldn't see a thing. His mother hadn't stopped crying all throughout. His father was plunged in thought with his arms folded over his chest.

"Don't cry, son," he said, tapping Homoi gently on the shoulder. "This isn't the first time this sort of thing has happened. You should count your lucky stars and be happy that you were given the chance to realize that. I'm sure your eyes will get better. Daddy will do everything in his power to see that they do. Hear me? Dry those tears, now."

The fog had lifted outside the window and the berries on the lily of the valley plants were sparkling. The dotted bellflowers were jingling and jangling and chiming and tolling their morning bells, pealing right up to the heavens.

The Twin Stars

It is popularly believed that Kenji is referring in this story to the Twins in the sky, Castor and Pollux; and, though he may have borrowed its title from the constellation of Gemini, Choonse and Pohse are actually two stars in the multiple star system Epsilon Lyrae, known as "the Double Double." The two most widely separated stars in this system can be discerned as two stars by the naked eye on a very clear night. This system is described in a textbook used by Kenji when he was a student at Morioka Agricultural High School.

The little boy named Tadashi, who finds himself on the Milky Way train after losing his life on the Titanic, tells Giovanni and Campanella that the two stars he sees out the window are two crystal palaces where the twins live. Tadashi says that they have an argument with a crow; and a reference is made to them playing the flute, as well as to a comet that comes "whooshing by." This is a classic incidence of one of Kenji's stories, "The Twin Stars," appearing in another, *Night on the Milky Way Train*.

The song for which Kenji both composed the music and wrote the lyrics forms a part of "The Twin Stars." It was thought, in ancient times, that the stars physically revolved around a point in the sky, and the song tells of this "journey." A more literal translation of the title would be "Song of the Circling Stars"; and in the translation of this song that I did decades ago, that is how I rendered it. But I now prefer to call it "Once Around the Stars" in English, which, while being a free translation, to me sounds better. In addition, there is some ambiguity in the first part of the Japanese title—"Hoshi Meguri"—which can indicate that someone is actually going from star to star, as the twins do.

There is some rather brutal violence realistically portrayed in this story. In fact, Kenji rarely beautifies the violence that humans and animals inflict on each other, regardless of species. He is above all a scientist who observes nature with a cold eye. He is not trying to protect us from nature's home truths, but rather examine them for what they are.

Self-sacrifice for the good of others plays a major part here as well. The twins have been dealt a bitter fate and find themselves at the bottom of the sea. But rather than rail against their fate, they accept it readily. Choonse says, "Seeing as we are unable to return to the heavens, we would be more than happy to do whatever is in our power to help everyone here."

"Ah, it is I who am humbled," says the king, "by your self-effacement. I will order the waterspout to take you back to the heavens forthwith."

The starfish have been sent to the bottom of the sea for their transgressions in one life or another. Yet no one has sinned so much that they cannot be forgiven and be permitted to transmigrate to another—better—world.

In 1996 the omnibus anime film "Kenji's Suitcase" was released in Japan. One of the stories depicted in this film is "The Twin Stars."

THE TWIN STARS

by Miyazawa Kenji

ONE

You can see two tiny stars no bigger than spores of the common horsetail on the west bank of the Milky Way. These are miniature crystal palaces where the twin child stars, Choonse and Pohse, live.

These two translucent palaces face each other. When night falls the twins invariably go home to their palaces and, sitting properly on their knees, they play their silver flutes throughout the night in tune with the song "Once Around the Stars." In fact, this is what they are there for in the first place.

One morning, while the sun was arising in the east at its usual awesome clip, Choonse laid down his silver flute and addressed Pohse.

"Pohse," he said, "that's enough, wouldn't you say? The sun has awakened and the clouds are bright and white. What do you say we go to the stream that runs through the western field?"

Pohse still had his eyes half shut, playing his flute as if there was no tomorrow, so Choonse went down the steps of his palace, put on his shoes and climbed up to the entrance of Pohse's palace.

"Pohse," he said again, "that's enough, wouldn't you say? The sky in the east is white, on fire, and down below the little birds all seem to be up and about. What do you say we go to the stream that runs through the western field? Wouldn't it be fun to make some fog using the windmills and send little rainbows streaking across the sky?"

"Oh, Choonse," said Pohse, surprised to see Choonse there and laying his flute aside. "Sorry about that. I didn't notice that the sun was up. I'll get into my shoes right away."

Pohse put on his white shell shoes and they crossed the silver celestial meadows together, singing as they went …

Oh white clouds, white clouds in the sky
Purify the path that the sun travels on
And scatter the light wherever you go

Oh blue clouds, blue clouds in the sky
Bury the rocks strewn on the path
Traveled by the sun, day in and day out

In no time at all they were at the celestial spring.

This spring is distinctly visible from below on clear nights. It is located some way from the west bank of the Milky Way and is encircled by little blue stars. Its pure water gurgles up from a bed that is blanketed in tiny blue pebbles, and a narrow current runs out of a pool on one side of it into the Milky Way. Take my word that birds like the nighthawk and the cuckoo, all skin and bones when drought strikes our world, look up in silence at the running water and just wish that they could gulp a few drops of it down. But there isn't a little bird that can make it up that high. For Corvus the Crow and Scorpio the Scorpion and Lepus the Rabbit, however, it's well within reach.

"Would you like to start by making a waterfall here, Pohse?"

"Sure, that's a good idea. I'll be right back with some stones."

Choonse slipped out of his shoes and stepped into the narrow current, while Pohse gathered those stones on the bank that were not too big for him to hold.

By now the sky was filled with the scent of apples. This scent was being breathed out by the silver moon still hanging in the western sky. It was then that they heard someone singing in a loud voice on the far side of the field.

Well of water in the sky
Just off the west bank
Of the Milky Way
Blue stars encircle all
From its heart of water

To its glittering bed
The nighthawk and the owl
The plover and the jay
They all want to get there
But it's too far away....

"Oh, that's Corvus the Crow," cried the twins.

And sure enough, that huge crow came strutting and swaggering and rustling right through the pampas grass in the sky, swinging his shoulders back and forth, decked in his jet-black velvet cape and jet-black velvet long johns.

"Well, how do you do?" said the crow, stopping in front of the twins and bowing to them courteously. "It's Choonse and Pohse, isn't it. Can't complain about the weather, can we. But, you know, when the sun comes out a crow gets a tad thirsty. Also, I think I was making a bit of a racket with my singing last night. Cheers."

Having said that, the crow plunged his head right into the stream's water.

"Please drink up to your heart's content," said Pohse.

The crow gulped down the water for a good three minutes without coming up for a single breath, then raised his head out of the stream, blinked his eyes and shook his head furiously, sending drops of water scattering through the air.

A gruff and harsh-sounding tune came wafting to them from the distance, and the crow became all shook up before their very eyes.

The red-eyed Scorpion in the southern sky
With his poisonous stinger and massive pincers
If you don't see them for what they are
You're more loony than any loony bird!

"That's about Scorpio the scorpion, a vicious beast if there ever was one. He's having us on with that business about being loony. All right by me. If he so much as gets near me, I'll pluck out those stupid red eyes of his!"

"Corvus," said Choonse, "you mustn't crow like that. His Majesty will get wind of it."

But no sooner had Choonse spoken than did red-eyed Scorpio come scurrying along, brandishing his two huge claws in the air and rattling his tail. The sound of this reverberated throughout the tranquil field of the heavens.

As for the crow, he was incandescent with rage. His body trembled and shook all over, and it certainly looked like he was about to pounce on the scorpion and clobber him. But the twin stars gestured frantically for him to hold back.

"Ah, my throat is parched and I need a drink," said the scorpion, crawling over to the bank of the stream while keeping close watch on the crow through a corner of his eye. "Well, top of the mornin' to you, Twins! Excuse me … I'm just gonna get myself a sip or two. Well, whadda ya know! For some reason or other, this water's all unclean … like *someone* I know. It's as if some jet-black birdbrain was just stickin' his filthy beak in here. Well, can't be helped. I'll just have to put up with it." The scorpion made a racket swilling down water for a good ten minutes, while flapping the poisonous stingers in his tail right under the crow's beak, to let him know what's what.

"Hey you, Scorpio!" shrieked the big crow, no longer able to hold it in and spreading his wings out wide. "I heard you badmouthing me a moment ago, calling me a loonybird or goonybird or something like that. I demand satisfaction from you right here and now."

"I say, did somebody say something?" remarked the scorpion, finally lifting his head out of the water and rolling his fiery red eyes. "You know, it doesn't bother me if someone's red or grey, I treat 'em the same, with this stinger in my tail!"

"Why you!" cried the crow, blowing his stack and leaping into the air. "Who do you think you are, eh?! I'm gonna whack you so hard you'll be flying right to the far side of the heavens, empty head first!"

The scorpion too was fuming with rage. He twisted his body around quick as a wink and thrust his tail, with its stinger, into the air. But this didn't deter the crow, who jumped up, evading the stinger, and came back down with its spear-like beak aimed smack for the scorpion's head.

There was no way that Choonse or Pohse could come between them. The crow inflicted a deep wound in the scorpion's head, and the scorpion had stung the crow's chest with its poisonous stinger. Both of them collapsed into a heap and, with a moan and a groan, lost consciousness. The scorpion's blood gushed out of its head into the sky, forming a nasty red cloud.

"Oh, heavens above, this is awful," said Choonse, hurriedly putting on his shoes. "The crow's been poisoned. We've got to suck it out right away. Pohse, would you hold him down for me?"

Pohse slipped into his shoes and went around to the other side of the crow to hold him down, as Choonse opened his lips over the wound on the crow's chest.

"Don't drink the poison, Choonse," said Pohse. "You must spit it out right away."

Choonse didn't reply. He just sucked and spit out the poison six times.

"Oh, I cannot thank you enough," said the crow, squinting his eyes open and gradually coming to. "I don't know what happened. I mean, I had that blackguard where I wanted him."

"Can you walk?" asked Choonse. "You must go to the stream and wash out the wound right away."

"There's that rat!" said the crow, standing on wobbly feet and quaking with fury again. "Vermin of the sky, that's what you are! You should thank your lucky stars you kicked the bucket up here!" The twins wasted no time in taking the crow to the stream, where they washed his wound clean and breathed on it a few times with their fragrant breath.

"Now, don't sprint or run, and make sure you get home before dark," they said. "And don't go doing things like that again, all right? His Majesty sees all, you know."

"I am deeply in your debt," said the crow with limp wings at his sides, feeling down in the dumps and bowing to them. "Thank you from the bottom of my heart. I'll watch what I do from now on."

And having said that, he made his way, dragging his feet, through the silver pampas grass field until he disappeared in the distance.

The two of them checked out the scorpion, who had a deep wound in its head. Its bleeding had already stopped. They scooped up water from the stream in cupped hands and washed the wound clean, breathing in turns on it.

The scorpion had managed to open his eyes a little by the time the sun had climbed to the very top of the sky.

"Well, how are you doing?" said Pohse, wiping his brow of sweat.

"Did that big lug of a crow die?" muttered the scorpion.

"You still going on about that?" asked Choonse, somewhat peeved. "If anyone was going to be a goner it was you. Now, pick yourself up, dry yourself off and get on home. You'll be in real trouble if it gets dark before you get there."

"Could I ask the two of you to take me there?" asked the scorpion with a strange glint in his eye. "You've been so kind to me up to now."

"I think we can do that," said Pohse. "Put your pincers over my shoulders."

"And mine," said Choonse. "The light's not going to be around forever. If you're not home by nighttime, we won't be able to complete our rounds."

The scorpion hobbled along, leaning on the twins' shoulders, which drooped down from the weight. The scorpion was very heavy and about ten times bigger than the twins. Even so, they managed to take one slow step after another, their faces bright red from the effort. The scorpion scraped its tail on the rocks as it toddled along and panted out pretty foul-smelling breath. All in all, they barely covered half a mile in the space of an hour.

The scorpion's heavy pincers dug into the twins' shoulders and chest, hurting like the devil. The celestial field glittered white as they crossed over seven little streams and passed through ten meadows. It got to the point that they were so dizzy that they didn't know if they were walking or standing still. And yet they persisted to take one step after another in silence. They had been walking like that for six hours and realized that it would still take an hour and a half more to get to the scorpion's home. The sun was soon to disappear behind the western mountains.

"I think we should shake a leg," said Pohse. "We've got to get home in the next hour and a half too. Are you in a lot of pain? Does it hurt?"

"I beg you," said the scorpion, crying. "We're almost there. Please have mercy on me."

"Yes, we're almost there," said Choonse, bearing up from the pain that seemed to be splintering his shoulder bones from the inside. "Does the wound hurt?"

The sun was quivering and sinking majestically beyond the western mountains.

"We really should have been home by now," cried Pohse. "This is awful. "Is someone here, I wonder, who can help us?"

But a hush lay over the entire field of the heavens and there was no reply. The clouds in the west were radiant and bright red, and the scorpion's sorrowful eyes, too, burned red. The brighter stars in the heavens were already appearing in the distant sky, singing their songs in their silver armor.

"Eureka, the first star!" shouted a child below, gazing up into the sky. "I'll be a millionaire!"

"Scorpio," said Choonse, "just a little bit further. Could you possibly shake a leg? Are you all tired out?"

"I'm knackered," said the scorpion, all miserable and wretched. "We're almost there. Please don't pike out on me now."

"First star? First star?" cried another child. "What d'ya mean? There's thousands and thousands comin' out now!"

Sure enough, stars were coming out one after the other, and the western mountains were but a shadow.

"Scorpio," said Choonse, his back so bent over that he was sure it would break in two, "we've already overrun our time. His Majesty is bound to tell us off. If worse comes to worst, we might even be turned into shooting stars. But it would be a catastrophe if you weren't where you're supposed to be on time."

"I'm so dog-tired I don't think I'm going to make it," said Pohse. "Scorpio, give it a bit more oomph so we can get you home before it's too late."

Pohse fell into a heap on the ground with a loud thud. This brought tears to the scorpion's eyes.

"Please forgive me," he said. "I'm such a blockhead. You have more brains in your baby fingernail than I have in my whole head. But I give you my word that I will make up for this. I promise you that!" No sooner had he spoken than did a bolt of lightning, decked in the brightest watercolor overcoat, come streaking toward them.

"I have come on the command of His Majesty to assist you," said the bolt of lightning, bowing ceremoniously to the twins. "Please hang on to my cape. I will have you back at your palaces in no time flat. His Majesty has, for some reason beyond me, been most delighted by what he has seen. And, as for you, Scorpio, no one has much taken to you ever, have they. His Majesty has bestowed this medicine on you. Drink up!"

"Well, Scorpio," cried the twins, "this is where we take our leave. Goodbye. Please take your medicine right now. And as for that promise you made to us, you've given your word, remember. Goodbye."

The twins grabbed hold of the lightning bolt's cape. The scorpion put his many feet together in gratitude and bowed reverently before drinking down all his medicine.

The lightning bolt blazed brilliantly again and in a flash they were at the stream they had left hours before.

"Now, please wash your bodies," said the bolt. "His Majesty has prepared new clothes and shoes for you. You have fifteen minutes."

The twin stars were delighted to bathe themselves in the cold crystal water flowing by them before donning beautifully scented robes of blue light and new shoes that beamed white. As for their weariness and pain, they were all gone. The twins felt rejuvenated.

"Well, let's be on our way," said the bolt of lightning.

The twins grasped the cape again and, in one streak of purple light, they found themselves back home at their palaces, and the bolt of lightning had vanished from sight.

"So, Choonse, let's get ready."

"Yes, Pohse, let's get ready."

The two of them climbed the steps to their palaces and, sitting on their knees facing each other, took up their silver flutes. The song "Once Around the Stars" could be heard all throughout the heavens.

The Scorpion with red red burning eyes
The Eagle with wings so gracefully unfurled
The Little Dog his eye so blue and bright
The long Snake of light shines in this world

Orion is singing brave and bold and true
While raining down his brilliant frost and dew
Andromeda's white nebula afloat
Fish with mouth agape up in the starry sky

And there where Great Bear stands up tall, remote
Five great steps his distance far away
From the Little Bear below the lone North Star
That guides us all … wherever near or far

The twin stars then began to play their flutes.

TWO

Two teeny-weeny blue stars are visible on the west bank of the Milky Way. Their names are Choonse and Pohse, and each has his own little crystal palace that precisely face each other. They both come back to their palaces every night without fail, sit properly on their knees and throughout the night accompany the song "Once Around the Stars" on their silver flutes. This is what they are there for in the first place.

The lower reaches of the sky had a pall of black cloud over it one evening, and under that pall it was raining cats and dogs. The twins were sitting up straight as usual in their palaces facing each other and playing their flutes when out of the blue a monstrous bully of a comet arrived on the scene.

"Listen, you blue twins!" said the comet, blowing a pale blue light of fog over them. "How about taking a little trip, eh? Tonight you don't have to do what you do all the time. Even the most seasoned sailor can't get his bearings from the stars when his ship's lost under a cloudy sky. The fellas at the observatory who check the stars have taken the night off and are about to doze off. The starry-eyed primary school kids who'd do anything on a dare have gone inside and are drawing pictures. The stars will go round and round without your blowing away on your pipes. Whadda ya say, eh? Get on the road. I'll get you back here by tomorrow evening."

"His Majesty allows us to not play on cloudy days," said Choonse, taking his lips from his flute. "We're playing because we like to."

"But I doubt that we'd be allowed to just go on a trip like that," said Pohse, also taking his lips from his flute. "It might clear up while we're on the road."

"No worries," said the comet. "His Majesty told me personally that it was okay. He said, 'Give 'em a ride when it clouds over.' Come on, let's be on our way already. I'm an awesome guy. They call me 'the celestial whale'. Heard that, haven't you? I gobble up all those wobbly little sardine stars and crunch down those black ricefish meteors. But the most thrilling thing of all is how I take a hairpin curve and circle right back in the direction I came from. My bones of light creak and screech and clatter. I go so fast and all but fly right out of my body."

"What do you say, Choonse," said Pohse, "shall we go with him? He says that His Majesty gave permission."

"But has His Majesty really done so?" asked Choonse.

"What?!" said the comet. "If I am not telling the truth, then may my head break up into little pieces and may it scatter, along with my torso and tail right down into the sea and turn into sea slugs! Why in hell would I ever be lying, eh?"

"Will you swear on the name of His Majesty?" asked Pohse.

"Sure, I swear," said the comet right away. "As His Majesty is my witness. I mean, um, His Majesty bequeaths on the twin stars one trip on this very day. How's that? Pretty good-sounding, wouldn't you say?"

"Uh-huh, that sounds good," they said. "So, let's be off."

"Okay then, grab hold of my tail right now," said the comet, with a grave look on his face. "Don't let go now. Got it? Ready?"

The twins held on to the comet's tail for dear life.

"Okay, off we go!" said the comet, blowing out a huge puff of pale light. "We're whooshing away in a puff of light!"

It's no wonder that the comet is called 'the celestial whale'. It sent the frail and fainter stars rushing to the corners of the sky. Before they knew it, the twin stars had covered an enormous distance, and their palaces were but tiny pale points of light in the back of beyond.

"We've come a long way from home," said Choonse. "Do you think we'll reach the place where the Milky Way drops off into a waterfall?"

"It's not the Milky Way that's gonna fall," said the comet in what was now a very unfriendly manner. "It's your own fall you oughta be thinkin' about! Ready, steady ... go!"

The comet shook his tail a couple of times with great force and, if that wasn't enough, swiveled his head around and hit the twins with a fierce blast of pale fog. This sent them hurtling down at breakneck speed into a blue-black abyss.

The comet laughed his head off.

"I take back all that swearing an' stuff I just did," he said … and he whooshed and puffed his way up, vanishing into the thinnest air.

The twin stars held tight to each other's elbows as they dropped through the sky, doing whatever it took to stay together. As they dropped dizzily down into the atmosphere, their bodies made the sound of thunder, sparkling and crackling bright red, before falling like an arrow through a layer of ink-like clouds and right into the black roaring waves of the sea.

The twins sunk deeper and deeper. But strange as it may seem, they were able to breathe normally underwater. The seabed was made of soft mud, and huge black things seemed to be asleep on it amidst the murky swaying seaweed. "Pohse," said Choonse, "we're on the bed of the sea, aren't we. I don't think we can get back to the sky from here. What are we in for now?"

"The comet pulled the wool over our eyes," said Pohse. "He even lied to His Majesty. He's really a revolting character, isn't he."

Just then a tiny little starfish glowing red spoke up at their feet.

"What sea or ocean do you two hail from?" he asked. "You've got the mark of blue starfish, you know."

"We're not starfish," said Pohse. "We're stars."

"Don't give me that!" said the starfish, fuming. "Stars?! Well, for your information, we starfish started out as stars. You two must be newcomers. Sure, you're greenhorn starfish, wet behind the ears and clearly up to no good. Listen, if you think you can just drop in down here like this because you've done something bad and you act all pigheaded and turn your nose up at all of us, you've got another thing coming. I'll have you know that I was a first-rate soldier when I lived in the sky!"

Pohse felt low and gazed upward. It had stopped raining, there wasn't a cloud in the sky, and you could see the sky through the seawater that was now calm and as clear as glass. The Milky Way and the celestial well and Aquila the Eagle and Lyra the Lyre were perfectly visible. You could even see the twins' palaces looking ever so tiny in the distance.

"Look, Choonse, you can see the whole sky and our palaces too. But, when you come down to it, we're starfish now."

"It can't be helped, Pohse. We can bid goodbye to everyone in the sky from here. I think we should apologize to His Majesty, even if we can't see him from here."

"Goodbye, Your Majesty. We are to become starfish from this day on."

"Goodbye, Your Majesty. We stupidly let the comet outfox us. We shall crawl on our bellies over the black mud of the seabed from this day on."

"Farewell, Your Majesty and all beings in the heavens. May you, I pray, prosper and be happy."

"Farewell, everyone. And to you, Your Supreme Majesty, please remain as you are forever and ever."

"Now, fork over those robes of yours!" babbled a large crowd of red starfish that had surrounded the twins.

"You two, hand over those swords!"

"Pay your taxes right now!"

"Stop bignoting yourselves!"

"Wipe my shoes, pipsqueaks!"

But then, out of the blue, a huge gigantic black thing passed over their heads, bellowing and roaring like there was no tomorrow. The starfish panicked and bowed low. The black thing was about to pass by them when it stopped dead in front of the twins.

"Well, well," it said, peering into their faces. "If it isn't two new rookies. Hasn't anybody taught you how to bow to your superiors?! Haven't you seen a giant whale before? They call me 'the comet of the sea'! Sound familiar? I gobble up all those wobbly little sardine stars and crunch down those black ricefish meteors. But the most thrilling thing of all is how I take a hairpin curve and circle right back in the direction I came from. The oil in my body is gooey. I take it that you two were banished from the heavens, so you must have documents to show it. Hand them over! Right this instant!"

The twins exchanged glances.

"We don't have anything of the sort," said Choonse.

The whale blew his top and shot a huge blast of water out of his mouth. This sent the starfish into a real tizzy and they all went hobbling here and there, but the twins maintained their cool and stood fast.

"No documents, eh?" said the whale, livid with rage. "You lowlife crooks! You'd be the first bad eggs to be sent down here for doing unspeakably evil things without being given papers. You're really the lowest of the low! Right. Say your prayers, because I'm going to down you in one gulp! Understand?"

The whale opened his mouth like a cave and got ready to swallow them up. The starfish and all the other fish around either swam away as fast as their fins would take them or dove straight into the mud, for fear of being swallowed up with them.

Just in the nick of time a silver beam of light shot through the water and a little sea snake appeared. This caused the whale to instantly clamp its mouth shut, as if he had been given a jolt.

"What are you doing here?" asked the befuddled sea snake, looking down on the twins from above. "You don't look to me like someone who's been banished down here from the heavens for committing some evil deed."

"These two little maggots have no official papers," piped in the whale.

"Shut your trap!" said the sea snake, glaring ferociously at the whale. "Who do you think you are, eh, calling these upstanding young ones maggots! You obviously can't see the halo that shines around the head of those who have performed good. Anybody can see the black shadow that gapes over the head of those who have committed evil. Please step over here, you two stars. I will take you to His Majesty.

And as for you, starfish … light up your lights. And as for you, whale, watch your step from now on or you'll be in for it!"

The whale scratched his head and bowed flat on the seabed. The twins were amazed to see that radiant red starfish had formed two rows, like lights lining a wide highway.

"Well, then, shall we go?" said the sea snake deferentially, shaking out a wave on his white hair.

The twins followed behind him on the road between the starfish lights. Before long they came upon the gate to an enormous white castle. The gate opened by itself and a host of upstanding sea snakes came out. The twins were taken to have an audience before the sea snake king.

"You're Choonse and Pohse, are you not?" smiled the king, who was a very old snake with a long white beard. "I've known about you for some time. The story of how you put your heart and soul into straightening out Scorpio's bent spirit has even made it down here. I took the liberty of including that story in our primary school textbooks. You must have been truly taken by surprise by the calamity that befell you."

"We are most humbled by your all-too-kind words," said Choonse. "Seeing as we are unable to return to the heavens, we would be more than happy to do whatever is in our power to help everyone here."

"Ah, it is I who am humbled," said the king, "by your self-effacement. I will order the waterspout to take you back to the heavens forthwith. And please remember me, the sea snake king, to His Majesty once you are back home."

"Does that mean that you have met His Majesty?" asked Pohse, delighted to hear what the king had said.

"Met him?" said the king, coming down from his throne in a flurry. "Dear, dear, not on my life. His Majesty is the only one I myself worship. He has been our teacher from time immemorial. I am but his humble and foolish servant. Perhaps you cannot fathom what I am saying now, but hopefully you will someday. Now, the waterspout must carry you home before the day breaks. Hey, you, is everything ready for them?"

"Yes, Majesty," replied one of the attendant sea snakes. "The waterspout is presently coiled in wait in front of the gate."

"Well, then, Your Majesty," said the twins, bowing politely to the king, "we bid you good day. We will send more formal expressions of our gratitude once we are up home. May this palace enjoy eternal prosperity."

"And may you two," said the king, standing in front of them, "continue to shine radiantly. I bid you good day."

The attendants all bowed reverently at the same time, and the twins walked through the gate. The waterspout lay coiled, fast asleep. An attendant sea snake lifted the twins up and placed them on the waterspout's head. The twins grasped its horns.

"Goodbye," shouted a host of radiant red starfish who had gathered around. "Please give our warmest wishes to His Majesty. Please ask him to grant us a pardon someday in the future."

"We'll be sure to ask him for you," said the twins in unison. "We look forward to the night when we will meet again in the sky."

The waterspout uncoiled itself in one fluid motion.

"Goodbye. Goodbye."

The waterspout thrust its head right out of the jet-black ocean … and in an instant was zinging noisily straight up into the sky at a furious clip, higher and higher and higher. It was still nighttime. The Milky Way was getting closer and closer, and the twin palaces, bigger and bigger.

"Get a load of that!" said the waterspout in the pitch dark.

The pale-blue luminescent comet had been smashed to bits, and his head and tail and torso were sailing down into the inky sea, flickering and flashing, as his head screamed insanely into the air.

"He's going to turn into sea slugs," said the waterspout in a soft voice.

Now "Once Around the Stars" could be heard, and the twins

arrived at their palaces.

"Goodbye. Be of good cheer," said the waterspout, easing them down, before shooting back down into the sea as fast as the wind.

The twins climbed the steps to their palaces.

"We humbly apologize for our careless behavior and for neglecting our obligations," they said, sitting up straight and addressing His Majesty, whom they could not see. "Despite this, we have been blessed by a miraculous turn of events, thanks to your benevolence. The ocean king has asked us to convey his most copious respects to you, and the starfish on the seabed have humbly begged for your mercy and forgiveness. And though it is far beyond our station, may we also ask you to forgive the sea slugs as well."

The twin stars took their silver flutes in hand. The sky was now golden in the east and the day was about to break in no time at all.

Barefeet of Light

"Barefeet of Light" is a lyrical story about death with very strong religious undertones. The bare feet themselves are, by inference, those of the Buddha.

Kenji was, from the time that he immersed himself in the reading and study of the Lotus Sutra while in his late teens, an ardent follower of the Nichiren sect of Buddhism. Nichiren was the thirteenth-century priest who based his teachings on the Lotus Sutra and the belief that all beings can attain Buddhahood in their current life. Kenji's deathbed wish to his father was that a thousand copies of the Lotus Sutra be printed and delivered to people.

That his father would comply was not a given, but he faithfully followed his son's instructions. Masajiro was not only a follower of the Jodo Shinshu sect, but one of the founders and pillars of the town's association for its propagation. Father and son fought bitterly over doctrine, as if that wasn't enough to fight over. After all, the father was an entrepreneur and landowner, and his eldest son just wanted to give everything away. The religious rift had not closed by the time of Kenji's death, but Masajiro did finally relent, converting some eighteen years later. He now rests at Shinshoji, a Nichiren sect temple.

"Barefeet of Light" was written around the time of Kenji's little sister Toshi's death in 1922, though, as with much of his work, he did make revisions as the years went on. A story like this of a death of a sibling could not be touching on any other event than that of his beloved sister's death. In fact, death and the surmounting of the grief that it brings is a frequent subject for Kenji. He knows that death can be severely painful and cause inexpressible sorrow; yet he also "knows" that this life is only one transient phase to another, the sparks that fly into the night sky and become stars, or, as he has it at the end of his beautiful poem "The Swordsmen's Dance of Haratai": "the rain of fire scattered into the Lion/Struck and passing on … a single life."

In his poem "Night," in which he writes about a time that "lukewarm new blood gushes" out of his mouth—he suffered, as did Toshi, from tuberculosis—he strives to overcome the pain and fear by saying …

This above all is the seminary of spring
Where Bodhisattvas have given up a hundred million lives
And the Buddhas have passed into Nirvana to reside
I have resolved time and again
To die alone
Unseen tonight by anyone
Leading myself by the hand.…

I cherish this image of him … leading himself by the hand. He hopes that he will be able to lead himself to a better place. That is the sole comfort of death.

The location of this story is the remote mountains of Iwate prefecture; the time, the dead of winter. This is a miserably poor family. The father is somehow able to feed himself and his two boys by making and selling charcoal. Like Kojuro in "The Bears on Mt. Nametoko," he sells what he can to a dealer, who no doubt passes it on at a substantial profit. The little brother Narao howls and weeps. He is afraid when he senses something ominous in what "the boy who flew in on the wind" said. Kenji doesn't name the boy, but we know who he is from another story. In this case, simply put, he is a harbinger of death, and Narao feels it in his bones. In fact, the three blue rays of light that cut across the room in the very beginning of the story already tell Kenji readers that they are in for a sad story about loss. The "beautiful scene" that they see is a glimpse into the next world, where there are countless suns that are mere gilded silhouettes …

the sun looking like a gigantic jewel with slivers of bitter-orange and green embedded in it, shining so brightly that they had to shut their eyes to its blinding light … and when they did, the sun continued to shine blue in the bluish pitch black that they could see, so they opened their eyes again and what they saw now was countless dark violet and gilded silhouettes of suns swaying and rolling against the sky.

Kenji has written any number of stories in which the person destined to die foresees the destiny. In "Barefeet of Light," the "shrill windlike whistling of the flute" that Narao hears coming from the top of the mountain is certainly akin to a death knell, and Narao weeps, sensing its import. In the late 1920s, Kenji wrote a cycle of poems titled "While Convalescing," thinking that he was going to die. One of those poems is "The Winds are Calling by the Front Door," in which those winds implore him to …

… keep your promise to marry
The one among us
Who sings in a beautiful soprano voice
In the blackened leafless forest
Above the giant jagged rock in the distance

It is the wind enticing him to the other world, the very same wind that Narao has heard.

The spindletree with its red fruit capsules in "Barefeet of Light" is called a *mayumi*, a melliflous word in Japanese that is also a female name, sometimes written, however, with various other characters. Though Kenji writes the name in hiragana to emphasize the lilting sound of the word, the characters for the name of the tree carry the meaning of "real bow." Bows for arrows were traditionally made from this wood and the tree was named after its product. (A similar phenomenon in English exists for the popular names rubber tree and lacquer tree.) The two brothers find themselves in the most horrifying of places. There is no doubt but that this is a Jigoku-e, a picture of hell, that genre of painting depicting the nether world. Ichiro and Narao are innocent children in both common senses of the word: They have little experience in life, and they have never committed a sin. But they are sent to hell for sins committed in previous lives. One of the demons tells them as much. This is a place of cruel torments and unspeakable tortures. Again, Kenji does not gloss over the details. We can hear the crack of the whip beside our ear.

But Ichiro's entreaty to whip him in his brother's place is heard, and the Enlightened One appears before them. All evil is drained of its ferocity; all darkness, swept away by light; and goodness, carried to you, with beautiful scent, on the wind.

"The timeless Buddha who bestows truth to all those who suffer ... There is no birth or death, no retreating or advancing ... no reality or unreality, no likenesses or differences...."

These form part of the lessons of Chapter Sixteen of the Lotus Sutra. Kenji's way of interpreting "no likenesses or differences" may be summed up in two lines from the first poem in his collection *Spring and Ashura* ...

just as everything forms what is the sum in me
so do all parts become the sum of everything that is

We all form separate entities, yet we are formed into one entity at one and the same time.

"Barefeet of Light" is surely one of Kenji's most beautiful and saddest stories. But it is also one that paints a distinct picture of what he called "the realm of light."

BAREFEET OF LIGHT
by Miyazawa Kenji

CHAPTER ONE
A Hut in the Mountains

Ichiro was awakened by a racket of birdcalls. It was long past dawn.

Three blue rays of light cut across the room from a corner of the hut, falling straight over the faces of the two brothers before shining on the woodman's knife and straw leggings hanging on the reed wall.

Bright embers of kindling were still burning red in the middle of the dirt floor. It was the smoke that was turning the sun's rays blue, taking on any number of forms as it twisted upward.

Ichiro turned to his little brother Narao, whose face was as red as an apple.

"Oh, the sun's way up," he whispered.

Narao was still dead to the world. His lips were slightly parted, so Ichiro reached out and flicked his brother's white teeth with his fingernail. Narao frowned without opening his eyes and, taking soft whistling breaths, fell right back asleep again.

"Get up, Narao! It's morning already. Get up!" said Ichiro, waggling his brother's head.

Narao scowled and mumbled something under his breath, finally squinting his eyes open.

"Yeah, I forgot, we came to the mountains," he murmured, as if realizing where he was for the first time.

"An' the fire went out sometime in the night. You saw it go out, didn't you?"

"Nope."

"An' it got so cold dad woke up and lit it again."

But Narao was off somewhere and just kept mum with a vacant

look in his eyes.

"Dad's doin' some work outside. Come on, get up, will ya!"

"Yeah."

The two of them got out of the single little futon they were bundled up together in and huddled over the fire. Narao made a face and rubbed his eyes, while Ichiro just stared into the glowing embers.

The river by the hut roared like a torrent and the birds were trilling loudly. Just then the door swung open, a golden shaft of light streamed right over Ichiro's feet, the snow on the mountains opposite the hut was alight and the shadowy figure of their father came through the door.

"You boys're up, that's good. You must have froze last night."

"We didn't."

"Fire kept dyin' out, so had to get up twice to keep it goin'. Narao, the food's ready, so go an' clean your teeth."

"Yeah."

"Better than home up here, ain't it?"

"Much better, Daddy, tho' there's no school up here to go to."

Their father chuckled, lifting the pot onto the fire. Ichiro stood up and walked outside, and Narao followed him.

They were met by a beautiful scene, with the glittering blue light of a radiant sky penetrating deep into their eyes and the sun looking like a gigantic jewel with slivers of bitter-orange and green embedded in it, shining so brightly that they had to shut their eyes to its blinding light … and when they did, the sun continued to shine blue in the bluish pitch black that they could see, so they opened their eyes again and what they saw now was countless dark violet and gilded silhouettes of suns swaying and rolling against the sky. Ichiro put his hands below the running water pipe. A thick icicle hung from the mouth of the pipe and drops of water falling off it shone in the sunlight, giving off steam that looked warm but was really freezing. Ichiro rinsed out his mouth and washed his face as quick as he could, raising his half-frozen fingers up to the sun, which didn't do much good, so he put them flat against his neck instead. Narao did exactly what his older brother did but gave up right away because he couldn't take the cold. His hands were all puffy and frostbitten red. Ichiro wrapped his palms around Narao's wet little hands to warm them up.

"Oh, they're so freezing, aren't they," he said.

The two of them went back inside again.

Their father was plunged into thought as he fixed his eyes on the fire, the lid clattered on top of the pot, and the two boys sat themselves down. The sun was well up in the sky, its three blue rays slicing through the hut on a sharp angle. The snow covering the mountain was etched against the blue sky, as if calling out to the heart to come to it.

It was then that something formless like smoke or a misty fog appeared out of the blue on top of the mountain, and in a moment the shrill windlike whistling of a flute came from there. Narao's lips curled downward, a strange look clouded over his face and, for no apparent reason, he started to sob. Ichiro stared at him, puzzled.

"What's got into you, Narao, eh?" said their father. "You gettin' homesick or somethin'? What is it?"

Narao just put his cheeks in his hands and bawled even louder, not saying a word.

"Does your tummy hurt? Narao?" asked Ichiro.

But all Narao did was howl and sob like before, as his father gently took his head in his hands and felt his forehead. This calmed Narao down, and now he was taking deep breaths between sobs.

"What're you cryin' for, eh? Wanna go home, do you?"

"Dunno," sobbed Narao, shaking his head over and over again.

"You hurtin' somewhere?"

"Dunno."

"Then what's all this bawlin' for, eh? I mean, a man doesn't bawl, ain't that right?"

Narao finally managed to eke out an answer between sobs.

"I'm afraid, Daddy," he said.

"What're you afraid of, eh? I'm right here and so's your big brother, an' the sun's up in the mornin', an' there ain't nothin' to be afraid of, eh?"

"I know, but I'm still afraid."

"But why?"

"'Cause of what that boy who flew in on the wind said."

"What'd he say, eh? That boy wouldn't hurt a fly. What'd he say?"

"He said, he said that you were goin' to put new clothes on me, Daddy."

At that he started to bawl again, and Ichiro felt a shiver run down his spine. But their father just laughed it off.

"That boy who flew in on the wind, is it?" he chuckled. "He sure knows what he's talkin' about, I'll give him that. I'm plannin' on buyin' you a new outfit in April, so there's no cause to cry. You can stop your bawlin' now."

"Yeah, no cause to cry, Narao," piped in Ichiro, trying to console him.

"That's not all he said," said Narao, rubbing his eyes until they were bright red.

"Not all?"

"He said that mummy would take a good hot bath with me, he did."

"Now, that's a bare face lie, I tell you. Imagine a big grown up boy like you takin' a bath with his mummy. That boy's just full of hot air, I tell you. Don't cry, don't cry!"

Their father forced a laugh and his face took on a bluish tint. As for Ichiro, he couldn't laugh for the strange tightness in his chest. And as for Narao, he couldn't stop weeping.

"Well, now, dry your tears 'cause it's time to eat," said their father.

"But then he went on to say that everybody was going to see me off," said Narao, rubbing and rubbing his little red eyes.

"See you off? Sure, he means that when you grow all up everyone will see you off when you leave us. There's nothin' bad at all in that. So, wipe away those tears, will ya? I'm gonna take you to the Morioka

Festival in the spring, so quit your cryin', eh?"

"What's so scary about that boy who flew in with the wind anyway?" said Ichiro, after staring into the fire now lucent in the sunlight. "He likes to pull the wool over people's eyes."

Once again Narao sobbed, but only from time to time, and his eyes had little black circles around them from all the rubbing in the sooty smoke. He looked like a racoon cub.

"Well now," said their father with a teary smile himself as he stood up, "you'll just have to wash that face of yours again, won't you."

CHAPTER 2
The Mountain Pass

The water in the roaring river had become more placid, peaceful and, it seemed, warmer by afternoon.

The boys' father was standing by the door to the hut endlessly discussing things with a dealer. The dealer had come by horse to collect the charcoal that their father made, to sell it on to others. The boys went to the door to watch the dealer strapping big straw bundles of charcoal onto his horse. The horse's brown mane was all frizzy as it chomped away at its fodder. Some kind of metal gear could be seen reflected in its bulging eyes and the boys felt really sorry for it.

"You boys stick with this man," said their father, "till you get back home. He's goin' as far as Narabana. I'll come for you this comin' Saturday, weather permittin'."

The boys had to be home to go to school by the next day, a Monday.

"Well, then," said Ichiro, "we'll be off."

"Yep. An' get your mum to fetch that saw—the big one—and hand it to someone who'll be comin' up this way. Got it? Don't forget, now. It only takes about an hour and a half to get home, so you little ones shouldn't take more than three and a half. But don't eat the snow, even if you're thirsty."

"Got it!" said Narao, now in such good spirits that he was hopping around in the snow.

"Well, I'll be headin' back now," said the dealer to the boys' father after he had finished strapping the bundles of charcoal onto the horse and tying them down securely with rope. "Think it best if they walk ahead of me, don't you?"

"No, let 'em follow you from behind," he said, bowing with a big smile. "Thanks so much for lookin' after them."

"All right then, off we go," said the dealer, gripping the horse's tethering strap and setting out. The horse trotted slowly, with its bells around its drooping neck tinkling and jangling in the air.

Ichiro let Narao walk in front of him. The snow on the road was smooth, hard and easy to walk on, but the sky was so steely blue as to look a bit frightening.

"Hey, some kind of bunches of things are dangling down on that tree over there," cried Narao.

"What was that?" asked Ichiro, who was too far behind to hear.

"That tree over there. It's got some bunches of things hanging on it."

Sure enough, there was a lone tree standing below the cliff and its branches were absolutely covered in clusters of brown fruit. Ichiro stood transfixed by the sight until he noticed that the horse had left them behind. The man leading the horse peered in Ichiro's direction, and when he saw him running to catch up, he turned ahead and started to walk again.

The road was still packed down with hard snow, but it was now so bumpy and lumpy that the horse stumbled over and over. Narao was so taken with what he was seeing that he too stumbled and tripped, almost falling over.

"Mind your feet!" said Ichiro to him each time he stumbled.

Before they knew it, the road had veered away from the river and was now winding up the side of a hill shaped like an enormous elephant. A number of chestnut trees with dry leaves clinging to their branches stood on the hillside, some birds flew off beyond them, clacking and jabbering away, the sunlight dimmed and the snow darkened, yet strangely gleaming more deeply than before.

That's when they heard the jangling of harness bells and saw a procession of horses coming their way. They all came together where the road led up to a stand of spindletrees decked out in red fruit capsules. The dealer's horse made room for the other horses and stood in the snowy shoulder, while the boys, still behind the horse, stepped off the road and found themselves knee deep in snow.

"Mornin'," said the dealer.

"Mornin'," said the men leading the horses past him.

The man bringing up the rear stopped short as his horse went a bit ahead without him.

"Whoa there!" he said.

The boys, the dealer and his horse all stepped onto the road again, and the dealer started conversing about one thing and another with the man who had stopped. The boys stood there waiting for the dealer's horse to continue the journey but, losing patience, started out on their own. After all, thought Ichiro, their house was just over the mountain pass in front of them about four kilometers from there, the sky had just about cleared up save for the odd cloud, and all they had to do was take the road straight home.

The dealer, who continued to talk with the other man, noticed out of the corner of his eye that the boys had gone ahead, but he figured that he could easily catch up with them. Narao, anxious to get home, forged ahead as fast as he could, while Ichiro kept glancing back to see the horse with its drooping head. All he could catch glimpses of was the two men deep in conversation and their big white gloves waving about in the air.

Even though the narrow road was now steeply climbing up the mountainside, Narao started horsing around, lifting up his knees and grunting on purpose, as if he was having a hard time with the climb.

"Hey, it's really steep here," said Ichiro, panting, from behind. "This is the path to the pass."

But Narao was soon exhausted, stopping so abruptly in his tracks that Ichiro smashed right into him.

"You puffed, Narao?" said, Ichiro, panting for breath.

From where they were the road behind them looked like no more than a thin track, and both the men and their horses were below the rise in the hill and were out of sight. Several stands of chestnut and oak trees were scattered on the blanket of snow that now gave off an inexpressibly gloomy light under the huge silver plate of the sun dimmed by a gigantic gauze of cloud.

"Look, a bird's whizzing across the sky!" cried Narao, catching sight of a hawk swooping right over their head and flying off into the distance.

"Let's get over the pass now," said Ichiro, after gazing around in silence. "It looks like snow's coming."

The moment he said that, the gentle darkening line of the mountain ridge lying below the radiant sky turned a milky white and a blanket of fine dry powdery snow enveloped the boys.

"Quick, Narao, get up to the top," said Ichiro, alarmed. "It's snowing already. It'll be flat on top and we can make it from there."

Narao sensed the alarm in his brother's voice and started to rush up the mountain in a flurry.

"Slow down! We'll be all right," said Ichiro, gasping for breath. "It's not all that far once we're at the top."

But, in reality, both of them knew that they had to hurry, and they scurried up the steep snowy slope at a dizzying pace, so fast that they were soon out of breath. It was now snowing thick and fast, burying everything around under a pall of white. The two brothers too were shrouded in white. Narao, weeping, clung to Ichiro.

"Should we go back, Narao?" said Ichiro, in two minds as he glanced down the mountain. "Maybe we should go back…."

But it was obvious that there was now no going back. The track below was no more than a long ash-colored pit. In contrast, the way up to the ridge was shining bright and they knew that they were almost there. The ground leveled off from there for a couple of kilometers and they had many times seen copper pheasants taking to the air and lots and lots of red and yellow berries growing on bushes and shrubs.

"It's not much more to go, so don't stop now," said Ichiro, looking straight into his brother's eyes. "It won't be snowing up at the top and the road flattens out, so just keep walking. There's nothing to be afraid of so long as we keep moving. The man with the horse will catch up with us, so stop crying. We don't have to rush to get to the top."

Narao smiled, wiping away his tears. Ichiro felt a lump in his throat when he saw tiny snowflakes landing on his brother's cheeks, then melting away. This time he started climbing ahead of Narao. The track was not all that steep now and the snow not that deep, though their straw boots sunk all the way down into it.

Black jagged boulders capped with snow lined the track as the two boys trudged up the mountain to the top, both of them ascending calmly, without speaking to each other, one step at a time. Ichiro brushed the snow off his body by flapping the cape around his shoulders. And, as luck would have it, they reached the top. "We made it, we got here," said Ichiro, looking back at his brother. "Narao, it's all smooth sailing from now on!"

Narao was out of breath, but a smile of relief passed over his beet-red face. A thick curtain of fine snow was falling between them.

"The horse is sure to be halfway up already. Let's call out."

"Yeah."

"Ready? One ... two ... three ... HELLO!"

But their voice just vanished in the thin air, and there wasn't so much as an echo, let alone a reply, as dark swirls of snow came whirling down on top of them.

"Right," said Ichiro, starting to walk again. "Let's get a move on. Shouldn't take more than half an hour to get down."

Just then a gale came howling down upon them, billows of smoky snow shot up from the ground, and the two boys could barely catch a breath as the freezing cold bit into their flesh through open seams in their clothes. They were forced to stop and cover their face with their palms until the wind finally passed over them. They started plodding ahead again, but they didn't get far before another powerful gust of wind struck them, making a terrifying flutelike noise, forcing them to double up into the wind as they began to lose their footing in snow that was now like a river flowing under them.

Up at the top it was not at all as they had imagined. Narao, at a loss for to what to do, tried to cling to his brother as he looked back down the mountain. But the wind had died down, and Ichiro had started to trudge through the snow again, leaving him to follow. Narao toddled along as best as he could, silently whimpering.

The heels in their boots were entirely seeped in snow, and though there were snowdrifts in their way from time to time they managed to get through them. Ichiro made good progress, while Narao did all he could to follow in his footsteps. Ichiro looked back often, but even so it was hard for Narao to keep up with him. When howling gusts of wind sent smoky swirls of snow into the air, Ichiro stopped to let Narao, who was rushing to him in small steps, catch up. And when he did, he grabbed Ichiro as if his life depended on it.

But by then they hadn't even covered half the distance across the ridge and the gigantic snowdrifts there were sending them tripping and stumbling. One of the snowdrifts was bigger than Ichiro had foreseen. He tumbled over himself and couldn't free his feet. His hands and lower body were completely buried in snow, and when he managed to free himself, even he thought it funny and blurted out a laugh. But Narao just stood back behind him and bawled like a baby.

"I'm all right, Narao," said Ichiro, taking some steps ahead. "Stop your crying."

Now it was Narao's turn to fall on his face. He thrust his hands into the snow and couldn't manage to get on his feet right away, staying like that with his head drooped down as if bowing to someone, crying his eyes out. Ichiro ran to him and lifted him up.

"We're on the last leg now," he said, brushing the snow off his brother's arms. "Are you up to walking?"

"I am, yeah," said Narao.

But he had a faraway look in eyes welled with tears, and his lips were curled down in a frown.

The snow didn't stop falling and the wind howled more threateningly than before. Now the two of them started to run, but this only caused them both to stumble and tumble until they couldn't tell if they were still on the track or not. All they saw was an enormous black boulder that seemed to appear abruptly out of nowhere beside them.

The wind rushed at them again, and Narao was beside himself with fright. The snow covered him like dust, like sand, like smoke. The track was gone, and facing them was another huge black boulder. Ichiro looked back, but all he could see was the hollow of footsteps that they had left in the snow.

"We took a wrong turn," said Ichiro, taking Narao's hand and trying to run. "We've got to retrace our footsteps."

But they fell on their faces into the snow at the first step. Narao burst into tears once again.

"Don't cry, Narao," said Ichiro, putting his arms around his brother as they stood below the boulder. "We'll stay put until it clears up."

But the mad wind beat against them with such ferocity, dumping so much snow over them that they could hardly breathe.

"It's no use," said Narao through his tears. "It's no use."

But his voice just scattered with the wind, as Ichiro took his cape off, wrapped it around him and hugged him tight, thinking that they were both bound to die from the wind and the snow. Countless multicolored lanterns of many shapes seemed to float before his eyes.

It was only the last New Year's holiday that they had been invited to the family's main house, and they all ate mandarin oranges together and Narao was stuffing one after another into his mouth and Ichiro had to glare at him to get him to stop and he saw that Narao had little red hands from chilblains like now and he felt so sorry for his little brother, as if some sort of poison was winding its way through his own body.

Ichiro sat there in the snow, not letting go of Narao for an instant.

CHAPTER THREE
The Realm of Dim Light

And yet … and yet despite all this, what transpired was as if in a dream.

In time the freezing needle slivers of snow turned somehow pleasantly warm, Narao was nowhere to be seen, and Ichiro found himself strolling all by himself in a grove of dark hazy light. It was all a gloomy yellow, so that you couldn't tell if it was the middle of the day or the middle of the night, and a host of plants that looked like wormwood and thickets of black bushes were growing here and there, breathing as if they were some sort of creature.

Ichiro looked down at his body. He couldn't for the life of him recall when he had put on the whole grey cloth that enveloped his body and, startled, he saw that his feet were bare and covered in deep wounds with blood oozing out of them, as if he had walked in bare feet a long long way. His heart and stomach felt drained of everything. He felt as if his body was about to break in half and, suddenly terrified, he began to wail.

What kind of a world have I come to, he wondered … but there was a hush over everything and no answer was coming to him. The sky was eerily vacant, and the more he looked to it for a sign, the more peculiar and anxious he felt. In an instant he felt a pain in his feet, as if they were on fire. Where in the world could Narao be, he thought.

"NARAO!" he cried out to the dark yellow sky.

Nothing but silence could be heard all around. That's when he couldn't stand it anymore and started to run, not caring at all about the pain in his feet. A wind rose, the cloth wrapped around him streamed straight back, and as he rushed ahead with tears in his eyes and bare feet, with the cloth, now in tatters, flowing farther back from his sides, he could picture the entire scene with himself in it and felt even more terrified than ever.

"NARAO!" he shrieked again.

A faint voice came to him from far far away.

"Ichiro…."

Ichiro, tears streaming down his cheeks, rushed to where the sound had come from, calling out his little brother's name over and over again. Sometimes he thought he dimly heard a voice answer him and sometimes he couldn't tell if he heard it or not. His feet had turned bright red, but he couldn't feel the pain. The blood oozing from his wounds was shining eerily blue.

Ichiro didn't stop running for an instant until he caught sight of a boy. The light coming off the boy was flickering like the flame on a candle about to go out. The boy was Narao, who was weeping with his face in his hands. Ichiro ran to his side, but just as he got there he lost his balance and fell down. He picked himself up with all his might and hugged Narao. But the light coming off Narao was now flickering on and off with such speed that Ichiro couldn't tell if he was embracing him or not, until he once more threw his arms around him and hugged him for dear life.

"Narao," said Ichiro, stroking his head, "where have we come?"

He was so choked up with tears that he was unsure whether he had said that himself or heard someone saying it in a dream.

"We just died," said Narao, sobbing.

Ichiro looked down at Narao's feet. They too were bare and covered in deep wounds.

"We can dry all our tears," said Ichiro, gazing around. The distance was bathed in a white glow and not a sound could be heard. "Let's see if we can make it to that bright place over there. There's got to be a home there for us. Can you walk?"

"Yeah. I wonder if Mummy's there."

"Sure she is. She's bound to be there. Let's go."

Ichiro took the lead. Perhaps some long arms would reach out to them from that dim and hazy yellow sky. The pain in their feet was now excruciating.

"We've got to make it there quick," said Ichiro, trying to endure the searing pain, as if his feet were white hot on fire. "We only need to make it there."

But it was obvious that Narao was in such unimaginable pain that he fell to the ground, unable to stop wailing.

"Hold on tight to me, Narao," said Ichiro, clenching his teeth from the pain and hoisting his little brother over his shoulder. "I'm going to make a dash for it."

And having said that, he ran like there was no tomorrow toward the hazy white light, bearing the pain that was ripping through his body. He fell down time and time again, but time and time again he picked himself up and started running again. The way behind him was now enshrouded in a bleary ash-colored mist and, briefly looking back, he caught a glimpse of something dimly red beyond the mist as he ran for dear life straight ahead.

Ichiro was so terrified he could barely get a breath out, yet each time he bore the pain and forced himself to pick up his little brother and run. Narao was slumped over his brother's shoulder as if totally unconscious.

"Narao, stay with me," cried Ichiro with all his strength. "Narao, it's me, Ichiro, your big brother."

Narao barely—just barely—managed to open his eyes, but his blackish pupils were not visible. Ichiro mustered all the strength he could and, lifting Narao over his shoulder, ran like the wind toward the dim light over and through what looked like flickering white flames. He fell over any number of times and felt like his whole body was being pulverized into glowing blue dust by a massive boulder, and when he ran, streaming tears behind him, he couldn't tell if his legs were actually moving or not. But he nonetheless didn't stop running, as if through a dream, never for a second letting go of his little brother.

When he finally came to the dimly-lit place he had his sights on, he saw that it wasn't at all the nice bright place he had imagined, and he just stood there frozen to the spot. There was a large hollow, like a valley, right before his eyes, and in it streams of wretched pathetic-looking children were being driven this way and that, back and forth, back and forth. Some of the children had a little cap on, while others had only an ash-colored rag over their naked body. There were pale skinny children with bulging eyes and tiny children with red hair, and children with bones sticking out who were rushing ahead with their knees bent. All of them were leaning forward as they walked, shivering and shaking from some kind of terror, never daring to even look to the side, breathing with deep heavy sighs and sobbing silently as they were being driven back and forth, back and forth. All of the children's feet had cuts and wounds like those Ichiro had on his own feet.

The most terrifying thing of all was the gigantic red-faced creatures with a human form, dressed in armor with jaggedy ash-colored thorns sticking out all over it. Their hair looked like it was made of flames and their bright-red eyes too were inflamed. They walked amongst the children wielding big thick whips, as the ground itself grated and rasped under their feet. Ichiro was frozen stiff in terror.

A curly-haired little boy like Narao, all wobbly on his painful feet, fell out of line.

"Mummy, it hurts so much!" he cried, about to tumble over himself.

At that, one of the terrifying creatures stood his ground and glared at the boy. The boy raised a hand and stumbled backward, trying to get away from the creature. But the creature was too quick for him and, with his lips twitching furiously, cracked his whip on him. The boy fell silently to the ground, writhing in agony. The children coming up behind him saw the whole thing and just stepped aside on their wobbly feet, passing him without making a sound. The boy on the ground continued to squirm and, doing his best to put the pain in his feet out of his mind, staggered to his feet.

As for Ichiro, he just stood there nailed to the spot, unable to move either forward or backward. That's when Narao blinked open his eyes.

"Daddy!" he screamed.

The huge creature standing in the hollow just below them glared up at them with its terrifying inflamed contorted eyes. Ichiro felt as if he couldn't even take a single breath.

"What in hell do you think you're doin' there, eh? Get down here this instant!" hollered the creature, brandishing his whip.

Ichiro teetered a couple of steps to the edge of the hollow as if being sucked down there by the glaring red eyes of the creature before stopping dead and hugging Narao with all his might. That's when the enormous creature's cheeks twitched and twinged and, with all his teeth bared, he started to climb toward Ichiro, howling and roaring all the while. In a flash, the two brothers were grabbed, and they found themselves in line with all the other children.

Ichiro felt full of pity as he watched his little brother, who could now walk, plod over the ground on feet wracked with pain. Ichiro called out over and over to his brother in a low voice as he was forced to make his way forward. But it appeared that Narao had swept his older brother from his mind. All he could do was hobble from the pain straight ahead, waving a hand behind him as if warding off terror.

It occurred to Ichiro then that these creatures forcing them to march ahead were demons, and he began to wonder what sin Narao and the other children could possibly have committed to condemn them to a place as awful as this. At that moment Narao stumbled to the ground over the bladelike red edge of a rock, and a demon cracked his big thick whip over his little body as if to slice it in two.

"Whip me in his place," said Ichiro, hanging on to the demon's arm and swinging from side to side. "Narao has never done a bad thing in his life."

"Sins are not punished for just one lifetime," shouted the demon, glaring at Ichiro, his lips furiously twitching away and his bare teeth blinding with light. "Get a move on!"

Ichiro broke out into a cold sweat, his spine tingled with pins and needles, and everything around him spun around him in a blue daze.

And so, the two brothers were force marched from then on, until they gradually seemed to get used to it and felt their pain easing. They watched, as if captured in a dream, as the others fell down on their lacerated feet. Then, without warning, everything there became dim and dark until there was black all around. The only thing that seemed to float up in the blackness was the pale line of marching children.

Ichiro's eyes became accustomed to the darkness and he could make out lots of black figures sitting perfectly still and glowing with a faint blue glow in the midst of a vast plain. All of them were enshrouded in long black hair, and all you could see was their white hands and feet sticking out. One of the figures seemed to budge a bit then abruptly begin to run, squirming all the while and screaming as if its body was being ripped to shreds. The next thing Ichiro knew, the figure fell silent and rolled onto the ground like a big ball of mud. Now he could see in the dark more clearly. The hair enshrouding the figures was actually made of the thinnest sharpest blades and they sliced into the bodies of the figures if they so much as budged.

The children walked farther and came to a place where it was a little lighter and the ground was bright red. The children in front of the line suddenly shrieked and wailed, the procession came to a halt, and the demons were cracking their whips and hollering in fury. It all sounded like thunder and hail had been let loose.

Narao was hobbling along right in front of Ichiro, and in front of him the field was blanketed with what looked like tiny slivers of agate that pierced the soles of the children who walked over it. The demons, though, wore shoes made of iron that crunched and pulverized the agate when they stomped on it. The air around Ichiro was filled with wails and screams, among them, Narao's.

"Where are they taking us?" asked Narao to the girl beside him. "Why are they punishing us like this?"

"I wish I knew," she sobbed, shaking her head from side to side. "Ow, Mummy … Ow … Ow!"

"Shut up!" barked a demon, cracking its whip behind them. "Your being here is all your own doing. Who said there's even gonna be an end place for you, eh?"

The blades of grass covering the plain grew rougher and sharper, and the children in front fell over again and again, barely managing to lift themselves up for the wounds on their feet and body. It got so bad that a single bark from the demons or a crack of their whip made them trip.

Narao looked back at his big brother, seemingly recognizing him for the first time, going to him and clinging onto him.

"Get a move on!" hollered a demon, bringing down the bite of his whip right onto Ichiro's arms that were embracing Narao.

Ichiro's arms throbbed and lost all sensation, but he kept the embrace around Narao, who was holding onto him for dear life.

"Please, I beg of you, don't hurt Narao," he cried to the demon who held his whip high above his head. "Please don't keep punishing him."

"Move it!" shouted the demon, his whip biting into the arms that shielded Narao.

Out of the blue Ichiro sensed some words that wafted to him like a faint breeze or a delicate fragrance …

"The timeless Buddha who bestows truth to all those who suffer … There is no birth or death, no retreating or advancing … no reality or unreality, no likenesses or differences…."

… and it seemed to him that what he was going through was easier to accept, and he repeated some of those words … "no birth or death … no likenesses or differences…." And when he did, the demon in front of him stopped dead in his tracks and stared at him, befuddled. The procession of children came to a halt too. There were no more cracking whips or screams. A hush fell over that entire realm. That's when they all saw an immensely tall and magnificent being coming their way across the dim red agate field that had been instantly transformed into a golden plain.

This gave them, for no reason that they could understand, some peace.

CHAPTER FOUR
Barefeet of Light

The feet of this being were an incandescent white as it walked with lightning speed and straight as an arrow toward them, its feet flickering at times until it came right up to Ichiro.

Ichiro was so blinded by the light that he didn't know where to look. The being's huge bare feet shined pure white, as if they were shells, with the radiant flesh around its enormous ankles hanging all the way down to the ground; and even though those feet had trod over bladelike slivers of agate and red-hot rising flames, there was not a single cut or scar on their soles, and the thorns sticking out of the ground remained unbent under them.

"You all have nothing at all to be afraid of," said the being with an absolutely imperceptible smile on its lips.

Its huge pupils were like blue lotus petals and they looked down on all of them with great dignity. All the children found themselves putting their palms together.

"You all have no cause for fear. Compared to the mighty power of virtue that encompasses the world, your sins are like the tiniest drops of dew on the tips of the thorns of thistles are to the light of the sun. You have no cause at all for fear."

Before they knew it they all found themselves forming a circle around the being, and every last demon there, so terrifying up to then, was standing behind them with their huge hands obediently clasped together and their heads hanging down.

"All of you have received terrible wounds," the being said, running its gaze around the circle. "You have only yourselves to blame for these wounds. Yet, in the end, that too is nothing."

The being gently stroked Narao's head with its huge pure-white palm. The two brothers could actually smell the faint fragrance of magnolia coming off that palm. Before long, the wounds and scars on the children's bodies had healed over and vanished. One of the demons wept and got down on bended knee before the being. It reverently lowered its forehead to the bladelike agate ground and reached out to touch those feet of light.

Once again a faint smile appeared on the being's lips, as a grand circle of golden light shone around its head.

"The ground you walk on here is made of sword blades that cut deeply into your feet and bodies. But that is only your illusion. The ground is actually perfectly smooth. Behold it."

The being leaned slightly forward and described a circle on the ground with its pure-white hand. All of them there rubbed their eyes and couldn't believe what they had just heard. The miserable ground that had up till then been made up of thorns of red agate and tongues of flames sending up black fire was transformed into the pure-blue surface of a lake, so perfectly smooth that not a single ripple was to be seen on it, and that surface appeared to sweep on and on, yet on the very edge were countless stripes of dark-green malachite and past the edge of that floating in the silence like a mirage that you could see in all detail, magnificent trees and grand buildings. The buildings were so tall that, even at that distance, the children had to raise their eyes to see roofs giving off a blue-and-white light and pennants displaying every color in the rainbow hanging down from them. Covered bridges with balustrades shining like pearls connected the buildings high in the air, and there were pagodas decked with bells and filigree studded with precious gemstones, with their slender finials shooting up into the sky. The water's surface mirrored these many buildings in perfect silence.

The countless trees there may just as well have been made of gems and jewels. Some had the shape of pure-blue alders, while others resembled willows bearing little platinum berries. An ethereal sound came off the gleaming and glistening leaves on all the trees as they brushed against each other.

Then they heard the music of a host of instruments floating down from the sky on fine multicolored dust, and amidst it they were startled to see magnificent beings filling the sky, some soaring through the air like birds. The long silver ribbon-like cords of their robes flew perfectly straight behind them without so much as a ripple in them, while the air carried the fragrance of a summer's dawn.

Ichiro realized that he and all the others were standing on that smooth-as-glass pure-blue water's surface. But, he thought, is this really a lake … no, it couldn't be made of water, it was all too hard for that, all too cold, all too smooth. In reality, it was a huge sheet made of blue gemstone. No, he thought again, not a sheet … it must be the ground in the end, though, he had to a admit, it was so placid and radiant that it certainly appeared to be the surface of a lake. Ichiro looked up to the being, who was now completely different from before. It now stood behind them smiling imperceptibly, with a magnificent diadem crowned in a golden halo, more noble and imposing than any other being ever visible to them. Angels bearing gold and ruby trays of exquisite flowers flew directly overhead, scattering deep gold and dark azure petals on top of them. The petals sunk downward from the sky as gently and quietly as air itself.

All the children were different from before and looked truly magnificent. Ichiro turned to Narao, who was now wrapped in golden robes with a diadem on his head. Then Ichiro looked down at his own feet. There was not a wound or a scar on them and they shone a radiant pure white. An exquisite scent was coming off his hands. The children were beside themselves with joy.

"It's really great here," said one of them. "Is that a museum way out there?"

"Well, there are definitely museums there," replied the grand shining being, smiling down. "Everything that ever happened or happens is collected there."

That was only the first of many questions.

"Do they have a library too? I really wanna read more and more stories by Andersen and things."

"I bet they've got a playground too where you can do anything. I bet if you threw a ball it would never stop moving!"

"I wanna have chocolate," said a little boy.

"You can have all the books here your heart desires," said the magnificent being. "There are even big books with lots of little books inside them, and there are the tiniest books that have all the books in the world inside them. You should read as much as you can. And as for the playgrounds, once you've learned how to run on them you'll be able to dash right through fire. And there's plenty of chocolate too, the best under the sun. Here you go."

The magnificent being raised its sights to the sky, as an angel came shooting straight down holding a stunning bowl decorated with yellow triangles. Once on the blue ground, the angel knelt before the grand being and offered it the bowl.

"Have a bite of this," said the grand being to all the children, handing a piece to Narao.

Before they knew it they all had a piece of the delicious chocolate in their hand. They took a single lick and felt a cool calming sensation rush throughout their body, and the tip of their tongue flickered and glowed like a blue firefly or a bitter-orange flame with an exquisite floral pattern. When they finished eating they felt full of energy, and an indescribably lovely fragrance came off their entire body. "Hey, Ichiro," said Narao, as if suddenly coming to his senses, "I wonder where Mummy is right now."

"I will show you your mother as she was before soon enough," said the grand being, turning toward Narao and stroking his head. "But first you must go to school here, and you won't be seeing your big brother for a time, because he's about to go back now to your mother. And you," he added, turning to Ichiro, "you're bound back to the world of before. You're a fine and innocent child, and it's most admirable that you stuck with your little brother through that field of thorns. Those bare feet of yours that were cut and sliced as you passed through that grove of evil blades will now take you anywhere you wish to go. Keep the spirit that is now in your heart forever. Countless beings from here have gone to live where you were living. Leave no stone unturned to find them and learn the proper and true way of how to live."

The being stroked Ichiro's head, and all Ichiro could do was keep his head bowed and his palms together. It was then that he heard beautiful and powerful singing voices coming from the sky, but those voices gradually faded into the distance as the entire landscape around him became enshrouded in a hazy mist. A lone white tree stood luminescent beyond the misty landscape.

Narao was standing there, shining magnificently, an imperceptible smile on his lips, stretching out his hand toward Ichiro as if about to speak to him.

CHAPTER FIVE
The Pass

"Narao!" cried Ichiro, or so it seemed to him, when he caught sight of something pure white. It was snow … and he could also see the blue sky shining bright above his head.

"He's still breathing! He's opened his eyes!" said a man.

It was the red-bearded man who lived next door, crouching right by Ichiro's head, time and again trying to wake him up. Ichiro finally opened his eyes wide. He was buried in the snow with his arms around his little brother. All he could see clearly against the brilliant blue sky was the faces and red capes and black overcoats of the people of his village.

"How about the little one, the little brother?" shouted a hunter in a jacket with a dog-fur collar.

The next-door neighbor grabbed Narao's little arm, as Ichiro looked on.

"It's touch and go for the little one," he cried. "Quick, light a fire!"

"Fire won't work," said the hunter. "Put him down in the snow …

in the snow." They gave Ichiro a hand to help him up. Ichiro looked down at his little brother, whose face was as red as an apple and whose lips were parted in an imperceptible smile, just as they were when the two were separated in the realm of light.

But his eyes were shut tight and he wasn't breathing anymore. His hands and his chest were as cold as ice.

Kenju Woods Park

Arguably Kenji's two most autobiographical stories are "The Life of Budory Goosko" (included in my collection *Night on the Milky Way Train*) and "Kenju Woods Park." Of these two, the main character in the latter closely resembles Kenji not only in his persistently geeky personality, but in his name as well. This story might just as easily have been titled "The Miyazawa Kenji Woods Park."

Kenju is a young man with an intellectual disability. Kenji identified with the disadvantaged in all spheres of life. Kenji's Kenju is looked upon as a bit of a blockhead, an epithet that Kenji was delighted to ascribe to himself. Kenju becomes ecstatic when he sees children playing happily around trees. He seems to fulfill Kenji's wish of the kind of person he wanted to be, oblivious when standing in a soaking rain.

But a wicked man appears. This is Heiji. Instead of presenting this narrative in terms of the clichéd fight of good over evil, Kenji deals with the confrontation in his own particular way. Good does not fight evil: Good embraces evil. The embrace is so tight that the yin of Heiji and the yang of Kenju become one. Both Kenju and Heiji fall ill at about the same time. They die together. Heiji could not survive Kenju's embrace. But neither could Kenju.

Kenji's stories are nearly totally devoid of the moral of the triumph of good over evil, with rare exceptions like "Obbel and the Elephant" (also included in that earlier collection). This is because the triumph of good over evil as both a literary device and a moral precept may give us the wrong kind of gloating satisfaction. Yes, we are happy to see a villain get their just deserts and die, even, as in Hollywood movies, when it usually comes to a horrible death, depending on how horribly they acted toward others in the movie.

But does the viewer of the movie or the reader of the story ever ask themselves, "Is the author only engendering a false and dangerous sense of self-righteousness in me?" or "Could I be the evil person in this story and the other guy be the good person?" I doubt it. People identify with the good person, particularly if that person is a compatriot of theirs or a member of their ethnic or religious group. So, when the awful villain dies, they feel not only satisfaction that "good" has triumphed; they feel *justified*.

Kenji knows that we all harbor bad karma in us. He felt a keen sense of guilt himself for his comfortable station in life. That is why we all must spend our life doing the ultimate good, rid ourselves of desire and cancel out evil not by killing it off but by absorbing it into our body and spirit. That is Kenji's core belief.

Kenju was dead for nearly twenty years when the professor returned home from studying in the United States. If we use the same time frame for Kenji, we revisit his hometown in about 1953. This was just about the time that Kenji's works were finally gaining the recognition that they deserved in Japan. Kenji, like Kenju, was being recognized for his achievements long after his death. The visiting professor who grew up under the shade of Kenju's trees says, "You know, sometimes it's hard to see the difference between the person who is a fool and the person who is very wise. Ah, the ways of this world are wonderful and mysterious." He is stating a truth that applies not only to Kenju and Kenji but to many people who are ahead of their times. If you are a true prophet and can foretell the future faithfully, for the good of all people, as so few can, then you may have to suffer in this life. People may think of you as excessively idealistic, naïve, foolish and even dangerous. That is the price that Kenju paid.

I doubt that people thought of Miyazawa Kenji as dangerous. But many people in his day did see him as excessively idealistic, naïve and foolish. They didn't "take him to heart," to use his own words from the poem "Strong in the Rain"; and yet he went on to say, "That is the kind of person I want to be." In other words, he absorbed their indifference and turned it into an aspiration.

Did he mind that he was being ignored as a writer? I think he minded very much. Miyazawa Kenji was an extremely ambitious writer and he craved recognition. He wasn't a selfless saint without an ego. He desperately wanted his voice to be heard. But I also think he felt in his bones that time was on his side.

He might be dismayed to learn, however, that while we have fully accepted him as a literary genius and a unique poetic voice, we are still guilty of the sins of destroying and contaminating the soil, water and air that sustain us.

Incidentally, Kenji went, in 1927, to Hanamaki Hot Springs, some eight-odd kilometers from the center of Hanamaki, to fashion the flower garden and clock made of flowers in a park there. They have been renewed over the years and can still be seen at the hot springs.

He sketched and designed eight little flower beds. My favorite is one he called "Tearful Eye." And that is exactly what it looks like. More than fifty years after his death it was planted on the grounds of the Morioka Shonen-in, a training and correctional facility for young people, for which it is now the symbol. Kenji and Kenju's posthumous fate are one.

KENJU WOODS PARK

by Miyazawa Kenji

Kenju was in the habit of taking his time when strolling through the forests or amidst the fields, his rope belt firmly tied around his waist and a big smile on his lips.

The sight of blue-green thickets and groves in the rain made his eyes blink with joy, and if he glimpsed a hawk sailing through the blue sky as far as it could go, he jumped up and down with delight, clapping his hands, and ran to tell everyone about it.

But as time went on he tried his hardest to stifle his joy, because all the other children mocked and scoffed at him.

When the wind roared through the leaves of the beech trees, causing them to sparkle with light, Kenju was so elated that he was beside himself. But he hid the elation in a huge forced yawn, unable to take his eyes off those trees. All he could do was just stand below them and gasp for breath. There were times, too, when he pretended to be scratching an itchy cheek while really chuckling under his breath.

From far away it certainly looked like Kenju was scratching the side of his mouth or yawning, but closer up it was clear to the other children that he was giggling through his twitchy lips. They could hear when he took those gaspy breaths and they didn't stop sniggering and making fun of him.

Kenju would have drawn five hundred buckets of water if his mother had asked him to. He would have weeded the fields in a single day. But neither his mother nor his father was ever going to ask such things of him.

Now, there was a disused field behind Kenju's house about the size of a big sports ground.

One year, when the mountains were still blanketed white with snow and the grasses and new shoots had not yet appeared, Kenju darted over to where his parents and elder brother were tilling the paddies.

"Mummy," he said, "buy me seven hundred cedar saplings, please?"

"Seven hundred saplings?!" she said, holding her hoe that was sparkling in the sun and looking him straight in the eye. "Where on earth could you plant seven hundred saplings?"

"In the field behind the house."

"No cedar's gonna grow there, Kenju," said his brother. "Why don't ya pitch in with the tilling here instead, eh?"

Kenju just stared down at the soil, fidgeting and squirming, as if he had said something wrong.

"Go and buy 'em for him, will ya," said Kenju's father from a short distance away, standing up straight and wiping the sweat off his face. "Kenju's never ever asked us for a thing, so go and get what he's askin' for."

At this Kenju's mother sighed a sigh of relief and smiled a big smile. As for Kenju, he dashed straight for the house, as happy as a lark.

Kenju wasted no time in taking hold of a hoe in the barn and going out to the field, where he got cracking in turning over the soil and digging holes to plant the saplings in.

"Kenju," said his brother, who had followed him there, "you gotta wait till you got your saplings before diggin' up holes. Give it another day an' I'll go an' buy 'em for you."

Kenju again felt awkward and a bit ashamed. He laid down his hoe.

The air was beautifully clear the next day, the mountains were gleaming in snow and larks were trilling, buzzing and churring as they soared higher and higher into the sky. Kenju was once again beside himself with joy and couldn't stop smiling as he dug holes where his brother said he should, starting on the northern edge of the field. He dug each hole at just the right distance from the next in rows as straight as arrows. And his brother was only a few steps behind him, planting the saplings one after the other.

That's when Heiji, the man who owned the field across the northern boundary, approached them with his little pipe between his teeth, his shoulders hunched over and his hands crossed inside his coat as if he was freezing cold. Now, Heiji was a man who only dabbled in farming.

He got most of his income from making life difficult for people.

"Listen, Kenju!" he said. "Get yer seedlings outta there, you dumb idiot. You'll be robbin' my field of sun."

Kenju blushed bright red and started to say something but couldn't get a word out. He just stood there with his heart in his mouth.

"Good morning, Heiji," said Kenju's brother from behind.

This sent Heiji off back from where he came, mumbling something or other under his breath.

But Heiji was by no means the only one to ridicule Kenju for planting cedar saplings in that weed-infested field. Everyone said, "Once a fool, always a fool," especially one who thinks that cedars will grow in that hard clay-like soil.

And they were absolutely right. Larger green saplings did spring up for the first five years, but they got all round and domed at the top; and even a couple of years after that, never grew to be more than about nine feet tall.

"Hey there, Kenju," said a farmer as a joke one morning, "shouldn't you be pruning those branches down?"

"Pruning? What's pruning?" asked Kenju, standing on the edge of the wood.

"You get yourself a machete and you chop off the lower branches."

"Yeah, well, I reckon I should do that."

Kenju dashed home to get a machete.

In no time he was chopping away at the lower branches of the cedars one after another, even though, needless to say, he had to bend right down to get to them, seeing as the trees themselves were only nine feet tall tops.

By evening all of the lower branches had been cut away, leaving only a few branches on top. Dark-green severed branches blanketed the weeds below and the trees above took on a bright, if bare, appearance.

Kenju felt terribly disturbed and deeply troubled by the bareness of the trees. His brother, who was just coming back from working the paddies, took one look at the wood and burst out laughing.

"Kenju," he said to his brother, who was clearly at a loss for what to do, "let's get all those cut branches together and make a really great bonfire. The wood looks really terrific."

This put Kenju at ease, and the two of them got down under the trees and gathered together all the severed branches.

The weeds below were now quite low and free of dirt, and, with the trees at intervals, the field looked like a go board made for long-lost hermits.

But the very next day, when Kenju was in the barn sorting out worm-eaten beans, he heard a huge uproar coming from the direction of the wood, with people barking orders left, right and center as if their voices were bugles, stomping on the ground and laughing so hard that the cackling sound sent birds fleeing off into the sky.

Kenju went to have a look and was shocked to see some fifty children tramping in lines like soldiers right down the rows between the trees, which took on the look of tree-lined streets. As for the trees themselves, they looked like they too had formed lines, decked out in blue-green uniforms, marching in step together. The children couldn't contain their glee at this, as they made their way between the trees, shrieking, with bright red faces, like shrikes.

In time, those rows took on names like "Tokyo Highway" and "Russia Highway" and, even, "Occidental Highway."

This delighted Kenju no end, and he enjoyed hiding behind a tree and laughing his head off.

It wasn't long before children started meeting there every day.

Rain was the only thing that kept them away.

On those days Kenju would stand all by himself outside the wood under the soft bleached sky getting soaked to the bone. "Keeping watch over the wood today again, are we, Kenju?" said passers-by with a smile, wrapped in their straw rain-capes. Dark brown cones adorned the branches, and cold translucent droplets of rain hung and dripped from their magnificent green tips. Nothing could drag Kenju away from there as he stood motionless for what seemed like an age, breathing heavily with his mouth agape, steam rising from his body into the moist air.

But then, one morning when there was a pea-soup fog …

Kenju had gone to gather reeds for thatching when he ran into Heiji. Heiji looked around to see if the coast was clear.

"Kenju! Cut down those damn trees!" he screamed, frowning like a wolf.

"Wh … why?"

"They're blockin' my sun!"

All Kenju could do was stare at the ground in silence. Even though Heiji claimed that his sun was being blocked, Kenju's cedars cast a shadow onto his land that was, at most, only about five inches long. Not to mention the fact that they formed a barrier against the strong winds from the south.

"I told ya to get rid of 'em. Now! If you don't…."

"I won't!" said Kenju vehemently, with his chin up.

Nonetheless, his lips were trembling, and it looked like he was on the edge of tears. Actually, this was the first and last time in Kenju's life that he ever stood up to someone.

As for Heiji, he wasn't about to let such a goody-two-shoes like Kenju make a fool out of him, and he completely flipped his lid. He yanked up his shoulders and punched Kenju right in the face and continued to slug him like that over and over again.

Kenju grasped his cheeks in his hands. He did not say a word and did not resist. But after a while he turned bright blue and began to teeter on his feet. This made Heiji somewhat nervous and he marched off into the mist with his arms folded over his chest.

Kenju contracted typhus that autumn and died. Hieji had died of the same disease about ten days before him.

But that didn't stop the children from coming together every single day in the woods.

The story moves quickly after this.

The railroad came to the village the next year and a station was built some three hundred and fifty yards east of Kenju's house. Big factories producing china, and silk mills were established in the area, and houses were built where there were fields and paddies. What was once a village was now a town. But Kenju's woods, for no apparent reason, stayed as they were, and though the cedar trees didn't grow much higher than nine feet, children still gathered by them every single day. A school was built beside the woods and the children there viewed them and the grass on their south side as a continuation of their sports ground.

Kenju's father's hair turned all white. It's what you would expect. After all, Kenju had been dead by then for some twenty years.

One day a young scholar who hailed from the village and who had been teaching at a university in America came home on a visit after being away for fifteen years.

Where had all the old fields and forests gone? Even the people living in the town were mostly newcomers from other places.

The scholar was asked to give a talk in the primary school auditorium to all the pupils about his life overseas, and after the talk he strolled with the principal and some others to the sports ground and over to Kenju's woods.

"Oh, nothing has changed here, I see," said the young scholar half to himself in amazement, fiddling with his glasses. "The trees are exactly where they used to be, though, if anything, they don't seem to be as tall as they once were. Children still play here, I see. You know, I think that my classmates and I were once among them...."

Then he appeared to have hit upon an idea and, with a big smile, turned to the principal.

"Is this here a part of the sports ground?" he asked.

"No, it isn't. These woods are on the property of that house over there, but the owners are perfectly happy to have children playing in them and they've left them as they were to that end. It may serve as a sports ground attached to the school but, in reality, it's not."

"That's wonderful, but I wonder why they do that."

"Well, it appears that people in the town put a lot of pressure on the old man to sell up, but that he just wouldn't give in, telling people these woods were the sole memento of his son Kenju and that they were here to stay, come hell or high water."

"Sure, yes, there was a boy named Kenju and we always considered him thick as two short planks. He was always chuckling and laughing under his breath. I recall him lolling about right here watching all of us play every day. He was the one who planted all these trees, wasn't he. You know, sometimes it's hard to see the difference between the person who is a fool and the person who is very wise. Ah, the ways of this world are wonderful and mysterious. These woods will be a children's park for time immemorial. Listen, how about calling it all 'Kenju Woods Park' and preserving it here just like this forever and ever."

"That's a brilliant idea," said the principal. "Nothing would make the children happier."

And that's exactly what happened.

A monument made of yellow-green olivine was erected right in the middle of the grass with KENJU WOODS PARK engraved in it.

People who had once attended the school and were now upstanding members of the community such as public prosecutors and military officers or owners of farms, big and small, a few of them overseas, sent many letters to the school, some of them including donations.

This all brought tears of joy to Kenju's family.

From that time on, countless thousands of people learned the nature of true happiness from the cedars in Kenju Woods Park, from their greenish black needles and their bracing scent, from the cool summer shade they provided and from the blanket of grass below the trees that shone like the light of the moon.

When it rained, cold translucent droplets dripped from them onto the grass just as they had when Kenju was still alive ... and when the sun shone, the trees were alive with new, beautiful and invigorating breaths.

The Ravens and the Big Dipper

Kenji began work on this story in 1921. With its military theme, it presents an unusual metaphor for him. But to appreciate it one must consider the general attitudes of the Japanese people toward the military in Kenji's day.

The brutality of the Japanese imperial forces and the untold misery they inflicted have remained vivid in the mind of the people of the world, as well as in the collective memory of the Japanese people themselves. But the Meiji-era military, created on the European model, was a highly respected and reputable institution in Kenji's day. The military attracted the best and brightest among Japanese young men; and in the wars of the era—Sino-Japanese, Russo-Japanese and the First World War—they brought much power and prestige, for better or worse, to the Japanese nation, power and prestige that were much admired and highly valued in the West.

Miyazawa Kenji personally was not a pacifist, although throughout his works he disdains any form of killing. He saw violence as one of this world's natural phenomena, natural to most animals. While he rails against the hunter, he does not condemn outright the killing of animals if such a thing is necessary for the survival of people, though he himself became a vegetarian from age twenty-one (save for the odd *torinamba*, chicken in soba soup, that he ate in his weaker moments). After his graduation from Morioka Agricultural High School he underwent a physical examination for the army. This was on 26 April 1918. He was twenty-one. The First World War was raging. Japan was an ally of the Western powers. The so-called Siberian Intervention, in which Japan purported to reinstate White rule in Russia, had begun in earnest in January of that year. It was dominating the news in Japan. Kenji fully expected to be conscripted into the army, to fight and, as was his wont of resignation, to die. He told his parents as much. He could also volunteer for a year to fight in Siberia and he seriously considered it. Conscription had been universal (for men) and obligatory since 1872, though primary householders and first sons, of which Kenji was one, could be exempt from conscription if they so wished (not, however, during the War in the Pacific). As it turned out Kenji failed the physical. He wrote at the time to his best friend Hosaka Kanai, "The doctor pressed his horn [stethoscope] against my chest and said, 'You've got a weak heart.' I said, 'Well, really?' But he had already gone on to the next fellow. I wouldn't really know if I have a weak heart or not, but I can climb mountains like the next fellow and not appear to be any the less for it."

Kenji's younger brother Seiroku passed his physical in May 1924, when he was twenty, and became a one-year volunteer soldier in December of that year. He was stationed up in Hirosaki in Aomori prefecture. Kenji visited him there in April and June of 1925; and the wonderful photograph of the two of them, Seiroku in uniform and Kenji in his fashionable homespun wool three-piece suit and open-collar shirt, dates from that time. Seiroku left service on 31 March 1926.

Kenji was certainly not what you would call a nationalist, but he was no opponent of Japan's burgeoning influence in the world. (What stance he would have taken as Japan further invaded Asia and the Pacific, triggering a war there, cannot be known, as he was mercifully dead by then.) He did fall under the spell of a man named Tanaka Chigaku, however, and became, for a time, an ardent follower in his organization, the Kokuchukai, or "Pillar of the Nation Association."

Author, preacher and chauvinist-activist Tanaka Chigaku is the type of fanatic warmongering religious advocate seen more commonly in Christian countries than in Buddhist-inspired ones. His version of what might be called "muscular Buddhism" led his organization to adopt ultranationalist stances. Kenji worshipped Tanaka. He went down to Tokyo and offered his services to his Nichiren-sect "Pillar of the Nation Association."

Takachio Chiyo, an instructor there, subsequently wrote of his first meeting with Kenji on 27 January 1921 in the entrance hall of the association's headquarters at Uguisudani in Tokyo, recalling him as "a sincere, honest and simple young man." Kenji, for his part, immediately apologized to Takachio for his inability to convert his father to Nichiren Buddhism, explaining that "it is due to the insufficiency of my self-discipline" and promising to throw himself into any activities assigned to him "to improve" himself.

Kenji spent nearly a year proselytizing for the Kokuchukai, distributing flyers and the like, not questioning at the time Tanaka's extremist militant notion that Japan would have to conquer other lands in order to establish an imperial order underpinned by the teachings of the Lotus Sutra. (The Kokuchukai, by the way, is still extant, claiming some twenty thousand followers today. Its founder Tanaka Chigaku died in 1939, never seeing, alas, what happened on 15 August 1945 to his glorious promise of victory.) From the mid-1920s on, Kenji lost his enthusiasm for the organization; but whether he thoroughly saw the light on it—and how far away he stepped from nationalism—is an open question.

The birds in "The Ravens and the Big Dipper" are large crows native to Japan. They resemble ravens, which is what I have chosen to call them here for both sound and literary associations.

The soldier ravens are so-called large-billed crows. They are bigger in size than the carrion crow that Kenji calls here a "mountain crow." The large-billed raven or crow of Japan produces any number of calls, one of them being a "cau," as opposed to a caw. Kenji transliterates this closely with ka-a-o. The story depicts a fight for territory and, hence, food, a theme that resonates with people in a poor region of the country like Iwate.

It is very possible that Kenji was inspired here by a story of Ernest Thompson Seton's. Seton was a British American author and wildlife artist. He published a collection of short stories in 1898 titled *Wild Animals I Have Known*. In this collection we find "Silverspot, The Story of a Crow." Old Silverspot is the leader of a band of crows who "are as well drilled as soldiers," have "lieutenants" and others who go on sentry duty, drill and forage. They also mate in the story and have honeymoons. Silverspot commands his troops by cawing out military orders. While a Japanese translation of this book did not appear until 1935, two years after Kenji's death, I believe, given the similarities, that he read it in English. (Seton's complete works were published in Japan in the early 1950s, and they subsequently became popular as manga and anime as well. *Wild Animals I Have Known* also contains a story about a rabbit who lives with his mother and interacts with squirrels.)

The ravens in "The Ravens and the Big Dipper" worship Majel, invoking this divine symbol ... "Ah, Majel ... Majel ... please transform this world into a place where it will not be necessary to kill an enemy, who should never be hated, and to attain that end, I am happy for my own body to be ripped to shreds." The image of self-sacrifice is unmistakable. Majel stands in for Myoken—the Venerable Star King—a Buddhist deification of the North Star and the Big Dipper in the Nichiren sect. The guiding principle behind this worship is that of the lessening of one's karmic retribution through acts of faith and practice. In this way humans can diminish their suffering for past sins that might otherwise torment them over a span of any number of lifetimes. If you were obliged to go to war and to suffer or die, then that was a natural feature of your life at that stage. Your sins could be diminished in their impact if you stayed on the straight and narrow, which to Kenji was the path laid by Nichiren.

Kenji does not often depict the kind of romantic love that pops up in this story. He was from a wealthy family and pursued the highly respected profession of teaching, which meant that it would not have been difficult for him to find a wife. In fact, he went through, however informally, two meetings that could be considered preliminaries for an arranged marriage. But the guiding principle of his life was *kinyoku*, or abstinence and the control of passion. There were rumors of a romance with a local girl from a soba restaurant, but these are unfounded. It is known, too, that he had a crush on Takahashi Mine, a nurse at Iwate Hospital in Morioka when he was admitted for an infection in the spring of 1914. He even wrote a few love poems about her. And his sweet poem titled "Romance" is about a boy and a girl …

The boy's lips smell of celery
The girl's cheeks a blossom of white clover

And the boy says to her at the end …

"I shall devote myself to you for all time"

It is sweet and it is romantic … but the boy and girl are both frogs.

"Mashili" in "The Ravens and the Big Dipper" refers to the planet Mercury; Sephira, or sapphire, to Saturn.

"The Ravens and the Big Dipper" was one of many works that was banned by the censors in the GHQ of the Allied Occupation (1945-1952) for its military theme. You would have thought that they had better things to do.

THE RAVENS AND THE BIG DIPPER
by Miyazawa Kenji

Cold ill-natured clouds were virtually skimming the earth, and no one could tell whether the light on the fields was coming off the snow or from the sun itself. The ravens of the Raven Volunteer Fleet were hemmed in by the clouds and obliged, for now, to form neat lines on a field of snow that resembled a vast sheet of tin. All the ravens in the fleet were berthed there, anchored firmly to the spot.

The velvety smooth pitch-black lieutenant and the young fleet commander stood fast, as straight as pins; and as for the superintendent, he didn't budge an inch, let alone sway in the wind. This raven superintendent was well up in his years. His eyes had turned grey and, when he cried, his cries came out in high-pitched coos and squeaks, like those of a poorly made doll.

"Hey, there are two ravens in this town with damaged voice boxes, d'ya hear?!" said a child unfamiliar with the way to tell a raven's age.

This was without a doubt wrong, for there was only one raven who cried like that and it was in no way because his voice box was damaged but rather derived from the fact that his voice had been all too deep and raspy from having shouted out commands in the sky for so many years. The fleet actually considered his voice, among all the sounds they heard, to be absolutely out of this world.

The ravens of the fleet looked like pebbles—or so many sesame seeds—anchored for this emergency, as they were, in the snow. But if you looked at them through a telescope you would see that there were big ones and little ones, like potatoes.

Night gradually fell.

The clouds started to float upward, enough for the ravens to find an opening to fly through. It was then that the superintendent shouted out the breathless command.

"Begin maneuvers! Take off now!"

The lieutenant raven was the first to strike the snow and take to the air. One after another, eighteen of his subordinate vessels took off, following behind him in evenly spaced formation. Thirty-two ships of the combat fleet departed one by one after that and, finally, the superintendent himself ascended majestically.

The lieutenant raven at the head of the raven fleet whirled about in the sky four times, sailed to the very edge of the cloud bank and made a beeline for the forest in the distance. Twenty-nine cruisers and twenty-five gunboats rose in rows, leaving the last two ships of the fleet to take to the air together. I must admit that this scene demonstrates the highly irregular manner in which the raven fleet sets sail.

The lieutenant raven turned left on his approach to the forest and the superintendent let fly his command.

"Cannons, fire!"

The fleet cawed out a thunderous volley. Among the ravens who had thrust a leg backward as they fired were those who had incurred injuries at the recent Battle of Natura-Naturata, and the nerves in their legs rattled with each boom.

"Depart stations!" cried the superintendent, circling four times. "Disperse!"

The superintendent then broke from the line and sailed down to his official residence in a cedar tree, as the rest of the fleet broke ranks and headed home to their barracks. The lieutenant raven, however, did not immediately return to barracks but rather glided by himself to the honey locust tree in the west.

Pale blackish clouds rested over the western mountains, with cloudy watercolor pools of sky peeking out through them in a soft glow, and the heavenly body known to the ravens as Mashili the Silver Messenger began to twinkle.

The lieutenant raven shot down like an arrow, landing on a honey locust branch. Another raven was already perched there, looking deeply worried. She was the gunboat with the best voice in the fleet and she was the lieutenant's fiancée.

"Caw-caw, sorry to be so late. Did today's maneuvers tire you out?" he asked.

"Caw! I got here before you and have been waiting for you. I'm not tired in the least," she replied.

"Right. That's good. Now, we've got to go our separate ways for a while."

"What? Why? Oh, heavens above!"

"The combat commander has ordered me to leave tomorrow and pursue mountain crows."

"But mountain crows are powerful, aren't they?"

"Yeah, their eyes are kind of popped out and they've got these narrow beaks and they look all hoity-toity and satisfied with themselves. But, you know, it's no big deal."

"Really?"

"Yeah, it's just a matter of course. But since war is war, there's no real knowing what a battle's going to be like and what might happen in it. If something does happen to me, our engagement's off and I want you to find someone else."

"Oh no, what will I do? That leaves me totally up in the air! How can you say such a thing to me? How can you! That's the last straw. Caw-cau … caw … caw …CAU!"

"Stop crying, will ya? You oughta be ashamed of yourself. Oh, someone's coming."

One of the lieutenant's subordinates, a chief petty officer raven, was rushing over. "Sir," he said, cocking his head to one side, "it's time for roll caw. Everyone is in formation."

"Fine. I will return immediately to the squadron. You may go now."

"Yessir!" said the chief petty officer, flying off.

"Come on now, dry those tears. We'll meet again tomorrow in line up. You've got to be strong. You should be at roll caw too, you know. I've gotta be off now. Give me your foot."

The two ravens grasped each other's foot. Then the lieutenant stomped on the branch and made a swift beeline to the squadron. The female raven didn't budge a feather. It was as if she was frozen to the branch.

Night fell.

Then … it was midnight.

Every single cloud disappeared from a sky that was like freshly forged steel, an ice-cold light filling its every corner and tiny stars imploding before exploding, and the axles of waterwheels creaked as if all hell was about to break loose.

At last a line started cracking in the light-blue steel sky, the sky broke into two equal halves and myriad long arms extended out of the crevasse, grabbing the ravens and trying to haul them beyond the roof of the sky.

The Raven Volunteer Fleet quickly combined forces, got into their long johns and flew about the air as if their lives depended on it. The veterans had no time to look after the rookies, and even ravens who were in love collided mercilessly with each other.

Well, sorry, that's not what really happened.

Not on your life.

In reality the waning halfmoon came out, rising a bit crushed in on itself and streaming with tears, over the eastern mountains. By that point the raven forces were feeling their oats.

A hush immediately descended on the forest. A young sailor took fright, lost his footing and let loose a half-awake cannon-like "caw."

As for the lieutenant, he was wide awake and not able to sleep a wink.

"I'm going to fall in battle tomorrow," he whispered, twisting his head in the direction of the forest where he left his gunboat fiancée with the beautiful young voice.

She was dreaming dream after dream in her velvety-black kelp-like treetop. She dreamt of how they were flapping together, flying wing to wing, and how they peered into each other's eyes all the time and how they climbed forever and ever up into the blue-black night sky. When the stars of the Big Dipper that the ravens call "Majel" came into sight, so close that they could even make out a pale-blue apple tree growing on one of them, their wings suddenly petrified, for some reason, and they tumbled headfirst toward the Earth. But when she opened her eyes and cried out "Majel … Majel" she found herself alone, to her shock, hanging off the branch of a tree. She quickly spread her wings again, stood up on the branch and looked over to where the lieutenant was, but soon found herself dozing off. The next thing she knew a mountain crow in pince-nez glasses had appeared, offering to shake with the lieutenant. The lieutenant waved his foot, refusing to shake outright with the mountain crow, who drew a shiny pistol and, in a flash, shot the lieutenant point blank. The lieutenant puffed out his silky black chest and began to teeter and fall, so once again she cried out "Majel … Majel," at which point she opened her eyes in amazement … and that was the long and short of it.

The lieutenant raven heard everything, from the sound his fiancée made when perched on the branch to her invocation to the celestial Majel. He sighed a big sigh and, gazing up at the seven radiant stars of the Big Dipper, softly prayed.

"Ah, it is beyond me to have knowledge as to who will see victory tomorrow, me or the mountain crow. But I do know that it is entirely up to your will, Majel, and that I will do battle with all the power that is given me and that whatever does transpire it will be as you have seen fit."

By the time he had finished praying, a little pool of silver light was welling in the eastern sky.

Suddenly a faint sound like keys jangling together reached him from far away in the cold north sky. The lieutenant raven grabbed his night binoculars and turned them toward the sound. He could see a single chestnut tree on the top of the ridge, lit a hazy white by the light of the stars. There was definitely an enemy mountain crow perched in the treetop, gazing up into the sky. This sight stirred courage in the lieutenant's heart.

"Caw … emergency, emergency! All ravens assemble!"

The lieutenant's subordinates immediately kicked off their branches, took to the air and circled him.

"Charge!" cried the lieutenant in the lead, shooting headlong to the north.

The eastern sky was already glowing white, like newly whetted steel.

The mountain crow kicked off its branch in a panic. He tried to flee toward the north, spreading his wings fully out, but the destroyers had him encircled before he knew it.

"Caw caw caw caw!"

The deafening cannons rang out. The mountain crow, its legs as wobbly as jelly, had nowhere to go but up. The lieutenant lost no time in the pursuit and, catching up with it, stabbed it right in its jet-black head. The mountain crow reeled and was dropping to the ground when the chief petty officer stabbed it again from the side. The mountain crow shut its grey lids as it lay, cold, on the snowy ridge at dawn.

"Caw … chief petty officer. Take the carcass back to barracks. Caw. Now, pull out!"

"Yessir!"

The chief petty officer, who was strong as an ox, carried the carcass off, while the lieutenant started back home to his forest with eighteen ships in his wake. By the time they returned, all the destroyers were puffing white breath from their beaks.

"You wounded? Any of you here wounded?" said the lieutenant raven, making the rounds and consoling them.

It was finally daybreak.

The peach juice of sunlight poured over the snowy caps, then gradually flowed downward, causing white lilies to bloom everywhere. The sun shone with a dazzling but sorrowful light, streaming along the snowy hills in the east.

"Attention! All assemble!" barked the lieutenant.

"Attention! All assemble!" roared all the squad leaders.

All the ravens lined up smartly on the snow-covered field. The lieutenant raven stepped out of rank and, nimbly stretching his legs over the gleaming snow, trotted straight for the superintendent.

"Reporting, sir!" he said, standing before the superintendent. "Today at dawn I noticed an enemy ship at anchor on Sephira Ridge. With haste I mobilized our fleet, attacked and sunk her. We have suffered no casualties. End of report, sir!"

As for the destroyers, they were overcome with joy, shedding steamy tears that trickled down their cheeks before falling onto the snow.

"Coo, squeak … coo, squeak," cried the superintendent raven, tears flowing from his grey eyes. "Well done. I'm proud of you. You deserve a pat on the back. Can't see why you shouldn't be promoted to lieutenant-commander. So be it. I'll leave the conferring of decorations on your subordinates to you."

The newly promoted lieutenant-commander recalled the mountain crow who had left its mountain in search of food and had been killed, surrounded by nineteen ships, and he too began to weep.

"Thank you, sir. Now, I would like to request leave to bury the enemy's corpse."

"Permission granted. Carry it out with all due honor."

The newly promoted lieutenant-commander raven saluted, took a step back and, rejoining his ranks, gazed up at the blue sky where Majel, the stars of the Big Dipper, would be. "Ah, Majel … Majel … please transform this world into a place where it will not be necessary to kill an enemy, who should never be hated, and to attain that end, I am happy for my own body to be ripped to shreds."

The stars of the Big Dipper poured a soft and serene blue light out of the blue sky.

All the while, the beautiful pitch-black gunboat raven stood motionless among the others in her line, shedding a stream of glistening tears. Her squad leader looked the other way.

Tomorrow she would be able to go on maneuvers with her husband-to-be. She opened her beak wide, over and over again, from joy, as it shone blood red bathed in the light of the sun.

But her squad leader looked the other way and let this, too, pass.

The Bears on Mt. Nametoko

We have witnessed Kenji's belief that cruelty to animals is a sin. There is no doubt but that he came to this belief as a result of his unwavering faith in the Buddhist cycle of reincarnated life.

But, for us in the twenty-first century, this metaphor of recycling our sins of commission and omission has come to be seen in a different light, one that Kenji, as a scientist, totally endorsed: All life is sacred because the destruction of one part of the net of interconnection leads to the destruction of another … and another, thread by thread. We must see nature as a whole, as a net of interdependence. The fact that humans are able to manipulate and destroy nature on a grand scale is, by nature, accompanied by a special responsibility to restore whatever they exploit.

We read the stories and poems of Miyazawa Kenji to find out what they say to us now. If Kenji's intentions were to have us convert to Nichiren Buddhism—and that was his primary intention—then that becomes Kenji's problem, not ours. I am not going to convert and neither, I suppose, are you. But I am going to continue to read his works to learn about my life and the lives of others around the world in the twenty-first century, not thanks to but despite his core intention.

Miyazawa Kenji is no longer the intellectual property of Hanamaki or Iwate or even Japan. He is a writer of universal truth who speaks to people in the present and future. The line he wrote in that first poem in *Spring and Ashura* may be applied to his stories and poems, that is, his entire literary legacy …

the light is preserved … the lamp itself is lost

In this case, the lamp is a single life and all that went into it. The light is, in Kenji's case, his works; in ours, whatever we leave behind. This will be shining brightly for centuries to come as it travels in all directions and through all time, never lost, in the universe.

"The Bears on Mt. Nametoko," one of Kenji's most loved stories in Japan, can be read today in this light. It tells us that we must protect our animals, or it will not be the animals that become extinct but us. The bears here are killed not for eating. It is for their gall bladder that provides an ingredient in medicine.

We may see bears as terrifying animals who we would rather meet up in a zoo than in a forest. But to Kenji they are neither bad nor good, as are all other animals and plants. They simply exist in nature. And that gives them the right to have a life and to express themselves. Virtually all of Kenji's animals speak, and some of them speak more cogently and wisely than humans. We are the ones who learn from them, not vice versa.

In the opening lines of this story, Kenji sets the scene … "The mountain inhales and exhales chilling fog and clouds almost every day of the year and it is circled by other mountains that look like bluish black sea cucumbers, turtles and sea goblins."

There are two things to point out here.

First, the mountain itself is breathing in fog and cloud. There are many descriptions in Kenji of inanimate objects breathing in and out. Kenji is telling us that everything around us is as alive in nature as we are, even the rocks on a mountain.

Second, the mountains are like sea cucumbers, turtles and sea goblins. In other words, this mountain range may as well be under the sea. To Kenji, the present encompasses the past and the future. He studied the history of the Earth by examining rocks, which, as I have mentioned, was his passion from childhood on. If you think of mountains as living things, you will respect them and not destroy yourselves by destroying them. They, in turn, will find themselves as part of a landscape or seascape or "lightscape" in the span of time.

Kojuro's death at the end of the story recreates a landscape of light, shadows and snow. The bears are there, as is Kojuro. But the scene is as unmoving and timeless as that of Stonehenge on Salisbury Plain in Wiltshire, England. Huge stone slab-like pillars stand there in a circle, as they have for four to five thousand years.

The circle around Kojuro is, like the circle of Stonehenge, frozen in time. It is a monument built by Miyazawa Kenji of Hanamaki Japan not to death but to renewal, the renewal that we must hope for in the century when humans possess more power than they ever have in history, the power to destroy, but also the power to preserve and protect.

This is one story of Kenji's that carries a social message as well as a moral one. That is evident in the way Kojuro, the master of the mountains, is treated and exploited by people in town. The driving force in this encounter is class brought by wealth. Kenji is no doubt thinking here of his own father's power over the poor farmers of the region. Class difference is also present in *Night on the Milky Way Train*. Giovanni comes from a poor home. His father is in prison and both he and his elder sister must work to sustain the household and care for their sick mother. Campanella's father is a scholar, and there are books in his home, not to mention a little train set that, in his dream, Giovanni becomes a passenger on to the stars.

Mt. Nametoko stands at a height of eight hundred and sixty meters, lying to the west of Hanamaki by the upper reaches of the Toyosawa River.

The magnolia makes an appearance here, as it does in a number of Kenji's stories and poems. It is a Buddhist symbol of purity.

Namari Hot Springs is located some seventeen kilometers from Hanamaki and sits alongside the Toyosawa River. The springs have been known for their healing properties since, some six hundred years ago, it was said that a white monkey was seen healing its sore foot in them. Another name for the resort is "White Monkey Baths." Kenji and Toshi frequented the bath in the Fujisan Inn at Namari Hot Springs. It is unique in Japan in that you stand in it as you bathe. At one-and-one-quarter meters in depth, it is the deepest hot springs in the country. I went there in the depth of winter, slipping and skidding in the snow to get to the inn, which was built before the Meiji Restoration, in 1841. Someone was playing the shamisen and steam was rising from the main building that housed the bath. Nothing had changed since Kenji's time; and I felt, as I slipped into that deep bath—one of the few *konyoku*, or mixed male-female, hot springs left in Japan—that I was being transported by the water in time.

The ages of Kojuro and his mother don't gell, but I'm sure that Kenji, had he lived long enough to see his fame, would have adjusted this in an editing process that was never to occur.

THE BEARS ON MT. NAMETOKO

by Miyazawa Kenji

Now, if you want to hear an intriguing story, listen to this!

Mt. Nametoko is a very tall mountain and the Fuchizawa River flows down it. The mountain inhales and exhales chilling fog and clouds almost every day of the year and is encircled by other mountains that look like bluish black sea cucumbers, turtles and sea goblins. The gigantic mouth of a cave gapes out about halfway up the mountain, and out of it spills the Fuchizawa River, forming a waterfall that roars some ninety meters down into a thicket of Japanese cypress and painted maple.

No one sets foot anymore these days on the tracks running through these mountains and everything is overgrown with butterbur and knotweed. Someone did put a fence up across a path to stop the cows from getting away and roaming about the mountain. If you climb up for some twelve kilometers you reach a place where the wind whips around the summit. It's there that you'll catch sight of something you can't quite make out … it's long thin and whitish, and it gives off smoke as it slides and winds down the slopes. That's Mt. Nametoko's Big Sky Falls, known, they say in these parts, as a place positively crawling with bears.

Now, I've never really and truly set eyes on either Mt. Nametoko or the gall bladder of a bear. I've just heard other people talk about them or, maybe, thought it up myself. I may be mistaken, but it's what I've come to believe. Be that as it may, the gall bladders of the bears on Mt. Nametoko are praised to the high heavens.

There's been a sign for as long as anybody can remember posted at the entrance to Namari Hot Springs and it says, "Get your Mt. Nametoko bear gall bladders here … They'll heal your wounds and are good for the stomach ailments that ail you!"

So you can be sure that there were bears roaming around there with their red tongues lolling as they crossed the streams and that their cubs were practicing sumo wrestling that broke, in the end, into paw fights. The man who caught them hand over fist was none other than the great bear hunter, Fuchizawa Kojuro.

Now, this Fuchizawa Kojuro was a gruff and prickly fellow with a rough reddish complexion, a squint in one eye, a chest like a small barrel and big bulgy palms like those of the Buddhist deity Bishamon at Kitajima, the one who can heal you by just laying on a hand. Summer would find this Kojuro in his leggings and his cape made of the stringy bark of the sacred Bodhi tree carrying a machete like the ones that wild tribesmen have and a big weighty musket like those the Portuguese used long ago. He'd roam freely with his trusty yellow dog, crisscrossing the region from Mt. Nametoko down to Shidoke Swamp, from Mittsumata up to Sakkai Ridge, and from the Mami Hole Woods over to Shirasawa.

The forests lining the ravines are so dense that you think you're passing through a bluish black tunnel, until you're suddenly dazzled by bright greens and golds, and the rays of the sun stream down as if the light was made of a carpet of flowers in full bloom.

Kojuro plodded and trekked through there, relaxed and taking his time as if walking through the rooms of his own home, while his dog sprinted ahead, darting along the ridges of the cliffs, splashing into the water, dog paddling with all its might through creepy deep muddy pools and, when finally making it up onto the rocks on the other side, shaking back and forth, wagging the water off its fur and, with a wrinkled up nose, waiting for the master to catch up. Kojuro would come wading through the water, putting one foot in front of the other like the needles of a compass, splashing little cliffs of froth from his knees up.

I trust that you will forgive me for telling you now that the bears on and about Mt. Nametoko were inordinately fond of Kojuro. As proof of this, when the bears saw Kojuro splashing and splattering his way through the rivers and streams or when passing along the flat narrow ridges lined with thistles, they stood in silence and watched him go. They paid close attention to him as they tightly gripped their branches at the top of the trees with both paws or sat on the clifftops holding onto their knees. Furthermore, when all is said and done, those bears were as attached to Kojuro's dog as they were to Kojuro himself.

It must be said, however, that when Kojuro got too close for comfort and his dog came shooting toward them like a fireball, and Kojuro, with a weird glint in his eye, pointed his rifle straight at them, they weren't so fond of him and his dog. At times like those, the majority of bears waved a paw at him as if to tell him they were greatly put out by this and would prefer him to stop what he was doing.

But there are bears and there are bears, and the fierce ones stood right up and roared ferociously, heading headlong for Kojuro with both paws outstretched, not thinking twice about crushing his dog underfoot. This didn't faze Kojuro one bit, however. Shielding himself behind a tree trunk and cool as a cucumber, he aimed straight for the white crescent-moon patch on the bear's chest and blasted it with a bullet. The entire forest screamed, and the bear thudded to the ground, making a shrill whining noise in its nose and spewing reddish black blood out its mouth, before dying. Kojuro rested his rifle against the trunk and, gingerly strolling up to the bear, said, "Listen, Bear, it wasn't no hatred that caused me to kill ya. I gotta earn a crust and the only way I know how is to shoot at you. Yeah, it'd be nice to have a job where I didn't have to commit an evil sin, but I ain't got no fields to my name an' from the outset all the trees belong to the higher ups, an' whenever I go down to the village no one'll even give me the time of day. So, I got no choice but to be a hunter. It's your fate to be born a bear just like it's mine to be born a hunter. So, hey, in the next life just don't be born a bear, that's all I gotta say."

The dog sat on the ground dispirited, with, nonetheless, what looked like a wan smile on his face. This is the very same dog that had seen Kojuro through his fortieth year, when every one of Kojuro's dearest had fallen ill with dysentery and both his son and his son's wife had, in the end, died from it. Kojuro took a sharpened knife from his inside pocket and made a clean slit from the bear's jaw through its chest and down to its belly, to separate the pelt from the body. It turns my stomach to describe what happened after that. Be that as it may, I can certainly tell you that Kojuro had the beet-red gall bladder of the bear tucked away in his little wooden backpack, had washed clean the pelt with its blood-soaked tufts in the river, and was soon trekking sluggishly down the ravine.

Now, Kojuro was pretty sure he understood what the bears were saying to each other.

In the early spring of a certain year, when not a single tree in the mountains was showing any green, Kojuro was making his way with his dog all the way up to Shirasawa. Toward nightfall he stopped on the track up to Bakkaisawa to spend the night at a little hut he had built out of running bamboo the summer before. But strange as it may seem and most unusual for him, he mistook one track for another. With a grim grimace on his lips and with both him the dog panting for breath, he retraced his steps any number of times, finally coming upon the hut, now half fallen in on itself.

He recalled that there was a spring just down from the hut and he went down the slope that led to it. But when he arrived he saw, to his astonishment, a mother bear and her cub who couldn't have been more than a year old. They were holding their paws up to their forehead exactly as humans do when peering into the distance, staring fixedly at the far side of the valley in the faint light of the waxing crescent moon. To Kojuro it surely looked like there was an aura surrounding the bodies of the two bears, and all he could do was stand there transfixed by the sight.

"I say it's snow, Mummy," said the cub, sounding like a pampered toddler. "I mean, look, only our side of the mountain's white. It can't be anything else but snow, Mummy!"

"That's not snow," said the mother bear, not taking her eyes off the mountain. "Think about it. Why would it snow only there?"

"I mean, it didn't melt and stayed there."

"That can't be. Mummy was just by there yesterday looking for thistle shoots."

Kojuro didn't take his eyes off them for a minute. The pale moonlight slipped down the slope, and everything there was as radiant as silver armor.

"Well, then," said the cub, after thinking it over, "it's gotta be frost if it's not snow. That's what I say!"

Kojuro thought to himself, "Yeah, a frost will be settling tonight for sure. The three little stars in Aries beside the moon are twinkling so pale in its light and, more than that, the face of the moon itself is like ice."

"Ah, Mummy knows now. That's all magnolia flowers."

"Yeah sure, magnolias. I know those any day."

"You certainly do not. You've never seen those before."

"I have so! I picked some of those just the other day."

"Those weren't magnolias that you picked. What you picked were yellow catalpa flowers."

"Was it?" said the cub, looking as if butter wouldn't melt in his mouth.

Kojuro felt a rush of emotion as he glanced once more at the snowlike flowers on the far side of the valley and at the mother bear and her cub perched there absorbed in the shower of moonlight before he slipped away, trying not to making a peep, back to the hut, pleading to the wind not to carry the sound of his footsteps in their direction. He was carried away by the scent of yellow spicewood intermingling with moonbeams.

Now, I cannot tell you how sorry I feel for this proud hunter Kojuro when he finds himself in town selling his bear pelts and gall bladders.

There was a big general store in the middle of town where they sold just about everything under the sun, from baskets and sugar to whetstones, from Golden Long-Nose Goblin and Chameleon brand cigarettes to flytraps made of glass. All Kojuro would need to do was put a foot through the door loaded down with his pelts and everyone in the store would smirk as if to say, "Well, look who's here!" And as for the proprietor, he'd pull out his massive bronze charcoal brazier in the next room and sit there like he was on a throne.

"Sir, I'm much obliged for your kind patronage," king of the mountain Kojuro would say as polite as he could on his knees with both palms flat against the tatami mat and his heavy mound of pelts by his side.

"Well, so what's it you want, eh?"

"I've, uh, got a couple more bear pelts for you, sir."

"Bear pelts? The ones you brought before are still in the back unsold, so's I won't be needin' no more."

"I beg of you, sir, an' hear me out. I'll give 'em to you real cheap, so please take 'em off my hands."

"I don't give a damn how cheap they are, I don't need 'em!"

The proprietor then would be cool, calm and collected, tapping the tiny bowl of his long-stem pipe on his palm. Having been told off like this, all Kojuro, the greatest bear hunter in those mountains by a country mile, could do was just anxiously screw up his face. What would he do for money to buy the rice needed to keep his family of seven, including his mother who was pushing ninety and his grandchildren, when all they had at their place was some chestnuts from the forest nearby and millet they could grow in the little plot behind the house? They couldn't even afford miso, let alone rice. People in the village grew hemp, but out at Kojuro's place the only thing even resembling fabric they could make was baskets woven out of the few wisteria vines they could string together.

"Sir, I beg of you," said Kojuro in a hoarse voice after a long pause, bowing low again. "You can set whatever price you wish, if you'll just buy my pelts."

"Right," said the proprietor after puffing on his pipe and doing his best to hide the smirk on his lips. "Leave 'em there. Heisuke, hand two yen to Kojuro, will ya?"

Heisuke would sit in front of Kojuro and plonk four big coins down between them, and Kojuro would respectfully hold them high in both hands with a big satisfied grin.

"Hey, Okino, fix something to drink for Kojuro here," said the proprietor, gradually becoming quite jolly and going on to chat in a breezy manner about one thing and another.

This would all make Kojuro as happy as a sandboy, and he'd sit up straight and tell the proprietor what he saw in the mountains and things, until someone in the kitchen said that the food and drink were ready and Kojuro would go through the motions of begging off but, in the end, be lured into the kitchen and once again bow low before all who were there. Before he knew it, someone would bring him a little black lacquer tray with salmon cured in salt, slices of squid and a jug of sake.

Kojuro would sit formally before the tray, lay a few slices of squid on the back of his hand and lick them over and over and, with all due politeness, pour himself a little cup of the yellowish sake. There wasn't a single person, however, who would think that two yen for a big mound of pelts from two bears was a fair price, even in a bear market. In fact, even Kojuro knew all too well that the price was just about as low as you can get. So why, you may ask, did Kojuro take his pelts to a general store like that one in town and not sell them one after the other to someone else?

Most people wouldn't know why, but it's because in Japan there's a game like Rock-Scissors-Paper called "Fox-Hunter-Proprietor." It's set up so the fox loses to the hunter and the hunter loses to the proprietor. In this case, the bears are fleeced by Kojuro and Kojuro is fleeced by the proprietor. And because the proprietors all live in towns, they're not generally eaten by bears. But I believe that these revolting slick proprietor characters will gradually vanish in time all by themselves, as the world moves forward. And when I write about such an upstanding man as Kojuro being brought down so shrewdly by someone so odious, the kind of man you never want to meet up with more than once in your life, I can tell you, it galls me no end. That was the lay of the land. Yet, it must be said that Kojuro never felt ill will toward the bears, even though his lot was to kill them. But then, something really odd occurred.

No sooner had Kojuro splashed and splattered up the ravine and hauled himself to the top of a boulder than did he catch sight of a very large bear climbing up a tree with its back rounded like a cat's right in front of him. In a flash he had his rifle ready to fire. His dog had dashed right up to the tree and was frantically circling its trunk.

It looked for a moment as if the bear was in two minds, whether to jump down onto Kojuro or stay where it was and allow him to shoot, when it suddenly let go of the tree and thudded to the ground. Kojuro approached the bear cautiously with his rifle pointed at it and was about to pull the trigger when the bear raised both its paws into the air.

"What are you killing me for?" it cried out.

"Oh, all I want from you is your hide and your gall bladder, that's all. It's not that I can take 'em to town and make a killing on them an', besides, I really do feel for you, but what am I supposed to do? An' now, when you put it to me like this, I tell ya, I feel like I should just eat chestnuts an' things, an' if I die from that, well then, maybe I should."

"Can I ask you to hold off for about two years? I'd be happy to die, you know, but I've got some vital things I need to take care of. So would you mind waiting for just two years? When that's over I'll even come right up to your house and die for you, and you'll be free to take my hide and my gall bladder then."

Kojuro was plunged into the strange thought of this and didn't move from the spot. And while he was plunged into thought, the bear planted its four feet on the ground and started to stroll away. Kojuro was still lost in thought, and the bear just sauntered away without so much as a backward glance, convinced that the last thing in Kojuro's mind was lodging a bullet in its back. And getting glimpses of the bear's wide reddish-black back catching the rays of the sun filtering through the branches, Kojuro moaned a heartrending moan and started on back across the ravine.

It was one morning exactly two years after that that Kojuro heard gales of wind blowing outside his house and he went out to see if any trees or fences had been blown down. The cypress fence was standing strong in the wind, but something reddish-black that he had seen before was lying beside it. Kojuro was taken aback. He knew that exactly two years had passed and was beginning to worry whether the bear would really come back or not. When he got closer he saw that it truly was the same bear. It lay there with a stream of blood oozing out its mouth. Kojuro found himself with his palms together in prayer.

Then, one day in January, this happened.

"Mum," said Kojuro, "I'm no spring chicken anymore an' for the first time in my life I really don't feel like gettin' my feet wet again."

His mother, who was pushing ninety, had set herself down in the sun on the veranda and was spinning thread. She lifted her eyes that could hardly see anymore, and you couldn't tell if she was about to smile or cry. Kojuro slipped into his straw boots, tying them at the ankles, rose and left the house.

"Granddad," called the children one after the other, poking their head playfully out the stable door, "don't be long!"

"I won't!" said Kojuro in the direction of his grandchildren, as he gazed up to the clear blue slippery sky.

Kojuro made his way along the hard-packed pure white snow toward Shirasawa. His dog was soon panting as it ran with its red tongue lolling, stopping from time to time to catch its breath. And by the time the grandchildren were back in the stable playing their game of tossing and picking up millet stalks, Kojuro's shadow had sunk beyond the far side of the hill.

He climbed up the bank at Shirasawa. The water was a pool as blue as blue can be, whose surface was frozen over like a sheet of glass, and countless icicles were hanging down like prayer beads around it, and red and yellow spindletree berries could be seen on both banks among them, as if the whole place was a kaleidoscope of blooming flower petals. Kojuro made his way up, keeping an eye on his own and his dog's glittering shadow as they mingled with the deep blue shadows of the wild cherry blossom tree trunks falling on the snow. He had made it a point the previous summer to visit the place over the ridge past Shirasawa and had seen a very big bear living there.

He entered the valley and continued to climb up it, crossing five narrow streams left and right, right and left, until he came to a little waterfall. He skirted the waterfall and started to make his way up to the ridges at Nagane. The snow was as bright as fire in his eyes, and he felt half blinded, as if wearing violet-lens glasses. His dog was not about to be defeated by the steep slopes and was digging its heels into the snow, despite slipping back down time and time again.

They finally managed to reach the peak and found a gentle flat slope dotted with chestnut trees. The snow there gleamed like white limestone right up to the tall peaks surrounding them.

Kojuro sat himself down on the summit when, out of the blue, the dog began to bark as if its tail was on fire. This startled Kojuro and he looked around. The huge bear from the previous summer was rushing toward him on its hind legs. Kojuro calmly adopted his stance and took aim at the bear with his rifle. But this didn't stop the bear from charging with its front paws outstretched toward him. Even the usually composed Kojuro turned white as a sheet.

Kojuro heard his rifle give off a loud bang, but this didn't stop the bear from getting closer, its massive black body storming ahead, swaying from side to side. The dog gripped the bear's leg in its teeth and wouldn't let go … but just then Kojuro felt a loud clang in his head, the world in front of him turned bright blue, and he heard these words coming to him from far away, "Oh, Kojuro, I wasn't going to kill you."

Kojuro was sure he was no longer of this world when he saw blue starlike lights gleaming and glittering all around him.

"This must mean that I'm dead. It's the flames you see when you die. Dear Bears, I beg your forgiveness."

I regret to say that I haven't the foggiest idea as to what Kojuro thought or felt after that.

Be that as it may, something else happened on a night three days after that. The moon was hanging in the sky like a great ball of ice, the snow was glowing pale white, and the waters there were giving off a soft phosphorescence. The stars of the Seven Sisters and Orion's Belt looked like they were breathing green and bitter-orange light in and out.

On the flat smooth plate of snow, surrounded by white peaks and chestnut trees, a number of large black figures had come to form a circle, prostrating themselves as if in solemn prayer, each one casting their own shadow in the snow. The black figures and their shadows remained like that, without moving for ever and a day.

Kojuro's dead body could be seen in the moonlight and the light of the snow. It was in a sitting position, with legs crossed, at the highest point in the middle of the circle. You wouldn't be blamed for thinking, if you gazed upon his serene frozen face and the almost imperceptible smile on his lips, that he looked as he did when alive.

And even though the stars of Orion's Belt moved from the very top of the sky tilting down toward the west, those big black figures stayed perfectly still, as if fossilized on that very spot.

Asahikawa

Kenji often felt a profound loneliness and at times sank into a depressive self-pity. Yet we think of his writing as being full of light, joy and hope. After we learn of the death of Campanella in *Night on the Milky Way Train* less than an hour passes before Campanella's father, standing on the bank of the river that took his son, resigns himself to the death. Giovanni, who has just lost his best friend in life, runs home at full speed to give the bottle of milk that he fetched earlier to his mother. This is a happy end to what is a story of personal tragedy ... or if not a happy end, one of contented resignation.

To Kenji, you can overcome your loneliness by realizing that you are not just a single solitary being in this life. Being a single solitary being you can nonetheless sense everything that is around you—all reality, the entire universe—together with all others like and unlike you, who also form a part of you.

We have a cosmic consciousness not only intellectually in our mind but as a concomitant part of our being, because each and every molecule in our body is interconnected, through our origins, with each and every molecule in others. And we all sense the universe together. I will quote again from the amazing and all important first poem in *Spring and Ashura* ...

Just as what is is but what we sense in common
So it is that documents and history ... or the Earth's past
Are nothing but what we have become conscious of

In other words, reality is that which we sense in common and is nothing more or less than that which we have become conscious of at any point in time.

I have chosen a poem to illustrate Kenji's solitude that is not well known in Japan. It is "Asahikawa."

Asahikawa is a town in Hokkaido some one hundred and forty kilometers northeast of Sapporo. Today's population is approximately three hundred thousand. At the time of Kenji's visit there were already about sixty thousand people living there.

If you go to the Higashi High School in Asahikawa (the Asahikawa Middle School in the poem) you will see a large stone monument of this poem, carved as it was written in Kenji's hand.

Kenji visited Asahikawa in early August 1923. This was only nine months after the death of his beloved sister, Toshi. Though he was still overcome by grief over her death, like Campanella's father and Giovanni, he understood that death is a normal phase of life, nothing more than a step in the cycle of existence; and this helped him, as it did those characters in *Night on the Milky Way Train*, to cope with it.

In this poem Kenji is alone in the early August morning. He is delighting in this carriage ride with the wind against his face, a wind reminiscent of a wind in October. (By calling it an October wind, he tells us by inference how fast the carriage is moving, for the autumn winds are brisk.)

Every trip that Kenji takes, be it one up a mountain, on a train or in a carriage, takes him on a journey through his consciousness. This is as he sees it: He is embarking on the journey *in order to* travel through his consciousness.

The important element in all of Kenji's stories and poems is the total sensory environment in which they take place. He argued with the publisher of his poetry collection that what he was writing was not poems. He called them "mental sketches modified." In other words, they are concrete depictions of his mental state at the time of seeing or writing, modified by the means of production, in this case words, paper and ink. This process is as vital as the narrative of the work itself.

The sensory atmosphere in this poem is created by the sound of the horse's bell, the driver's whistling, the black fabric tossing in the wind and, more than anything, the mane tossing like flames. Kenji often sees something elemental, in the natural sense, in a thing or object. The mane appears to him as fire, one of the elements. Here again he is telling us that that which we see is connected to something elemental (fire) in nature.

In the second half of the poem the poplars are swaying blue, and the sky is cold and white. The final image is the dew, just like the dew on Indra's net, an image he invokes in a story with that title of a net that connects every single molecule in the universe to every other. Our meager physical presence is a part of a vast, cold, white and blue, eventually otherworldly, universe.

Our consciousness as single individuals is bound up inextricably in the sounds, colors and forces of nature. Knowing and *sensing* this allows us to overcome our solitude and to relate to the world and the universe.

This is the origin of hope and joy in the works of Miyazawa Kenji: the possession and awareness of this consciousness. We all have it by virtue of us being born as human beings. You do not learn this from your parents or in school. It is the essence of the human condition. Knowing this, I suppose, is why the two men at the end are smiling, just as we should be smiling in spite of the cold of the sky that hangs above our heads all our life.

The three plants named at the end—Babylon willow, Chinese plantain and dianthus—are all natives of East Asia. The willow grows tall, while the other two plants are low on the ground, emphasizing that they all appear as equals out of the same soil and dew, the latter being a Buddhist symbol of the transience of life.

ASAHIKAWA

by Miyazawa Kenji

The early morning delight of riding alone
In this little colonial-style horse-drawn carriage!
"Take me to the Agricultural Testing Station …
It's at 6-jo 13-chome"
The horse's bell rings   the driver whistles
The black fabric swings in this virtually October wind
A troop of cavalrymen leads a line of horses
This horse turned out to be a hackney
Its mane tosses like flames
Ah, how agreeable is the shaking of this carriage
The black fabric glides excessively
This agile little horse should be reined in
I race through this town so early
Without fail stretching to the pinnacle of Enlightenment
Now at 6-jo, turning
Oh, larch tree   Japanese larch tree
And blue swaying poplars
A row of colonial-style official residences
The Asahikawa Middle School
All flourishing
The carriage roof striped yellow and red
Truly in the gypsy fashion
Who wouldn't want a carriage like this one?
Two men approach on horseback
The sky is cold, white
Yet the two men are smiling a toothy white smile
Babylon willow Chinese plantain and dianthus
All rise in the cold morning's dew

Drawing Water

Nineteen twenty-seven was a particularly intensive year for Kenji in terms of the production of poems, many of which are truly wonderful and among his best. He had turned thirty in August of the previous year and wasn't always well. In March of 1926 he had given up his teaching position, of his own volition, at Hanamaki Agricultural School, and in November of that year had spent several days in hospital. When out of hospital he began teaching at the Las Chijin Kyokai. (This was an organization that he created out of the two-story house the Miyazawas built just above the Kitakami River, the one that became famous for the board by the back door where Kenji wrote, "I am in the field below." Chijin Kyokai loosely means "Farmers' Association," and Las comes from the Polish word for "forest.")

In December 1926 he traveled to Tokyo (his seventh trip to date to the capital), taking his cello with him. Though not entirely recovered from his weak lung condition, he took the trip to improve his playing of the cello and the organ, to further his knowledge of Esperanto and raise his proficiency at typing on a typewriter.

The absolutely prodigious outpouring of poems in 1927 lasted until about the end of the summer of that year. Even if he had just written those poems and nothing else, they would have been sufficient in number and quality to form a collection that would have secured him a reputation among the greatest of Japanese modern poets. After that, however, he wrote much less. In August 1928 he spiked a high fever; and in December, he was hospitalized with acute pneumonia. For the next two years he was too fragile in health to do arduous physical work.

"Drawing Water" carries the date 23 March 1927. This puts it between "Around the Time when the Diluvial Period Ended" (included in my Bloodaxe Books collection *Strong in the Rain*) and "Black and White Cells" (see page 202). It is an amazing poem that reveals much about Kenji's mental state, how he senses nature and the role of human beings in it.

It comprises a simple narrative.

Kenji is drawing water from a well when he spots a lone moth in his bucket. The moth is drowning. No doubt its wings have soaked up the water, preventing it from flying.

Kenji occasionally writes about moths. They are not as beautiful as butterflies and not particularly loved in Japanese art. But to Kenji the life of each and every living thing is sacred. His aesthetic of beauty encompasses all creatures big and small. He takes up the moth in his poem from May 1924, "The Sun Sheds Slivers of Topaz." That poem portrays a realm between this world and that, where the moth is a kind of messenger "sent adrift, shakily, forlorn, faint white in the day, across the air's indefinite shoreline" ...

> *with the water being mercury*
> *and the wind carrying such balmy aromas ...*

In "Drawing Water" the moth is trapped by the water and cannot be "sent adrift." So what does Kenji do? He scoops it out of the water. Immediately the moth comes to life and takes off. Its course, written in English in the original, is a "zigzag." There is no predicting the route taken or the chaos caused by the wings of a moth. Its journey into the air cheers up the desert. But there is a fascinating connection in this poem with a world far away ... in the United States.

I will follow thee alone,
Thou animated torrid zone!
Zig-zag steerer, desert-cheerer,
Let me chase thy waving lines,
Keep me nearer, me thy hearer,
Singing over shrubs and vines.
Insect lover of the sun,
Joy of thy dominion!
Sailor of the atmosphere;
Swimmer through the waves of air,
Voyager of light and noon;
Epicurean of June,
Wait, I prithee, till I come
Within ear-shot of thy hum,
All without is martyrdom.

This is part of a poem by Ralph Waldo Emerson titled "The HumbleBee." (Humblebee is another word for "bumblebee"; and "prithee" comes from "I pray thee" and means "I ask you.") This poem is an idyll dedicated to the "insect lover of the sun," animated and free flying. Kenji must have become enamored of Emerson's bee and would have loved the phrases "sailor of the atmosphere" and "voyager of light and noon."

Emerson was a major force in Meiji Japan, particularly through his widely read 1841 essay "Self-Reliance." It appealed, with its emphasis on individualism and nonconformity, to the Japanese youth of the new modern nation state, Kenji among them.

For Kenji the subject is not a bumblebee on a voyage of pollination but a single living animal of another sort, a moth, coming back from the edge of this world. Or is it a messenger from the other world caught on its way between that world and this? This moth and Kenji's rescue of it are symbols: that our role on Earth is to save animals, even a single moth, just as we would save a drowning child. Our altruism is our most important attribute as humans, and we should exercise it at all times and toward all things, seeing as everything is beautiful, everything has a role to play.

The strawflower in this poem appears in the original in its Latin name, Helichrysum. Kenji often uses the Latin names for plants and rocks of all sorts, making it difficult for some readers to identify with the object and what he is trying to describe. But he is as much the scientist as he is the poet; and naming things with their "real names" is important to him. The common Japanese name for the strawflower is "straw hat daisy." The strawflower has stiff papery petal-like leaves that many people mistake for petals. It is an Australian native plant! Kenji would have known it for its decorative use as a dry flower. Here its corolla acts as a metaphor for the moth on the surface of the water, along with the metaphor of the sea as a shellfish (reinforced by the epithet of the sealike air).

The indentations of the lines appear here as they are in the original. Kenji often indents when he wishes to make a parenthetical statement in metaphoric or dialogue form. The lines depicting the taking off of the moth are written this way to help us visualize flight. The moth "sails," further underscoring the merging of the worlds of air and water. Finally, "indeterminate clouds" is a reference to the threshold of the world beyond.

DRAWING WATER
by Miyazawa Kenji

The bucket of water that I have drawn
From the rhomboid shadows of the well
Emerges into the amber light
Brimming with the sparkles of waves
And plenty of foam A lone moth
… captivating shellfish …
… strawflower corolla …
Had been drawn into my bucket
The moth is drowning
Due to the smooth powerful surface tension of the water
I'll scoop this early spring intruder
Into the warming glowing sealike air

Oh, right away a tiny spray of water
        iridescence
        spring moth
                    takes off
                takes off
            takes off
        zigzag steerer   desert cheerer
It's now sailing between the dark-brown tufts of the forest
And indeterminate clouds

Black and White Cells

Back in 2008 I received an email from Prof. Tani Jun at the Institute of Physical and Chemical Research, or Riken, in Saitama prefecture. Prof. Tani was attached to Riken's Research Center for Brain Science. This was the first contact I had ever had with Prof. Tani, an eminent researcher into the mysteries of cognition and the workings of the brain.

He asked me if I would translate one of Kenji's poems, which he wanted to introduce to a nonJapanese audience of specialists at a conference to be held in the United States. He said that this poem, written on 28 March 1927, arguably marked the first time in the world that anyone had stated that our emotions, dreams, ideas and feelings stem from the functioning of our nerve cells.

I had read the poem a long time before then but hadn't realized how epoch making it might have been. In fact, I must confess, I didn't understand the poem either. But once I translated it I found that it is not all that difficult to understand.

Compassion and pity and mercy and empathy and love are main preoccupations for the man and the poet called Miyazawa Kenji. But where do these feelings reside? Many Japanese writers would say "the heart." Japanese has a word that does not translate well into some other languages: *kokoro*. Kokoro is, in English, a combination of heart and mind, with the spirit, care and sympathy thrown in. Kenji's worldview originates in the brain, the brain that not only thinks but senses the inner and outer world. As I mentioned earlier, he called his poems "mental sketches modified."

Many Western writers, particularly the Russians, place emphasis on something they call the soul. Superficially, it might look like Kenji, being a devout Buddhist, also looked to something akin to a soul for understanding of the self and its fate in this world and beyond.

But a careful reading of the poem that I translated for Prof. Tani shows that Kenji views the self and its cognitive recognition as emanating in and from our neurons alone. Our emotions, dreams, ideas and feelings are created and triggered by physical phenomena. Everything in the natural world can and should be explained on the basis of scientific "observation and experience." (His otherworldly reveries are visual metaphors that are there for their religious or moral purposes, not as metaphysical constructs.) States of being, incidents and events may look supernatural or surrealistic, but they are not. All phenomena that take place in Kenji's world are natural and realistic to his mind. Many years ago I coined the term "Kenji realism" to counteract the notion, entertained by some Japanese critics, that Kenji is an author of "pure fantasies."

In 1994 Nobelist Francis Crick, co-discoverer of the structure of the DNA molecule, published a book that caused a sensation, *The Astonishing Hypothesis*. In this book he wrote, "You, your joys and your sorrows, your memories and your ambitions, your sense of personal identity and free will, are in fact no more than the behavior of a vast assembly of nerve cells and their associated molecules."

So much of modern psychology and psychiatry had been based chiefly on an analysis of our behavior from the social—that is to say, environmental—or genetic viewpoint. What are our parents like? Our education? What environmental factors in our upbringing lead us to take the actions, for better or for worse, that we take? Crick's astonishing hypothesis of the 1990s was that if we want to understand how we see the world and act within it we need also to study the nerve cells in our brains.

The truly astonishing thing, however, is that an unknown poet and scientist living in a small provincial town in Tohoku in Japan had said the very same thing nearly seventy years earlier.

Another note on what he meant by "mental sketch modified."

"Mental" here signifies that all of our observations of the outside world are processed in the brain, through our five senses. To Kenji, the senses process nature in more complex ways than each separate sense might indicate. That is why, for instance, he hears music when the wind blows against electric wires and touches the universe when he puts his hand into a flowing river.

"Sketch" signifies the fact that Kenji went outside into nature in order to commune with it. He did not merely sit in his study and read books about natural phenomena, although, needless to say, he was an inveterate bookworm and a studious researcher. As I wrote, he knew the Latin names of plants and rocks, and often used them in his writing. Naming things properly is very important to Kenji, as it is to all scientists.

Kenji did not sit on a veranda watching the passage of the seasons and lamenting on the fleeting nature of life, as many Japanese poets have done for centuries. He does not sing of the seasonal changes in nature in the way many poets in Japan have done since Heian times. A change of season is a mere instant in his world; and our emotions are shaken up by things on a much grander scale than a cherry blossom in full bloom about to fall or a maple leaf turning color before leaving its branch for the earth.

Kenji resembled, in one sense, the French impressionist painters Monet and Pissarro, and the American artist Winslow Homer. They all painted *en plein air*. These artists went outside and created their art there. This is what Kenji means by "sketch." He was happiest when roaming the countryside with his sketchbook, making notes on what he saw. Put "sketch" together with "mental" and you get his understanding of the outside world: a sketch of nature—including all interconnecting phenomena in it—processed through the brain, that is, the senses. You understand nature by sensing and processing it. Poetry is the jotting down in words of this process. Like Thoreau Kenji chose to be "on the deck of the world," where he could observe everything before him.

Finally, the third word in the phrase, "modified." Once the senses sketch nature in its sights, sounds, smells, textures (touch) and tastes, these phenomena are processed in the brain. However, just as the image of an actor in a film is captured by a lens and stored on film, what we see in the cinema is not the actor himself but that image after it has passed through a medium. Similarly, the very process of writing down on paper using the medium of ink alters the image of the natural phenomenon as sensed and described. It can never be the same as the thing itself. It is only a representation of it by the artist or poet, altered by the very action of writing it down. It may not be nature itself, but it's the next best thing: an x-ray of the poet's brain at the prolonged instant of sensing and writing.

"Black and White Cells" is only six lines long. What is Kenji saying here?

The key phrase in this poem is "the flow of consciousness." Our consciousness—that is, the thing that allows us to be ourselves and sense things outside ourselves—derives from the cells in our brain and what he calls their "myriad permutations." The cells, for their part, "derive" from "electronic permutations." In other words, the reason why we can sense things—the reason why we have a consciousness— is entirely physical. There is nothing supernatural here, no place for a soul. You will only find neurons communicating with other neurons.

Note the difference between my self, as two words, in line five, and myself, as one word, in six.

First there is the self, which may also be called "consciousness." This is defined solely by the electrical impulses in our brain. How we then sense this consciousness and how we go on to express it in word and action defines me and you and everyone else: This is us, that is, ourselves. This is the person I see when I meet you and that you see when you meet me. It all starts and ends with our own private neurons and their myriad permutations.

Why "black and white cells?" There is no such thing as a black cell in the brain.

Kenji is putting two opposite-meaning words together to suggest, allegorically, a binary-like functioning of cells. It could just as well be translated with "off and on." Here his concept of the brain resembles today's computers. Just as he compares his own light to an alternating current, so he sees his self as a thing that is now on (light, life), now off (total blackness, death in this life). His frequent use in his works of the word for "flickering" illustrates this binary quality of our state.

So, we are just a bundle of neurons interacting with another bundle of neurons. Kenji wonders: Why don't we just kill each other then? Why are we nice to each other? Why do we empathize with each other when, say, there is a terrible disaster like the Great East Japan Earthquake and the tsunami that followed? What is the mechanism of morality and compassion in Kenji's world, its most crucial component? That is something that Kenji thought about and agonized over constantly in his short life.

First of all we must ask ourselves this question: Why do we all sense the world in the same way, at least in terms of its reality, a reality that Kenji, being a scientist, called "data"? Of course, once we sense these data, we immediately differ on what we think they mean. Countless questions of interpretation of the "data" exist, and this is a cause of dissension and conflict.

Kenji is concerned with the data in nature. After we process these data, we must have our own view of the universe that allows us to form our own opinions on their meaning. He was a man of deep, even dogmatic, conviction. But despite his dogmatism, which had a religious underpinning, he wanted all of us to form our own viewpoint, so long as it was based on proper observation and knowledge of the universe. He says this verbatim in one of his poems. This allows us to form our moral compass.

For Kenji the plate of the compass encompassed the entire universe, not just his family, his hometown, his country or even his species. This is what makes him unique for his and our time. His moral compass was one that included all other animals and plants and inorganic substances like rocks, air, light, the stars and galaxies far beyond our own Milky Way.

For this reason, it is not compassion that motivates him to write what he writes and do what he does, although compassion is surely a manifestation of his behaviour: It is the way in which he senses everything around him, near and far, and the way in which this informs his "self" and how he is motivated by that self, as a matter of consequence, to act.

This is the key that opens up the immense treasure chest that is the world of Miyazawa Kenji: We are connected to each other through our senses. If we observe and study nature, we will all come to know our proper place in it as human beings. Only then can we all work together for the betterment of humankind.

The plate of our moral compass should be as big as the universe. The hand of the compass will point us, as a natural expression of our consciousness, in the direction of goodness, mercy and love, as we see them in our own unique way.

BLACK AND WHITE CELLS

by Miyazawa Kenji

Black and white cells form a myriad of permutations.
They sense these permutations in and of themselves.
The flow of consciousness is derived from this.
Those cells themselves are, in turn, derived from many
    electronic permutations.
In the end, what is called my self
Consists of an electronic system that I sense as myself.

Is it Only in Hienuki

There is a small stone monument at Toyagasaki Shrine in Hanamaki. Into this monument is engraved the second last poem that Kenji wrote.

Hienuki is a district in Hanamaki. In fact, Hanamaki Agricultural School was originally called Hienuki Agricultural School. (Hienuki is coterminous with Hanamaki.) When Kenji was appointed to the teaching staff there in December 1921 it carried the Hienuki name; and in April 1923, while he was still on the staff, it acquired the Hanamaki name.

A festival to celebrate a good harvest was held at Toyagasaki Shrine between 17 and 19 September 1933. Kenji was too weak to go to the shrine at that time. He sat in a chair outside his home and watched people on their way to the festival. Though that night was apparently quite cold and he was in some pain, he stayed outside there for a long time.

Unable to breathe normally, he must have known that he was not long for this world. Nonetheless, his pain was trivial and bearable in light of the joys of the revelers. He found happiness in the thought that others would go on to plant rice, invent new inventions, sing songs, live and care for each other.

Miyazawa Kenji was a very complex man. He was now ecstatic, now deeply depressed; now wracked with anger, now full of a hunger to express unbounded devotion. But he was never bitter. When I think of the expression fixed on Kenji's face for an eternity it is that expressed in his poem "Strong in the Rain": "A constant quiet smile on his lips."

His very last poem, written with a brush at the same time as "Is it Only in Hienuki," reads: "This is the life I am now losing through illness/But I would be full of joy/If I were to be useful to the harvest." It is under the clear sky shining everywhere in "Is it Only in Hienuki" that Miyazawa Kenji, age thirty-seven, died, two days after writing these short poems, at 1:30 pm on 21 September 1933.

IS IT ONLY IN HIENUKI
by Miyazawa Kenji

Is it only in Hienuki and its region
That the ears of rice have ripened so brilliantly
With a bumper harvest for the three-day festival?
This festival sky is clear and shining everywhere.

PART TWO

Works by Other Authors

Hanako

By Mori Ogai

Mori Ogai (1862-1922), novelist, essayist, translator and one of the towering figures of the literary world in the Meiji and Taisho eras, was a master stylist. His prose style could not be farther away from the flowing, often seemingly random and excessively emotional, style of Miyazawa Kenji. It is controlled, concise, rational, formal, and chockablock with erudite Japanese and foreign historical references, the latter being chiefly classical Chinese and modern German. His style exerted an astounding influence on modern Japanese literature, inspiring an author born less than three years after his death, Mishima Yukio. Mishima, a master of clear and rich style in Japanese, took the pen directly from Ogai's hand.

Ogai himself was inspired by his encounters with German culture. He was sent to Germany to study hygiene, particularly for its uses in the military. (Ogai was later promoted to surgeon general in the Imperial Japanese Army, becoming head of the Medical Division of the Army Ministry.) He arrived in Europe at Marseille on 7 October 1884 and went from there to Berlin. He spent his first year of study in Leipzig, going on to pursue his studies in Dresden and Munich. Before leaving Europe he stayed in Vienna, London and Paris, leaving, once again from Marseille and arriving back in Japan on 8 September 1888, for a span outside Japan of some four years.

The story "Hanako" appeared in print for the first time in the 1 July

1910 issue of "Mita Bungaku" (Mita Literature). Mita is the district of Tokyo where Keio University is located. The journal was established in that year at the university's Literature Department by Kubota Mantaro, who had been taught by Ogai.

Ogai had heard third hand about the encounter between Rodin and Hanako from his son, who was told about it by his private tutor, the interpreter. The interpreter plays a major part in the narrative. Ogai's oblique method of presenting it—in a sense the encounter between the two "main" characters takes place on the edge of the narrative—is fascinating. By looking askance, one can see the center more distinctly, a Japanese observational device recognizable in the woodblock print.

We don't learn much about Hanako herself from the story that bears her name. Her real name was Ota Hisa and she was born in 1868, the year of the Meiji Restoration. Hanako was her stage name. Dying in 1945, exactly four months before the Japanese surrender, she spans the most tumultuous period, save perhaps for equivalent decades in the Heian period, in her country's history. (The home in Gifu that she was living in was destroyed in an American air raid and she passed away not long after it.)

Hanako joined a traveling troupe of actors and left Japan for Denmark in 1902. Her most significant encounter was with American dancer Loie Fuller, the so-called Goddess of Art Nouveau. Fuller also knew Rodin, who was enamored of her moving figure, as well as were Toulouse-Lautrec and Alphonse Mucha, for whom she modeled. It was Fuller who suggested her stage name of Hanako.

Hanako modeled for Rodin in 1906, after which she became friends with him and his wife. There are fifty-eight works of his based on her modeling, and two of them, both masks, were gifted to her. She took the two masks back to Japan, where she arrived in December 1921. Thanks to her selling them to a dealer in Tokyo, they were not destroyed in the bombing of her home. She was able to hold a single pose for a long time, maintaining the tension, and this impressed Rodin.

Rodin had spotted her on stage in Marseille on 18 July 1906. This encounter at the Colonial Exhibition occurred thanks to his having seen the Khmer dancers of the Cambodian Royal Ballet previously in Paris. (The dancers had accompanied King Sisowath, who had ascended to the throne two years earlier, on an official visit to France and the Exhibition.) Rodin was so taken with the dancers that he followed them from Paris to Marseille, making some one hundred and fifty drawings of the dancers, some of which he subsequently filled in in watercolors.

In Marseille he stopped in at a Japanese dramatic performance with the intriguing, if somewhat chilling, title "Revenge of the Geisha." Hanako was the geisha. It is said that Rodin was inspired by her expression when she faced death by harakiri; but as women were not allowed to commit this ritual act (a privilege reserved for the presumably gutsier sex), I cannot vouch for the authenticity of the expression she managed to maintain. At any rate, Rodin requested a meeting with her and that led to the encounter described in "Hanako."

The Hotel Biron, where Rodin maintained his studio, has had several names over its history. In 1916 Rodin bequeathed the studio and its contents to the French government, who opened it as the Rodin Museum dedicated to him and his work three years later. It is still there, on the Rue de Varenne in today's Paris.

The contrasting way in which Kubota speaks to Rodin and to Hanako is very telling of Japanese society then and, to some extent, now. Though he is speaking French to the sculptor, Kubota's dialogue is, needless to say, in Japanese in the story and is formal and highly respectful. The register drops like an elevator in free fall for Hanako, whose profession is totally deplorable to the educated interpreter's mind. He is decidedly uncomfortable with this task and prefers the company of the books in the next room. Ogai is telling us as much about the Japanese male as he is about the Japanese female.

I have in my desk drawer a typed-out translation that I did of "Hanako" dated 1973 (not the translation below, which is a new one).

The thing that I have always loved about this story is its remarkable point of view. You will look at many of Hokusai's views of Mt. Fuji and not immediately focus on the mountain. He leads you to view it through the everyday life of the people of the district depicted as a part of nature as a whole, that side-glance of the Japanese aesthetic.

Hanako is here for Ogai to comment on the aspiration of the artist; to get under the skin; to recreate the world inside the object, or person, under examination; to probe what makes a toy move; to expose what makes a human being tick.

"Hanako" is a beautiful example of a writer's peripheral vision. Ogai, like Hokusai, looks to one side, then another in order to reveal the essence in the middle.

HANAKO

By Mori Ogai

Auguste Rodin entered his atelier in the Hotel Biron. The morning sun filled every corner of the spacious room.

The hotel was originally a luxurious structure built by a tycoon, but until not long before then had served as a convent for Sisters Servants of the Sacre Coeur. The young girls of Faubourg Saint-Germain would be assembled in this room and be led in hymns by the Sisters. The girls lined up in a single row and sang out with their pink lips parted like the mouths of chicks in the nest about to be fed by their mother. But you could no longer hear their animated voices now. A different variety of animation, a different kind of life, now reigned in this room. This was a life without voice. And though it was devoid of voice, it nonetheless was a tempered, intense and palpitating life.

Mounds and lumps of clay sit on various pedestals and tables; and there are rough, angular pieces of marble elsewhere in the room. Rodin is in the habit of working on a number of projects simultaneously, turning to them as his spirit dictates, allowing them to grow naturally in the sunlight as flowers do on their plants. Some mature gradually; some, more swiftly. The power that his will exerts on form is astounding. His works come to life even when his hands are unmoving on them. From the instant he sets to work, he is able to muster the kind of concentration that normally would require hours of tedious labor in others.

Rodin, beaming, surveyed the half-finished head that he was working on. Its wide forehead. A bulbous knot of a nose in the middle. An ample white beard about the chin and jaw.

There was a knock at the door.

"Entrez!"

His vigorous voice, entirely unlike that of an old man, disturbed the still air in that room, and a thin man in his thirties with dark-brown hair and the look of a Jewish professor opened the door and entered.

"I have brought Mademoiselle Hanako for the appointment," he said.

Rodin's expression remained impassive as he watched this man enter and listened to what he had to say. He recalled the time that the Khmer king had visited Paris. The king had brought dancers with long slender limbs and supple bodies that, when they moved in their ways, bewildered and allured the observer. Rodin had held onto the dessins that he had hastily drawn of them at the time.

Every race, in this manner, has its own beauty. Rodin believed that it was up to a person to discover that beauty with his eye; and, hearing that Hanako was appearing in the variety theater in Paris, he had contacted her agent and asked for an appointment. The man who stood before him now was that agent, in a word, an impresario.

"Have her come in," said Rodin.

The fact that he did not so much as point to a chair was not merely an indication of how little time he had.

"An interpreter accompanies her, sir," said the impresario, respectfully.

"Who's that? Is he French?"

"No, sir, he is a Japanese, a student at L'Institut Pasteur. He learned from Hanako that she would be visiting you, sir, and offered his services."

"That will be fine. Let them both in."

The impresario bowed and left the room. Two Japanese entered immediately. Both of them were exceedingly small. They were followed by the impresario, who shut the door behind him. Though Rodin was by no means a tall man, the two Japanese barely came up to his ears.

A deep furrow appeared between Rodin's eyebrows whenever he scrutinized objects, and so it did on this occasion. His gaze shifted from the student to Hanako, where it now lingered.

The student greeted Rodin and grasped his outstretched hand with its raised tendons. This was the hand that created Danaid, The Kiss and The Thinker. The student took his name card out of his card case and proffered it to Rodin: M. Kubota, Bachelor of Medicine.

"You are presently studying at L'Institut Pasteur?" said Rodin, glancing down at the name card.

"Yes, I am."

"Have you been there long?"

"For three months now."

"Studying hard?"

Kubota got a start. It was widely known that Rodin was in the habit of asking all students this very same direct question, and now it was his turn to answer it.

"Yes, very hard, sir," he answered, vowing in his heart at that instant that he would apply himself to his studies and work until the day he died.

Kubota introduced Hanako. Rodin grasped her small sturdy hand as he ran his eyes down her little firm body, reading her, in this one long glance, from her clumsily set "butterfly" coiffeur to the tips of her toes visible in her thonged sandals.

Kubota could not help but feel a certain degree of embarrassment. He would have preferred to have been able to introduce a somewhat finer example of Japanese womanhood.

One can appreciate his embarrassment. Hanako was no great beauty. She had suddenly appeared on the stages of Europe, calling herself a Japanese actress. The Japanese living in Europe had never heard of such an actress, and, needless to say, this included Kubota. Far from being a beauty, she had the looks of a scullery maid, if I am not being too unkind to her. The skin on her limbs was soft and smooth and, by all appearances, she could not have done very much heavy work in her life. She was only sixteen and, as they say, in flower; and it is somewhat of a stretch to think of her as a housemaid. She rather resembled a girl just out of her childhood.

Rodin was pleased beyond all expectation. Here before him was a healthy, active young woman possessing a sturdy muscular frame without an ounce of fat below her thin pale skin, with muscles of evident tensile strength, a small face with a compact forehead and jaw, and an exposed neck. Rodin was delighted as well with the fact that the muscles in those gloveless hands, arms and entire body seemed to be throbbing with energy.

He put out his hand to her and she, well accustomed to European ways, grasped it with an amiable smile on her lips.

Rodin offered them both chairs.

"May I ask you to wait in the drawing room?" he said, turning to the impresario.

After the impresario left the two Japanese sat down.

"Are there mountains in Mademoiselle's birthplace?" asked Rodin, opening a box of cigars. "Or is the sea nearby?"

Hanako, as a woman making her own way in the world, had a series of set phrases prepared to answer people's questions, much like the little girl in Zola's *Lourdes* who gets on the train and recounts the miracle of how her leg was cured. Hanako's story thus resembled one written by a novelist practiced in routine. But Rodin's unexpected question had fortunately shattered this pattern.

"The mountains are quite far, sir. We are by the sea."

Rodin was pleased with this answer.

"Did you often go boating?"

"Yes, I did."

"Did you row the boat yourself?"

"No, my father did. I was still little then."

Rodin conjured a picture in his mind's eye. He fell silent for a few moments. He was a man of few words.

"Mademoiselle is familiar with my profession, I trust," he said without transition, turning to Kubota. "Would she remove her kimono for me?"

Kubota did not reply at once. For anyone but Rodin he would have refused outright his services as an intermediary for such a thing as asking a Japanese woman to pose unclothed. But seeing as this was for Rodin, he had no objection. He did not feel obliged to give it another thought. He simply hesitated because he was unsure as to what Hanako would say.

"I will ask her and see."

"Please do."

"The master has something he wishes to ask of you," he said to Hanako. "He is the world's greatest living sculptor and he sculpts people's bodies. I mean, even you know that much. That's what he wants to ask you, if you'll pose without your clothes on for him. So, what do you say? I mean, take one look at him. He's such an old man. He's pushing seventy. As you can see, he's past the age of foolishness. So, you up for it?"

Kubota fixed his eyes on Hanako, wondering whether she would blush from bashfulness, assume an affected air or, perhaps, protest.

"I will oblige him," she said candidly, without blinking an eye.

"She has consented," said Kubota to Rodin in French.

Rodin's entire face lit up. He rose from his chair and placed some paper and chalk on the table.

"Do you choose to remain here?" he asked Kubota.

"In my profession I have been called upon at times to decide whether my presence is necessary. However, in this case I feel it might make Mademoiselle Hanako uncomfortable."

"I see. We should be finished in fifteen or twenty minutes. Please be so kind as to wait in the library," he said, indicating a side door. "And do help yourself to a cigar."

"He says that it'll take only fifteen or twenty minutes," Kubota told Hanako.

He took a cigar for himself and receded into the library.

*

There were doors on both sides of the modest room that Kubota entered, but only a single window with a plain bare table below it. Bookshelves lined the walls on both sides of and opposite the window.

Kubota stood stationary for some moments, running his eyes over the lettering on the leather spines of the books. They were in no special order; and it looked very much as if they had been placed according to the chance of their acquisition. Rodin was a dyed-in-the-wool bookworm who had collected books from the time he had wandered Brussels as a poor young student. Among the old and soiled books there were those that obviously had a special meaning for him; and that is no doubt the reason why he had brought them there.

The ash from his cigar was about to drop, so he walked to the table and flicked it into an ashtray. He picked up a book that happened to be there. It was an old book in a gilded leather binding, and he took it to be the Bible. But when he opened it, he realized that it was a pocket edition of *The Divine Comedy*. Another book, lying on an angle in front of it, was a volume out of the complete works of Beaudelaire.

He opened the book to the first page, with no particular desire to read it, to find that it contained the essay on "The Philosophy of Toys." Out of sheer curiosity he began to read.

When Beaudelaire was a little boy he was taken to someone's home where a little girl lived. This little girl had a roomful of toys. The essay goes on to say that the girl invited him to play with any one of them.

When a child plays with a toy, he inevitably feels the need to break it open. He will want to see what makes it the toy that it is. In the case of a moving toy, he will want to find out what drives it. Children turn from the physical to the metaphysical. They are intrigued by metaphysics more than by physics.

Kubota found himself caught up in this fascinating essay of a mere four or five pages' length.

It was then that there was a knock at the door, and it opened.

"I beg your forgiveness," said Rodin, sticking his hoary head through the doorway. "You must be frightfully bored."

"Not at all. I have been reading Beaudelaire," said Kubota, returning to the atelier.

Hanako was already making preparations to leave. Two sketches lay on the table.

"What of Beaudelaire were you reading?"

"The Philosophy of Toys."

"The form and structure of the human body, as with those toys, is not interesting as form and structure. It is a mirror of the spirit. What is interesting is the flame inside, the flame that one can see in the form."

Kubota discreetly stole a glimpse at the sketches.

"They're much too rough for you to tell anything," said Rodin, adding, after a long pause, "Mademoiselle has a very beautiful body. She has no fat, and her muscles float to the surface, each one remaining a separate entity. They are like the muscles of a fox terrier. Her tendons are firm and thick, and the joints in her arms are as large as those in her legs. Her legs are so sturdy that I have no doubt but that she could stand forever on one leg with the other leg thrust out on a right angle. She is like a tree with its roots deep in the earth. She is unlike the Mediterranean type with broad shoulders and a wide waist. She is also unlike the Northern European type with wide waist and narrow shoulders.

"She embodies an aesthetic of strength."

The Tale in the Woods

By Ishikawa Takuboku

The Illusions of Self is my volume of translations of Takuboku's tanka, published by Balestier Press. It contains much information about his poetry, life and times. He was—and still is—the most brilliant creator and foremost advocate of that traditional genre of Japanese poetry.

The two great poets of Iwate, Ishikawa Takuboku and Miyazawa Kenji, were born fifty kilometers and ten years apart (1886 and 1896). They went to the same middle school in Morioka. They both died young of tuberculosis: Takuboku at twenty-six in 1912; Kenji at thirty-seven in 1933.

Takuboku was already on the way to being mega-famous during his lifetime, while Kenji did not receive superstar status until many decades after his death. Both are today considered voices for progress and activism in many spheres of social activity. Takuboku is more political than Kenji; Kenji more aware of the natural and cosmic forces determining our fate than Takuboku. Had Takuboku lived longer, it is very possible that they would have met. As it is, they are the soul brothers of Meiji Japan.

"The Tale in the Woods" was published in the 20 September 1907 issue of the alumni magazine of Morioka Middle School, the present-day Morioka First High School. Kenji wasn't to enter the school until a year and a half later. But judging by the tenor of the stories he subsequently wrote, "The Tale in the Woods" clearly influenced him.

This Takuboku tale takes up the arrogance of the human being as the self-styled lord of all creation. Environmentalism was certainly in the air in late Meiji. The word "ecology" was used by Meiji scientist Minakata Kumagusu (about whom I have written at length in *My Japan*). It is the monkey in the story who reminds us of the importance of the natural environment to us humans who, in his words, "don't have the brains you were born with."

The polemic described in this story, now more than a century old, goes on....

THE TALE IN THE WOODS

By Ishikawa Takuboku

I have recorded here a tale that takes place in the woods.

A man walked into the woods.

A monkey sitting on a branch of a very tall tree posed a question to the man.

"We share ancestors, so why do you human beings look down on us?"

The man answered the monkey this way.

"We're clever, unlike you stupid monkeys. Would we human beings have produced so many great heroes in our history if we came from the likes of you?"

The monkey spoke again.

"Oh, you human beings are so pathetic! You have all simply forgotten the past. Don't you see that the very fact that you are alive right here and now is because we have the very same ancestors? Those who have forgotten their past will have no future. There will be neither progress nor happiness in the future if you get too big for your britches and think that you're the cleverest animal and that now is the best time ever. I really pity you. It probably won't be long before human beings are wiped from the face of the Earth."

The man spoke up in anger.

"What the hell are you talking about, damn monkey! You haven't got brains as big as ours, so how could you possibly ever be a match for us humans? You monkeys don't have houses like us. And you don't even wear clothes like we do, right? Don't you know that we're eating much more delicious things than the nuts you feed on?"

The monkey laughed and spoke again.

"Ha ha ha! Our hair is natural clothing that keeps us healthy during the four seasons. If you human beings had the brains you were born with, you'd be living lives in tune with nature."

The monkey didn't stop there.

"Our home is the entire forest. And not only these woods but all the woods all over the world are our 'home sweet home'. Do you really think that suddenly waltzing into our home without so much as a how-do-you-do is something that a proper human being does?"

The human being's voice now became rough and hoarse.

"Get down from there! Come on down! I'm tellin' you to get yourself down here and say once more to my face what you just said!"

The monkey spoke.

"My, you're a guest with a beastly way of talking, aren't you! I happen to be the master of this house, I'll have you know. No one can tell the master of his house what he must do. You're the guest here, sir, so I suggest you start by paying your respects to the master of the house. Now, how about coming on up here and feasting on some horse chestnuts with me?"

The man looked up into the tall tree and saw the monkey in the branches looking down on him and beckoning him with his paw. All he could do was look up like that, seething with anger at the monkey who was beyond his reach.

The monkey spoke again.

"Oh, you human beings are truly pathetic! Humans can't stand on their own two hands. They can't grasp things with their feet. Look, our four legs are not only legs but hands as well. If you look at the way the arms and legs of human beings are attached, it's plain as day that they could once do whatever we can do. But the fact is that you can't do it now. The history of your limbs, if you take a step back, is just that: history. Someday the time will come when your limbs won't be good for anything at all. That'll be the result of human beings being such sloths!

"The only progress that humankind is making day in and day out is progress in the history of carelessness and neglect. Look, the mechanized civilization that human beings brag about so much is, in the end, run by the very diabolical hand that is turning all of you into a race of lazybones!"

The man screamed out his words.

"How dare you, you cocky beast! Come down right this instant!"

The monkey spoke.

"There's no animal in this world as backward as the human being. Take a look at us. We share ancestors with you. Not only can we move with complete freedom on the ground, we can move up and down at will. You're stuck on the ground. Sure, you once could live in trees, but that was donkey's years ago. Then you slid down to the ground with your fellow snakes and toads. If that isn't a 'come down' I don't know what is. Think it over and ask yourself: Which is closer to Heaven, the horizon that human beings stand on or the trees we sit in … and which is closer to Hell?"

The man screamed his words out again.

"Ponder this, revolting little beast! All we'd have to do is chop down the trees all over the world. Where would your home-sweet-home be then, eh? If we did that, you'd have to stand on bended knee in front of us, bow your head low and beg us for your salvation."

The monkey spoke.

"Ah, so finally a human being has spit out his most evil thoughts. Human beings throughout their history have plotted their hateful rebellion in every corner of the world, snuffing out Nature, brutally butchering everything that is true and beautiful, chopping down trees, digging away mountains and burying rivers to make their flat roads. Yet those roads—the borders between all that is true and beautiful and all that is not—do not lead to the heights of Heaven but rather to the gates of Hell. Human beings have forgotten where they came from and have turned their backs on Mother Nature. Oh, could there be a more cursed and doomed animal in this world than the human being?"

Having said that, the monkey felt deeply sorry for human beings.

As for the man below the tree, he may have sensed that there was some truth behind the monkey's pity for his kind, but it didn't mean that he was prepared to recognize it as truth. So he started to walk out of the woods, grinding his teeth in fury.

The monkey watched him and spoke.

"Sir, where are you heading?"

The man's voice trembled.

"Stay where you are. I'm gonna make you sorry for what you just said. I'm goin' home and I'll be back with my rifle."

But before the man had finished speaking, several huge horse chestnuts sailed down from somewhere, clunking hard against his head.

The man flew off the handle.

"What in the hell do you think you're doing? I'll get you for this, you … animal!"

In a flash the branches of the trees creaked, the leaves rustled … and the old monkey was no longer to be seen in those woods.

He had jumped from branch to branch and flown through the air until finding refuge far far away deep in mountains into which the sun slips out of white clouds and disappears.

The Spider's Thread
By Akutagawa Ryunosuke

Akutagawa Ryunosuke (1892-1927) is perhaps best known outside Japan as the author of the short story "In the Grove," one of two of his stories on which Kurosawa Akira based his classic film "Rashomon." Akutagawa achieved considerable fame in Japan during his lifetime.

Many of his works hark back to Japanese legends and folktales, although they often pivot around a very modern focal point of light parody and dark humor. His novel *Kappa*, a biting satire on Japanese society, is still read today by Japanese of all ages, and a number of his short stories appear in school textbooks.

"The Spider's Thread" is Akutagawa's most well-known short story. It is an allegory about good, evil and redemption. Kandata, the wicked criminal sent to Hell for his sins, is given a chance to save himself, thanks to the Buddha remembering that Kandata had once spared the life of a little spider. But Kandata's fate is sealed for all eternity when he tries to save himself at the expense of others.

Akutagawa distilled this story from three sources, two Japanese and one Russian. The Russian one is the so-called parable of the onion that appears in Dostoevsky's *The Brothers Karamazov*, which Akutagawa finished reading in English in 1917, the year before he published "The Spider's Thread." In Dostoevsky's novel, Grushenka, who represents the Slavophile ideal of the Russian woman, recites the parable to Alexei Karamazov, telling him that she heard it as a child from the household cook.

A very wicked woman is sent, upon her death, to Hell and flung into the Lake of Fire there. But when an angel informs God that during her lifetime the woman had done a good deed by pulling an onion out of the ground and giving it to a beggar, God, not known to be averse to the odd fatal wager, proposes that an onion be given to the woman to pull herself out of Hell and up to Heaven. If it breaks, however, she will find herself back where she started.

The onion appears and the woman begins to pull herself up by it. But when she sees that other sinners are attempting to extricate themselves using "her" onion, she hollers, "This onion is mine, not yours" … at which point the onion breaks and the woman plops back down into the lake, to burn there for an eternity. The angel, seeing this, weeps.

"I know this story by heart, Alyosha," says Grushenka, "because I myself am that wicked woman."

Her honesty and the story itself symbolize Christian redemption for both her and Alexei, a novice in a monastery, the youngest of the Karamazov brothers and himself a symbol of forbearance and lovingkindness.

In a sense Akutagawa was, perhaps, less a teller of stories than a reteller of them. But the tradition of piecing together old tales and fables, often in the form of parody, long preceded him. The two Akutagawa stories that Kurosawa based "Rashomon" on are both "borrowed" from the Heian compilation of "tales new and old," the *Konjaku Monogatari*. Akutagawa's short story "The Nose" is closely based on the Gogol story of the same title. He borrowed from old and new, Japanese and foreign. His lyrical and economical prose style, however, redeems both him and the stories, of which "The Spider's Thread," which exquisitely transforms Dostoevsky's Christian parable to a Buddhist one, may be the most sterling example.

THE SPIDER'S THREAD

By Akutagawa Ryunosuke

One day some time ago, the Buddha was taking a stroll by himself along the edge of the Lotus Pond in Paradise. The jewel-like lotuses in the pond blossomed pure white, their golden stamens in the center of each flower giving off an indescribably heavenly fragrance that wafted ceaselessly throughout the air and beyond. Another day was about to begin in Paradise.

Before long the Buddha was standing on the edge of the pond and gazing between the lotus leaves covering the surface at the state of affairs below. Seeing as the Lotus Pond in Paradise was directly above Hell, the Buddha could see down to its very depths, and make out every detail—as if peering into the crystal-clear water through glass—of the River Styx and the Mountain of Needles.

At that very moment the Buddha caught sight of a man named Kandata squirming along with all the other sinners. Now, this man Kandata was a thief on a grand scale who had murdered people, set fire to houses and had committed just about every wicked deed under the sun.

Yet the Buddha remembered a single good deed, too, that this man had to his name. One day, you see, while Kandata was passing through a dense grove of trees, he happened to spot a little spider crawling on the path.

He wasted no time in lifting up his leg to trample on the little spider when he gave it a second thought, telling himself, "Naw, this little creature has a life too. After all is said and done, it deserves pity and shouldn't have its life taken away from it just like that." So, in the end, he let the little spider live.

The Buddha looked down at the goings-on in Hell, recalling that Kandata had spared the spider's life. And, in return for this good deed, he wished to do anything he could to rescue him from Hell. As fortune would have it, he looked to one side and saw a spider, who had come to live in Paradise, spinning the threads of an exquisite silver web over the jade-colored leaves of the lotuses.

The Buddha slipped one of the spider's silver threads into his hand and let it fall between the jewel-like white lotuses, straight down to the very depths of Hell far below.

Now, the Pool of Blood in the very depths of Hell is full of sinners, Kandata among them, who are now floating, now sinking in it. Every which way you look you see only pitch darkness; and if you do catch a glimpse of something in the dark, it can only be the glint of a needle on the terrifying Mountain of Needles. The utter helplessness of the people there is, in a word, indescribable. On the surface the Pool of Blood is as quiet as the grave, with only the feeble grieving sighs of sinners breaking the silence. The sinners who have committed evil sufficient to get them this far down have already passed through a variety of other Hells, whose tortures have left them without the strength to cry out. So naturally even master thief Kandata, choking on the blood of the pool, could do no more than squirm and writhe like a toad in the throes of death.

Then it happened. For no particular reason Kandata raised his eyes and looked up at the sky above the Pool of Blood. He couldn't believe his eyes. A single thin silver spider's thread, gleaming in the still darkness, was silently dropping, as if avoiding all human gaze, from the farthest heavens above, gliding down to a spot right above his head.

Kandata found himself clapping his hands. If only he could hang onto the thread, he could climb his way far up and out of Hell. If things went well, why, he could get himself right up into Heaven. And no longer would he be driven up the needles of the Mountain of Needles or be submerged in the blood of the Pool of Blood.

With this in mind he wasted no time in grabbing the thread and starting to climb up, fist over fist. After all, for a master burglar like Kandata this was child's play.

The distance between Hell and Heaven, however, was tens of thousands of miles, and however much he rushed, he didn't seem to get any closer. After a short spell of climbing Kandata felt completely worn out, unable to put even one more fist over the other. There was nothing left for him to do but to take a break; and, hanging off the thread, he glanced far down below him.

The Pool of Blood that he had only just been in was, thanks to his prodigious climbing, now lost in the depths of darkness. The terrifying Mountain of Needles was dimly glowing far below his feet. At this rate it wouldn't be long, he now figured, before he was well clear of Hell. Kandata, entwining the spider's thread around his hands, hollered with a laugh he hadn't produced in the years since falling into Hell, "I've done it! I've done it!"

But just then he noticed that countless sinners, like a long line of ants, were clambering up the spider's thread that he was on. All Kandata could do was hang there, roll his eyes and drop his jaw like a complete idiot, and look downward, astonished and terrified. How, he wondered, could such a thin spider's thread, barely able to bear one person without snapping, hold up under the weight of so many? If, by chance, the thread broke now, he thought, I, the main person here, who had taken such pains to get this far, would be tossed back down into Hell. That would be a total disaster.

All the while hundreds and thousands of sinners were making their way, in a single line, slowly but surely up the thin gleaming silver thread from the black depths of Hell. It certainly looked like the thread was about to snap in two, if something wasn't done soon. At that point, Kandata hollered out.

"Hey, you sinners! This spider's thread's mine. Who told you you could climb up it, eh? Get down. Get down!"

At that very instant, the spider's thread that had seemed perfectly fine up to then snapped clean in two just above the place where Kandata was hanging from it. There was nothing he could do about it. Before he knew it, he was cleaving the wind, falling head first like a spinning top toward the dark depths below.

All that was left was a short thin shred of the spider's thread of Paradise hanging down and gleaming brightly in the moonless, starless air.

The Buddha, who had been watching this from its beginning to its end from the edge of the Lotus Pond in Paradise, was visibly saddened when Kandata plunged like a stone back into the Pool of Blood. He began to stroll along the pond's edge once again. He saw it as just punishment for Kandata, a man whose heart knew no mercy, a man who believed that he alone was worthy of escape from Hell.

As for the lotus blossoms in the Lotus Pond in Paradise, these occurrences meant nothing in the world to them. The jewel-like white flowers at the feet of the Buddha danced in the wind, waving their stamens, which gave off an indescribably heavenly fragrance that wafted ceaselessly throughout the air and beyond.

It was approaching noon in Paradise.

Cherries

By Dazai Osamu

"It's not that I'm weak, it's that the suffering weighs down on me too heavily."

This was said, in 1938, by a writer whose life and death are noted with public attention every year in June. The popularity of this author has hardly waned over the decades in Japan. Crowds gather on 19 June in a ritual of celebration and mourning: Given the personality of this man, it is not easy to separate the two.

He is Dazai Osamu, author of such postwar classics as *Ningen Shikkaku* (*A Shameful Life*) and *Shayo* (*The Setting Sun*). The leading publishing house Shinchosha long ranked the former its second most popular novel, while the latter is its tenth most popular. In fact, Dazai is also extensively published by numerous other major publishers, including Chikuma Shobo, Kadokawa and Iwanami Shoten. A large number of his novels and stories have been made into feature films, the latest in 2019.

Young people today are particularly drawn to his works, and it is easy to see why. Dazai is the King of Dysfunctionality. His heroes are—as he fancied himself—proudly and defiantly behind the eight ball, having put themselves there in a stance of diffidence, as if waiting, with perverse anticipation, to be knocked down a hole, into a gutter and out of the game.

The themes in his novels, short stories and essays are those of dejection, illicit love, drug dependency and a morose, aimless alienation; his method, utterly—often to the extent of being maudlin—confessional. He puts the reader in the confession box as priest, then, on the other side of the little window, opens up his heart—and his veins. (In the postwar era Dazai was lumped together with Sakaguchi Ango and Oda Sakunosuke, both of whom also dabbled in drugs. The three are referred to as the "Buraiha," or "The Dissolute Ones." That aimlessness and irresponsibility became emblems of Japanese youth after the war is understandable. During the war they had been nothing more than ammunition.)

There is much in common in Dazai's literature, in a more contemporary context, with the themes and characters in the fiction of Murakami Haruki. People are having relationships, but they never seem to "get it together." It is only habit and the magnet of social decorum that keep them parallel until the attraction weakens and they drift away from each other.

"I'm the joker in the family. Let me put it this way. All I can do is put a jolly face on the huge amount of anxiety and mental anguish I feel. And no, it's not only at home that I do this. Whenever I come into contact with people, no matter how depressed I am, no matter how much physical pain I am in, I do my frantic best to create a pleasant mood all around. Then, after parting, I reel with fatigue and think only of money, morality and suicide."

This is what Dazai wrote in what is arguably his most pathetic look into his own heart and the life of his family, the short story titled "Cherries" that follows. He portrays himself in a hopeless and self-piteous light. It may be this brutal honesty, coupled with a kind of self-centered sadsack coyness, that appealed to young people in the immediate postwar period and continues to appeal to those in a generation today who seek both to lose and, at the same time, identify themselves in measured doses of cyber-disclosure.

Dazai was born on 19 June 1909 into a very well-to-do family in Aomori prefecture, at the very top of Honshu. By the time he was a young man he was feeling intense guilt over his wealthy background, while Japan was experiencing the worst effects of the worldwide Depression. A number of suicide attempts (there were three between 1930 and 1937) followed, one in which a young female companion died.

Left-leaning intellectuals like Dazai were persecuted in the 1930s, as fascism became the norm throughout Japanese society, and Dazai recanted. But was this recantation, too, a pose, just like his self-styled Marxism? His charm, even today, lies in the fact that you cannot tell pose from reality. Was his honesty merely a ruse to engender sympathy in the reader? It doesn't matter to us anymore. We are engaged by his lovable helplessness and his always-say-die decadence.

One of his most enduring and attractive books is *Otogizoshi* (*Otogizoshi: The Fairy Tale Book of Dazai Osamu*). This book consists of four well-known ancient Japanese tales retold by Dazai as he awaited the end of the war in 1945, spending part of the time on the run from the bombing and another part in a dugout shelter with paper and pen in hand.

The retelling of ancient tales, as I have mentioned, has been a common genre of Japanese literature for centuries. Dazai worshipped the most famous modern proponent of story-retelling, Akutagawa, and, to a certain extent, fashioned himself after the master. Even more so than Akutagawa, however, Dazai spins the old stories around his little pink wounded ego.

In one story in *Otogizoshi*, "The Stolen Wen," Dazai writes of the hero who is inordinately fond of drink: "Drinkers tend to say inane and obnoxious things when they're drunk, but most of them are in fact harmless, innocent souls." This is no doubt how Dazai wished to view himself, "harmless and innocent"; although, from the point of view of the ladies who accompanied him on his suicide missions, this innocence might well seem seriously disingenuous. Perhaps the old Japanese adage *hige mo jiman no uchi* (too much self-deprecation is a kind of boasting) applies to the characters in Dazai's works who are fun-house mirror images of himself. No one relished personal insipidity—and relished apologizing for it—like Dazai.

He cruised from one personal crisis to another, frequently being bailed out, financially and morally, by a member of his family. He suffered depression and despaired of living, troubled by thoughts of death his entire life, virtually everything else—love, family, literature—turned into an excuse to hurry it along.

"It's a hell of a thing to stay alive in this world," he wrote in the not-very-veiled autobiographical "Cherries." "Wherever you go you get tangled up in chains; and if you so much as budge, blood spurts out."

This story centers around an on-going argument, exacerbated by the children, between him and his wife. There is a saying in Japan, *Fufugenka wa inu mo kuwanai.* An English equivalent of the meaning is: Marital rows are best left alone. But I prefer the literal meaning of the Japanese for this story: Even a dog won't eat an argument between husband and wife.

Dazai suffers from a seeming lack of ability to commit to anything, be it causes or women. He flirted with both, vacillating, plunging into one after another, then slithering away, leaving his former skin behind. It is this very anguished flight instinct in him that links him to a certain strain of male behavior today ... and by no means only in Japan. What passes for "white male behavior" in the West is alive and kicking all over the world. He has got to be the world's most noncommittal literary man! But he is brutally honest in a way that few male writers are about themselves. His self-knowledge is his redeeming feature and a brilliant force in his literature.

He always seems to be in need of guidance and help. I am not being facetious when I say that this is one thing that engenders in some female readers the instinct to mother him back to normality or in some male readers the itch to identify with his brazen independence and couldn't-care-less egoism. But, poor little rich boy that he was, his colleagues and acquaintances were not always okay with his constant kvetching. Even his most precious personal relationship outside family, that with the remarkable author Ibuse Masuji (1898-1993), could not be sustained for his inability to shed his self-obsessiveness. Ibuse was like a father to him and wrote about the relationship himself in any number of works. Ibuse was his life support. He was there for many serious breakdowns.

But in his suicide note, Dazai called Ibuse *akunin* (a wicked, evil man). It was so shocking to Ibuse and to the public that even today many people think the note was written by the woman who died with Dazai in the canal. There is no doubt in my mind, however, that Dazai himself wrote this note. Perhaps he resented Ibuse for being such a kind mentor and, as such, keeping him alive as long as he did.

Dazai jumped into the swiftly flowing waters of Tokyo's Tamagawa Canal on 13 June 1948, together with Yamazaki Tomie, a woman for whom he abandoned his wife and children. Their bodies were recovered six days later.

The fact that the discovery of Dazai's body coincided with his birthday was not lost on the public of the time. That birth and the acknowledgement of death occur on the same day of the year is an immaculate irony in Dazai terms. This is why the celebration and the mourning that take place every year on 19 June are displays of perfectly matched sentiments. After all, wallowing in self-pity was, for him, a way of life and a luxury; and luxuriating in self-pity has become a part of his legacy.

And yet ... he is a master raconteur! I spoke often about him and his literature with Inoue Hisashi. "Dazai speaks personally to his reader, intimately," Hisashi told me. "Reading him is like listening to a friend talking. This is a rare talent and probably the main reason why his popularity has been sustained for so long."

Dazai opens "Cherries" with a truncated quotation from Psalm 121, the entire first line of which is "I will lift up mine eyes unto the hills, from whence cometh my help."

CHERRIES

by Dazai Osamu

> *I will lift up mine eyes unto the hills*

Parents, I would like to think, are more precious than children. You may sanctimoniously believe, as did the moralizers of old, that you live for the children, but let me tell you, children are much stronger than their parents. At least that's true for my family. Don't get me wrong. I'm certainly not harboring any secret and shameless desire to have my children look after me when I'm old. Yet, you wouldn't know it, because the parents in this household are at the constant beck and call of their children.

Now, my children are far from grown up. The elder daughter's seven; our son is four; and the younger daughter's just one. Even so, each in their own way has got it all over their parents, who have every appearance of being their hand servants.

We cram ourselves into a three-mat room in the summer for our raucous, chaotic dinners, as daddy … that's me … wipes the sweat streaming down his face and grouches under his breath, "There's an old ditty about how gross it is to sweat your way through a meal, but what can a father who's so refined do but drip with sweat when his kids are such pains in the neck?"

Their mother, who's running about like a madwoman with the one-year-old at her breast, waiting on them hand and foot, picking up after them, blowing noses, and wiping them and picking up the spilled food, says, "Father's the one with the wettest nosey … he spends all his time wiping his nosey".

Father forces a smile.

"So where are you all wet? Between your legs?"

"Oh, such an elegant father."

"Huh? Nothing of the sort, my dear. Just medical talk. Nothing to do with elegance at all."

At that, mother turns all serious.

"My ... my breasts. This place between them ... is the vale of tears...."

The vale of tears.

That one shut me up, so I just went on eating.

I'm the joker in the family. Let me put it this way. All I can do is put a jolly face on the huge amount of anxiety and mental anguish I feel. And no, it's not only at home that I do this. Whenever I come into contact with people, no matter how depressed I am, no matter how much physical pain I am in, I do my frantic best to create a pleasant mood all around. Then, after parting, I reel with fatigue and think only of money, morality and suicide. And no, it's not only when I have met with people. This happens when I write as well. It's when I'm sad that I strive to create stories with a light, jolly air. I mean, here I am trying to give people exactly what they want, and they just don't see it, coming out with contemptuous things like, "Dazai's lost his edge ... he's lightened up too much ... he's trying to attract readers with facile humor."

Is it a bad thing for one human to give people what they want? Is it a good thing to be a pompous sourpuss? The fact is, I just can't stand it when someone's a killjoy, when people get all humorless and out of sorts. So, at home I keep coming out with one jokey comment after another, some of the jokes treading on pretty thin ice. I might be betraying one portion of my readers or critics by doing this, but let me assure you that the mats on the floor of my room are new, my desk is neat and tidy, my wife and I treat each other with consideration and respect, and furthermore, it goes without saying that I have never struck her, nor have we ever had violent quarrels where one or the other of us screams "Get out of this house!" and one or the other of us leaves, because this daddy and mummy adore their children to pieces and the children, for their part, are attached to their parents in a most cheery fashion.

But, it's not that way on the inside. Mummy bares her breasts and we get the vale of tears … and as for daddy, he sweats like a stuck pig at night. They are well aware of the other's anguish, but they both take pains not to aggravate it, with daddy telling his jokes and mummy laughing at them.

And yet, when mummy came out with her vale of tears this time, it shut daddy right up, and, with the best will in the world, he couldn't think of a single clever thing to say. Daddy's clamming up just sent things from bad to worse, and, though unaccustomed as a "man about town" to get all heavy, he muttered, with his heart in his mouth, "Get some help in. What's stopping you?" He was doing his damnedest not to hurt her feelings.

As I said, three children. When it comes to housework, daddy is a write-off. He can't even lift a futon into the closet. He makes do with his stupid jokes. He doesn't know the first thing about rationing, registering and stuff like that. It's almost as if he's living in an inn or something. When a guest comes, he treats him like a king. And there are times when he leaves the house with a packed lunch to go to work at his private little office and doesn't come back for a week. He calls it "work," but if he manages two or three pages a day it's a lot. The rest of the time, he drinks. When he drinks too much, he looks like death warmed over and just tries to sleep it off. Besides that, it appears as if he's got young "lady friends" scattered about.

Now, the kids. The seven-year-old and the little one born this spring are a trifle prone to colds, but, well, they're no worse than anybody else's kids. But the four-year-old boy is as skinny as a scarecrow, and he can't even stand up yet. He's unable to speak. All he does is make a funny noise or two. He doesn't understand what people say to him. He just crawls about the place and won't be toilet trained. Even so, he eats like a horse. And yet, he doesn't put on weight, is really small, has thin hair and refuses to grow.

Mummy and daddy avoid getting into deep discussions about their son. The reason is that it's all too distressing to admit to each other that they've given birth, in a word, to a boy who's severely handicapped.

Sometimes mummy grabs him and holds him tight. And daddy often thinks of getting hold of him and, in a fit, jumping into the river with him and ending it all.

Man Murders Mute Son. In the afternoon of such-and-such a day, Mr. So-and-so, age 53, dealer in x at number y, z street, split open the skull of his 18-year-old son with an axe, then shoved scissors into his own throat but was transported to a nearby hospital where he is in critical condition, and recently his 22-year-old daughter was married to a live-in husband, and his motive was to get rid of the son, who was not only unable to speak or hear but was also not very clever, out of love for the daughter.

It's newspaper articles like this that plunge me in a drunken stupor.

Oh, if only it was a simple case of retarded development! If only the boy would suddenly shoot up and resentfully ridicule his mummy and daddy for all their needless worry! We've hidden everything from relatives and friends, hoping in secret that this will come about, teasing our son playfully and putting a good face on it.

Mummy tries her best to keep her head above water, and daddy's no different. It wasn't as if he was the most prolific novelist in the world from the outset. He's a timid little coward to the core of his being, and his words stutter onto the page, making this as plain as day to the public. It pains him so much to write things down that the only thing that saves him is drowning his sorrows in drink. When you drown your sorrows in drink, you can't remember what it is you were trying to say. You drink because things are tedious and annoying. The people who are always able to express clearly what's on their mind never get dead drunk like that. (This explains why women don't drink much.)

I've never known an instance when I've won an argument. I'm always the loser. I'm overpowered by the strength of my opponents' conviction, by the scale of their self-assurance. I just clam up. It does dawn on me on reflection that my opponents might be arguing totally out of selfishness and that I may not always be the one in the wrong; but the thought of insisting on a reopening of the verbal hostilities once I've given in is pretty dismal, and, besides, these arguments leave a grudge as horrible as a fist fight, so I just laugh it off even though I'm shaking with rage, shut my mouth and, with my head full of all sorts of things, drown myself in drink. Let me put it straight. I could beat around the bush like this till the cows come home, but the fact is that this story is about an argument between a married couple.

"The vale of tears."

That's what lit the fuse. This married couple, as I have already noted, are an exceedingly civilized pair of people who do not indulge in violence or swearing at each other. And yet, this very thing is what courts danger and leads to an explosive situation, the danger when neither says a word because they are both gathering evidence of the other's faults, the danger that each is playing their cards close to their chest, stealing a look at one card then another, preparing to get the jump on the other and to lay all their cards triumphantly on the table. That's what's behind the coy reserve with which they treat each other, if you must know. I'm not sure about the wife, but I do know that this husband is so full of bulldust that you couldn't beat it all out of him even if you wanted to.

"The vale of tears."

The husband takes a very jaundiced view of that. But he doesn't want to start an argument either. So he keeps his trap shut.

"You're saying that to spite me, aren't you, eh? But, you're not the only one crying, you know. I'm just as focused on the kids as you are. I care a lot about my family. When the kids so much as cough once in the middle of the night, I wake up and I can't stand it. I want nothing more than to move to a nicer place so that I can make you and the kids happy, but I'm up to my neck and I just can't manage it. I'm doing all I can to keep my head above water. I'm not some mad devil, you know. I don't have what passes for 'nerve' to sit back and watch my wife and children wither away before my eyes. It's not that I'm oblivious to things like rationing and registering. It's just that I don't have the time to learn about them."

That's what daddy muttered inside to himself, not having the self-confidence to say it out loud. He realized, too, that if he had said it, mummy would have come back with something that threw him for a loop and he'd be left totally speechless again, so he just mumbled, barely able to offer an opinion, "Get some help in."

Mummy doesn't say much either, but when she does, she does it with a cold confidence. (This trait is by no means limited to this mother. All women generally display it.)

"But it's not so easy to get someone who'll take the job."

"You'll find someone if you look. It's not so hard to get someone to come. What's hard is to get someone who'll stay."

"Are you inferring that I don't know how to handle people?"

"Why would I...?"

Daddy clammed up again. Actually, I did think that. But I wasn't about to spell it out. Oh, if only she'd hire someone to help us out! Daddy has to look after the two eldest when mummy puts the baby on her back and goes out to run her errands. And I've got about ten guests coming to see me every single day to boot.

"I'd like to go to my office."

"Now?"

"Yes. I've got something I have to get written down before tomorrow, come hell or high water."

That wasn't a lie. But the main reason was that I had to escape the gloom of the house.

"I was planning on visiting my sister tonight."

I knew that. Her sister was seriously ill. But if she went, then I'd be left with the children.

"That's why I'm tellin' you to hire someone..." is what I started to say, but I stopped myself. If I even broached the subject of a member of her family, the mood between the two of us would go sour.

It's a hell of a thing to stay alive in this world. Wherever you go you get tangled up in chains; and if you so much as budge, blood spurts out.

I stood up without saying another word, took the envelope with my manuscript fee from the desk drawer in the six-mat room and slipped it into the sleeve of my kimono. Then I wrapped some blank paper and a dictionary in a big black cloth and blew out of the house like a gust of wind. Writing was the farthest thing from my mind. What I wanted to do was kill myself. I made a beeline for a bar.

"Oh, Mr. Dazai!"

"I wanna drink. Ah, you've got on that striped kimono I like so much…."

"Suits me, doncha think? I put it on to please you…."

"Had it out with the missus again today. I've got so much pent-up emotion in me I can't take it any longer. Get me something to drink. I'm stayin' the night here. Yep, nothin's gonna stop me from stayin' right here."

Parents, I would like to think, are more precious than children.

Children are much stronger than their parents.

Cherries have appeared before me.

The children in my home are not given the luxury of eating such things. My kids have probably never seen a cherry. They'd be thrilled to eat one, though. They'd be overjoyed if I brought home some cherries for them. If you strung them together with thread and put them around your neck, it'd look like you had a coral necklace on.

But daddy gets through a whole plate of them, eating them as if they tasted awful, spitting out the pits, eating and spitting out, eating and spitting out … all the while muttering to himself, putting up a bold front, "Parents are more precious than children."

The Water Letters

By Inoue Hisashi

On 9 April 2010 my dear and wonderful friend Inoue Hisashi passed away. He was seventy-five. Over a period of more than thirty-five years I considered him not only my best friend but something of a big brother. When I was living in Australia, I stayed often with him and his family on visits back to Japan. He was kind enough to put me up at his home in Ichikawa in Chiba prefecture, a short train ride across the Edo River from Tokyo.

I was able to invite him, his wife and three daughters to Australia in 1976. Hisashi graciously accepted the position of visiting lecturer in the Department of Japanese at the Australian National University, where I was teaching at the time. He stayed in Canberra for five months, living in a flat across from mine on Northbourne Ave., and during his stay we met every day. I also managed to get an invitation for him to speak at Writers Week at the Adelaide Festival of Arts that year.

Hisashi had not been overseas until then and was famous for his dislike of flying. Nonetheless, he enjoyed his stay in Australia, I believe, and said as much in many articles and some books. The stay outside Japan gave him that distant but distinct objective view of his country that all of us who live overseas acquire, to a greater or lesser degree, of our own country. Hisashi wrote one of his best plays, "Ame" ("Rain") in two weeks while living on Northbourne Ave. It is still popular in

Japan and had its most recent production in September 2021.

All in all I translated only a small number of his works. The first was his novel based on the time he worked backstage at the France-za vaudeville theater in Asakusa, Tokyo, *The Fortunes of Father Mockinpott*. It was serialized over several months in the Mainichi Daily News, becoming the first Japanese novel to be serialized in Japan's English-language press. I also translated his comic novel *Boon and Phoon*, which appeared in the Japan Quarterly, an excellent journal then published by the Asahi Shinbun. There were two other works: his play about Hiroshima, "The Face of Jizo"; and the novel about the sixteenth-century Portuguese missionary, Luis Frois, *My Friend Frois*. Both "The Face of Jizo" and *My Friend Frois* were published by the publishing arm of the theater troupe that he established to produce his plays, Komatsu-za.

My Friend Frois is a remarkable piece of fiction written in the first person, as if it was the diary of Frois himself. I originally translated it in 1983 for serialization in the Mainichi Daily News, where it ran as a serial before coming out in book form. Though it does not have the reputation of some of his other more popular novels, I consider it among his best works. It is full of witty and wise social commentary about Japan then and now.

An incident relating to the process of the translation of that novel tells something about Hisashi as a writer of fiction.

My Friend Frois contains quite a few references to the names of foreign missionaries, ships and the like. These were written in Hisashi's original in katakana, the script used for foreign words. As almost all of these were Portuguese I had little way of knowing how to transcribe them into the alphabet. Needless to say, there was no internet; and I had no access to a big library. I phoned him to ask if he could possibly send some of the materials he used to research the novel. They might show the names in Portuguese.

A couple of days later a cardboard box, heavy and coming up to my waist, arrived by courier. It contained about thirty books of an historical and technical nature. All of them, I could tell, had been examined or thoroughly read; about half of them had slips of colored paper throughout pages that had been marked with a marker pen. Thankfully, all of the references that I required in Roman letters were there.

"Thank you so much for sending all those books," I told him on the phone that day.

"That was just about one-third of the books I used for research," he said. "Should I send the rest?"

"No, no! That's enough!" I said.

I have not known another Japanese author who delves so deeply into the context of their stories. He was an inveterate bookworm and often spent days in his little study without leaving the house. He compiled an enormous library over the years and gave it to the "Mental Block Library" that he established in Kawanishi-machi, the present-day name for Komatsu-machi, his birthplace in Yamagata prefecture. In all he donated two hundred thousand books to them.

I have written extensively about him in both my memoirs, *My Japan* and *The Unmaking of an American*, so I will limit the rest of this introduction to a discussion of "The Water Letters."

Hisashi came relatively late to an interest in the environment. He was never the outdoor type. But his ardent advocacy of the cause of rice farmers led him, I believe, to delve into ecology. In addition, his favorite author was Miyazawa Kenji (we had that too in common), and the love of his works drew him naturally into Kenji's natural world.

He wrote "The Water Letters" for the opening of the Yamagata City Sports Center on 4 October 2003, where it had its premiere, before being published in "Subaru" magazine, the literary journal of the major publishing house of Shueisha, in their December issue of that year. It is a play meant for recitation on stage.

In September 2010 the Japan PEN Club hosted, in Tokyo, the seventy-sixth International PEN Congress, and I was asked to translate it for that occasion. Japanese actors performed the play for the delegates from all over the world. Copies of the translation were given to them so that they could follow the narrative on stage. The theme of that year's congress was "Environment and Literature." Alas, Hisashi had passed away five months earlier.

"The Water Letters" takes up a group of letters read to the audience, urging them in the end to link the condition and fate of the water where they live to the condition and fate of the waters of the world. The people reading the letters are: a brother and sister in Uzbekistan who are forced to leave their village because the Aral Sea is drying up; an old man bemoaning "the endless stretch of mud and the feeble flow" of his beloved Colorado River in the United States; a twelve-year-old Chinese boy who is scared because the Yellow River is just "vanishing away"; a girl in Mexico City whose school is teetering on its foundations because the government has been pumping up too much underground water ... and others. With its reference to linked global problems, this drama conveyed the perfect message to authors from all over the world.

It may just be that those months in Australia in the 1970s were resonating with him for decades before he came to this issue of how one Japanese might raise the consciousness of the people of the world about water. Or, I would like to think, perhaps it expresses another kind of link, one with another author from Tohoku, who died in 1933, just a little over a year before Hisashi was born: a link between the nature that surrounds us and our own nature.

If that is so, then we come right back to the world of Miyazawa Kenji, ending the commentary in this book in a full circle.

THE WATER LETTERS
By Inoue Hisashi

1 We Are Water

Many voices are heard murmuring in the dark. After a while, a group of readers can be seen standing together in a corner as the lights fade up. Three words can be made out in the murmuring: Earth . . . Water . . . Planet. Suddenly those three words come together, and the group speaks as one.

All This Earth that we inhabit is a planet of water.

Boy It's called a planet of water.

Girl It's called a planet of water because . . .

Boy and Girl . . . it's brimming with water.

Hearing their words, the members of the group individually say "Water . . . water . . . water" until, again, their voices merge.

All The earth is brimming with water. (*They begin to take this further.*) For instance . . . the astronauts who have seen the Earth from space speak with one voice.

Youth The Earth is an all-blue sphere. It looks like a gigantic blue drop of water just about to fall.

All It's true. Two-thirds of the Earth's surface is covered by seas.

They are seas swelling with water, and from those seas the ancestors of humans came onto the land. Even every one of us was born into this world from the waters . . . of the sea in our mother's belly. And for this reason . . . there is water, just water . . . in every part of us.

Boy Sixty percent of our body is water.

Girl Eighty percent of our blood is water.

Youth Eighty percent of our brain is water.

Middle-aged Man In other words, humans are water with clothes on, weeping, laughing, loving and showing affection toward each other.

All Not only humans. Every living thing on the Earth is a mass of water. Ninety percent of a tomato is water. Eighty-five percent of an apple is water. Seventy-five percent of a fish is water. All living things are masses of water.

Middle-aged Man The trees and the flowers all live on water. When a tree grows in height, it sucks up water with the force of a hand pump. The source of a tree or a flower's power to grow toward the sky is water . . . only water.

All In this way . . . all of us live on water. We are all given life by water. More than that: We are all nothing but water. I am water. Water is me. We are nothing but water.

Girl I am water.

Boy Water is me.

All We are nothing but water.

Old Man And yet it's said that nowadays strange things are happening to water in any number of places in the world.

Middle-aged Man Water seems to have caught a disease.

Boy Water has caught a disease.

Girl We have caught a disease. (*The group huddles together.*)

Youth We will now present to you water letters sent by the world to Yamagata.

All The water letters.

2 The Lake Has Vanished

Sister My older brother and I are about to be taken away from the village by our mum. The three of us are going to live in one room of an apartment in a faraway town. But I wonder if there's work for mum in the town. I'm worried sick over it.

Brother A long long time ago, a number of roads went from China through Central Asia to Europe. These are generally referred to together as "The Silk Road." My little sister and I are primary school pupils in the Central Asian country of the Republic of Uzbekistan, right in the middle of The Silk Road. We've always lived in a fishing village there on the shore of the Aral Sea. The Aral Sea was the world's fourth largest lake up until my grandfather's time.

Sister They say that lots of fish were caught in the old days.

Brother But about the time our dad was a young man, they took the water from the rivers that feed the Aral Sea to grow cotton.

Sister That's because they could make more money growing cotton than catching fish.

Brother The government had made it a policy to grow cotton. But it takes huge amounts of water to grow cotton. You have to rain water on cotton fields every day. So now, forty years later, the Aral Sea is half the size it used to be.

Sister The cotton fields snatched the water away from the Aral Sea.

Brother The sea was very salty in the first place, so when the water was reduced to half, its saltiness got two or three times worse.

Sister Lots of fish just died . . .

Brother Dad started spending more and more time fishing. If he hadn't pushed himself like that, he couldn't have caught enough fish. Dad got high blood pressure from taking in too much salt and . . . last year . . . he died.

Sister That's why we have to leave the village. And it's not only us either. The only people who will be left after we leave are the head of the village and his family.

Brother I learned at school that if you go east on The Silk Road as far as you can go, you come to a country called "Japan," where they get the most or the second-most amount of rain of any country in the world. That's why all of us in class admire Japan. Uzbekistan is a desert country. We long for rains like that.

Sister All I want is to walk just once in the rain. (*to her brother*) Can we go to Japan someday?

Brother (*after some thought*) With a little bit of luck.

The readers chant the following five lines in a whisper from a corner.

All Water vanishes from the village. People disappear from the village. Water vanishes from the village. People disappear from the village. Not a soul is left in the village.

3 The River Has Vanished

Old Man The Colorado River . . . it's a long river. It's a big American river, starting in Wyoming and flowing through the six states of Colorado, Utah, New Mexico, Arizona, Nevada and California before emptying into the Gulf of California in Mexico. I was born and raised in a small Mexican town in Sonora at the mouth of the Colorado River. I turn seventy-four this November.

Boy The Yellow River is twice the length of the Colorado. If you put seven or eight Yellow Rivers end to end, you'd create a band that stretched once around the globe. It's really long. I live in the city of Lijin by the mouth of the Yellow River. I'm twelve years old.

Old Man When I was a young man the Colorado River formed dozens of lush green deltas in the Gulf of California. But now they've all dried up, leaving nothing but an endless stretch of mud and a feeble flow that makes the most pitiful sound as it trickles into the sea. Can you believe it? The great Colorado has no mouth!

Boy The mouth of the Yellow River is gone, too. In the twelve years that I have been alive, the river has emptied into the sea only twice. All that's left to see now is just a huge flat of yellow sand.

Old Man Along the way there are enormous dams and immense farms, and not so far away are big cities like Los Angeles, Las Vegas and San Diego. The river generates electricity and provides water to irrigate crops, water for millions of people to cook and shower with, and water to quench their thirst with. So there's nothing that can be done, and yet . . . every time I gaze at the dried-up mouth of the river, I feel uneasy, as if something crazy's going on.

Boy It's normal for a river to get wider as it approaches the sea. After all, there's more water near the mouth, right? But not the Yellow River. The closer it gets to the sea, the less water it carries until, in the end, the river itself vanishes away. It's scary.

Old Man I'm scared too.

4 And The Ground Sinks

Girl I'm a primary school pupil in Mexico City, the capital of Mexico. A little while ago a huge commotion occurred when the school's gymnasium started teetering and leaning to the right. (*She approaches Old Man and Boy.*) Mexico City is located on a tableland two thousand and two hundred meters above sea level. With cool summers, it's really a great place to live. The one trouble is, it doesn't rain very much. I read in our geography book that Japan gets an average of two thousand millimeters of rain per year. Mexico City doesn't even get a fourth of that. So the city has to pump water up from below ground for its almost twenty million inhabitants. But they have pumped up too much water. The water level of the underground water has dropped twenty meters in the last fifty years, and that has caused the ground to sink. It probably won't be long before the gymnasium falls over or buildings around the city teeter and lean to one side. I can't sleep, thinking about that sort of thing. I'm scared.

Old Man beckons Girl and they hug each other.

5 Islands Sink

Youth steps forward.

Youth There's a small country in the Indian Ocean made up of twelve hundred coral islands. It's the Republic of Maldives, population about three hundred thousand. I support myself in the Maldives making dried bonito fish. Our dried bonito is exported to Japan, so some of you out there may even have eaten it. The land of the Maldives is, well, not more than about two meters above sea level at its highest point. Coconut palm groves gently cover land that's as flat as a tray. And when it comes to the delicious taste of the coconut juice you drink while you're sitting in the shade of those trees with the cool sea breezes . . . well, please come and see for yourselves. The sea is beautiful, too, and it has lots of fish. Fifty thousand Japanese tourists visit the Maldives every year, and they all agree that it's as close to paradise as you can get on Earth. When I hear that, I'm filled with mixed feelings of joy and sorrow and fear. That's because . . . if people from developed countries keep on burning oil and coal like they do now, this paradise will be transformed into a living hell. If you keep on burning oil and coal, the Antarctic ice will melt off the land, adding water to the ocean and readily raising the sea level by about one meter. What will happen when the sea level goes up a meter? . . . eighty percent of the land mass of my country will sink into the sea, turning a blessing into a curse. When that day will come depends on the amount of oil and coal you can cut down on. (*to Old Man and Youth*) Help us.

Youth kneels in front of Old Man and Girl.

Old Man It seems, when you look at it, that we humans are indifferent to the suffering of others . . . that we are creatures who survive on apathy.

Youth Are you telling us to give up?

Old Man is silent. All Old Man can do is take their hands in a consoling gesture.

6 Water Goes Around

A woman in her thirties steps forward.

Woman in her Thirties I do research on water at a university in Venice, Italy. Venice is a city crammed with stone buildings built on reclaimed land, so you can imagine their weight. These days you can see with the naked eye how much the land has subsided because too much ground water has been withdrawn. The Piazza San Marco, so popular with tourists, is underwater four days of the week, and people have to walk on fifty-centimeter-high platforms laid out on the square. My research has showed me, however, that pumping up ground water isn't the sole cause of the sinking land. It's also due to global warming caused by the excessive burning of fossil fuels. The surface temperature of the Earth is rising, and when terrestrial ice in the Arctic and Antarctic melts, the sea level will rise, causing the Piazza San Marco to be submerged under water. In other words, the fate of the Maldives will be the fate of the world. If the sea level goes up by one meter, not only Venice and the Maldives but Tokyo and New York and every city on a seacoast will share this fate. That is to say, we all share the same water. Japan's own scholar from the Edo period, Hayashi Shihei, said: "The water of the Sumida River is linked to the water in the Thames." These are true words of wisdom. All the water in the world is linked, forming one body of water. (*She approaches Old Man and the others.*) The water of Venice is the water of the Maldives.

Youth The water of the Maldives is the water of Mexico City.

Girl The water of Mexico City is the water of the Yellow River.

Boy The water of the Yellow River is the water of the Colorado River.

Old Man The water of the Colorado River is . . .

Group … the water of the Mogami River.

All The water of the Mogami River is the water of the world. The water of the world is the water of the Mogami River. Water goes around, it goes around the world. Water is a single body … the world is a single body.

7 The Faraway Well

A mother in her thirties steps forward, holding hands with her nine-year-old son and seven-year-old daughter, blurting out . . .

Mother The well is so far away! The three of us live on a savanna in the Republic of Chad in central Africa. My husband left home to work on laying an oil pipeline and has not come back. I work from eight in the morning till four in the afternoon making plain rubber sandals.

Son Every morning at seven, my sister and I take our lunch with us and head out to draw water from a well.

Daughter My brother has a big bucket.

Son My sister has a little bucket.

Mother The well is eleven kilometers away, so they both walk twenty-two kilometers to fetch water. They get home after three. The well is so far away.

Daughter The bucket is so full on our way home, I have to stop and rest every hundred meters. My arm feels like it's coming off. I wish the well was closer.

Son There was a well in the village a long time ago, wasn't there?

Mother We haven't had rain for twenty years, so the nearby wells dried up . . . but the thing that I worry about most is that you two can't go to school because of the water.

Son Drawing water is important work for children. It can't be helped.

Daughter But I'd like to go to school just once.

Son We need water to live. That's why it can't be helped.

Mother The head of the village told me that in Japan and America and Europe they have toilets that flush with water, and that every time you do your business in the toilet, water flushes it away, and the amount of water used each time is the same amount we use in a day.

The two children look up at their mother in amazement. She embraces them.

Mother What stopped the rains from coming down?

8 The Rain That Withers Roses

A female high school student steps out to a different place.

Female Student People of Yamagata. I am a high school student in Paris. Something happened recently that shocked me. The potted roses that I had put out on my veranda in the middle of the day had completely withered by evening. It turned out that the culprit was the afternoon rain. Apparently, Parisian rains carry a lot of sulfuric and nitric acid. Our chemistry teacher at school told us, "The smoke that comes from factories and airplanes and cars and things that run on oil or coal has sulfur and nitrogen in it, and these become sulfuric and nitric acid in the atmosphere and get into the rain, which becomes acid rain when it pours down." Sulfuric acid and nitric acid destroy trees and forests and everything. There's a bronze statue of Victor Hugo not far from our house. He's the great author of *Les Misérables*, and it's a custom of the people around here to bow their head a little to the statue every time they pass by it. But lately the tip of Victor Hugo's nose seems to be corroding away. It turns out that the culprit here too is acid rain. What about Japan? Are the bronze statues of Yamagata also corroding away?

Female High School Student walks out of the light and Middle-aged Man 1, an employee of the United Nations, comes into it, speaking as he enters.

9 The Fight over Water

Middle-aged Man 1 People all around the world are continually fighting over water, saying, "This water is ours!" and "No, it's ours!" It's terrifying to think that people are fighting over water in a hundred places every day. I deal with water issues for a special United Nations agency. My time is taken up running on a daily basis from one fight over water to another, looking into the details and mediating. Today I want to tell all of you in Yamagata about an incident that occurred at the Euphrates. The Euphrates. It's the length of twelve Mogami Rivers put end to end. It flows parallel to the Tigris and, it is said, was the cradle of the world's first civilization, that of ancient Mesopotamia. But the river is a source of trouble, too. Its source is in Turkey, but it courses through Syria and then Iraq before joining the Tigris and flowing into the sea. It is an international river. Turkey, Syria and Iraq have all built a number of dams along the river that is their lifeline. Think of a river that's been dammed in thirty places! Syrians hear that the Turks, upriver, are damming the river, and get all hot under the collar. Iraqis learn that the Turks and Syrians, both upriver from them, are building dams, and blow their stack. It's commonplace to see soldiers from those countries staring each other down over the river. The Euphrates has been dry this year due to a lack of rain. Syria sent troops to the Turkish border, threatening the Turks and demanding they open the floodgates and let more water through. The Turks came back with, "The part of the Euphrates that runs through Turkey is Turkish!" They too sent troops to the banks of the river, and the soldiers of the two countries glared menacingly at each other. This is dangerous. It could easily lead to an exchange of fire. Fearing this, children joined hands and entered the river up to their knees. A hundred Syrian children. A hundred Turkish children. They joined hands in the middle of the river and cried out, "Don't make the water in our river run with blood!" No shots were fired. A bullet might have struck a child crying, "Don't dye our river red!" Then, some of us from the U.N. went in, and the two governments began to talk things over. Those children were worried sick about the fighting over water that goes on year in and year out. That's what prompted them to put themselves in the line of fire and find a peaceful way to solve an international problem. These days so many awful things are happening in the world, but it's at times like this that I feel some hope for the future. This concludes my report.

10 There's Water Here Now

Three children—Boy A, Boy B and Girl A—stand in a separate area.

Boy A Our village is in northern Afghanistan.

Girl A It's at the foot of the Hindu Kush, west of the Himalayas.

Boy B Every year there has been less and less snow, and the water from the melting snow is not reaching us. The ground water is also going away and our well has dried up.

Girl A I think the snow has gone away because the world is getting hot like a greenhouse.

Boy B It'd be good if we could dig a deeper well, but we don't have the money for it. So more and more people are leaving the village.

Boy A But volunteers came from Japan this year and dug a well for us.

Three Together That's why there's water here now.

Girl A I thanked the head of the Japanese group from the bottom of my heart. This is what he said ...

Boy A "We're digging the wells for ourselves, you know. The water here flows into the Kabul River and from there into the Indus River and then into the Indian Ocean. Without a doubt, the water is carried on the ocean currents to Japan. So it's the same as if we were digging for ourselves."

All The water of the Kabul River is the water of Japan. The water of Japan is the water of the world. Water goes around . . . it goes around the world. Water is a single body . . . the world is a single body.

11 The Astronaut

Middle-aged Man 2, an astronaut, stands alone, reading his letter.

Middle-aged Man 2 So long as I live I will never forget gazing at the Earth from the space shuttle. The Earth was an all-blue sphere. It looked like a gigantic blue drop of water just about to fall. It was floating in the jet black of space as if about to burst out of the gossamer-thin atmosphere that surrounds it and scatter throughout the sky. Something occurred to me in the corner of my mind as I stared at our lovely planet. It was words from a play I had once read. "It is said that there are one hundred billion suns . . . one hundred billion stars … in our galaxy alone … and our galaxy is only one of many billions of galaxies. If each star in our galaxy has, on the average, two planets going around it, then there would be two hundred billion planets just in our galaxy. How many planets among those might be blessed, like the Earth, with a temperate climate and water? Probably not many at all. So the very existence of a planet with water like the Earth is a miracle. Of course, just because there is water on a planet does not mean that life will occur. Yet at one time in the past, the smallest forms of life did appear on Earth. This too was a miracle. That these forms of life went through countless ordeals and trials to evolve into human life shows that there is no end to miracles. And the fact that you are one of those humans is yet another miracle. You and I are here as the result of billions and trillions of accumulated miracles. The very fact that we are here, alive, is a miracle of miracles. That we are talking to each other, loving each other, fighting each other . . . every one of these things is a miracle. Humankind itself is a miracle. Even our slightest gestures are miraculous. That's why we must survive. It's miraculous that the Earth is a planet with water, that the water has given birth to life, that we live on the planet of water. And because our existence is so miraculous, we must survive … we must survive with our water. That's exactly what I felt as I gazed at our brilliant blue planet, a newborn child. I could not stop nodding my head at the truth of this.

12 I Am Water

The members of the group, each saying a line, gather around the astronaut.

A The planet of water . . . Earth.

B Our planet blessed by water.

C On the planet, always the same amount of water.

D Only so much water on the planet.

E Earth continually renews the water.

F It renews old water.

G This means, Earth is a brilliant recycler.

H The King of the Recyclers.

All The Earth is the King of the Recyclers.

We are given life by its powers.

And yet . . .

I Humankind destroys the continuous cycle.

J Humankind gets in the way of recycling.

K It gets in the way.

L People . . .

M Factories . . .

N Cars . . .

O Fields...

P Rice paddies . . .

Q Airplanes . . .

R People shampooing every morning . . .

S People throwing away things that water can't dissolve . . .

T More . . .

All More ... more ... more ... (*The group continues with this chant as* *individuals speak.*)

U We've got to think of something to do.

V We've got to come up with something.

W Think of the Earth as a planet of water.

A The planet of water . . . Earth.

B Our planet blessed by water.

C On the planet, always the same amount of water.

D Only so much water on the planet.

E Earth continually renews the water.

F It renews old water.

G This means, Earth is a brilliant recycler.

H The King of the Recyclers.

All The Earth is the King of the Recyclers.

We are given life . . .

By its powers.

But, more than that . . .

We were born of water and that's why . . .

We are water ourselves.

Water ourselves . . .

Water ourselves. (*At some point the smallest child in the group cries out.*)

Smallest Child I am water.